A Lover's Secret

Howard Reiss

Praise for the Novels of Howard Reiss

P Town is a 2016 Readers' Favorite Silver Medal Winner in the Contemporary Romance category.

Readers' Favorite gives *P Town* 5 stars and calls it an "unforgettable read."
"This book grabbed me from the very first page and kept me obsessively reading until the end. Author Howard Reiss has done a beautiful job in creating characters that his readers will connect with, relate to, and care about. If that isn't a hallmark of a great author, I am not sure what is."

--Readers' Favorite on *P Town*

IndieReader gives *P Town* 5 stars. "Beautifully written from beginning to end, *P Town* is endearing and inspiring."

--IndieReader on *P Town*

P Town won the 2016 Los Angeles Book Festival in the Spiritual category.

Readers' Favorite gives *The Laws of Attraction* 5 stars. *The Laws of Attraction* is "a very insightful and quirky legal thriller" where "nothing is what it seems at first." "The strange testimonies discussing the eternal soul and reincarnation, the various revelations about Susannah's past, and the way everybody's beliefs are tested all make for a page-turner." "This intelligent mystery" is a "guilty reading pleasure."

--Readers' Favorite on *The Laws of Attraction*

Howard Reiss is skilled "at making characters seem real and lovable in the space of a few pages or paragraphs."

--Readers' Favorite on *The Laws of Attraction*

Readers' Favorite calls *The Year of Soup* "a wonderfully insightful read" and recommends it to "anyone who loves mysteries, emotional fiction, and self-discovery." "Howard Reiss is able to deftly weave story into sustenance and create a plot that is beautifully original without straying too far from classic themes of this sort of genre."
The Year of Soup is "a hands-down, great read."

--Readers' Favorite on *The Year of Soup*

BookBub calls *The Year of Soup* "a heartwarming read."

--BookBub on *The Year of Soup*

"*The Year of Soup*, as with his first novel *A Family Institution*, clearly establishes Howard Reiss' credentials as an especially gifted storyteller with a knack for creating fully developed characters and original storylines that engage the readers complete attention from first page to last. *The Year of Soup* is highly recommended and thoroughly entertaining, making it an appropriate addition for community library contemporary fiction collections."

--The Midwest Book Review on *The Year of Soup*

"*The Year of Soup*, mixes a fine stew of intelligence and wisdom, while also at times stirring in a sharp wit and a pinch of genuine, heartfelt charm and humanity."

--IndieReader on *The Year of Soup*

A LOVER'S SECRET

The Year of Soup received the Silver Medal for Best Fiction in the North-East Region at the Independent Publisher Book Awards in 2013.

"By understanding our family history we can understand our future. A frank novel of family and what binds us all through our troubles, *A Family Institution* is a choice pick for general fiction collections."

--*The Midwest Book Review* on *A Family Institution*

"The dialogue and the physical descriptions of characters ring with truth."
"If you liked *Where We Belong* [by Emily Giffin], you'll love.... *A Family Institution* by Howard Reiss."

--*IndieReader* on *A Family Institution*

Copyright © 2019 Howard Reiss

All rights reserved.

Published by Krance Publishing

ISBN-13: 978-0999511848

DEDICATION

To my mother . . . Rose . . . whose loving memory blooms deep in my heart.

TABLE OF CONTENTS

	Introduction	11
1	The Internet is for Time Travelers	19
2	Facebook Lies	45
3	After the Breakup	63
4	The Proposal	95
5	Lies Goes On	113
6	Baseball is Forever	129
7	Going Home	149
8	The Shadow Boxes	169
9	Can You Ever Really Know Someone	185
10	Recognition and Remembrance	205
11	Daisies Again	237
Sample: *The Year of Soup*		241
About the Author		245

INTRODUCTION

Life is a fairy tale . . . or at least it should be. That's pretty much the way I looked at the world and my life in it from the moment I became conscious of myself until I left my teens behind. Maybe I'm exaggerating, not exactly a fairy tale but something pretty close to it. I think I kept hold of the remnants of that fairy tale philosophy into my early twenties, although too much time has passed for me to really recall. Still, I have little doubt I thought like that, even if it was only subconsciously, at least until the summer I graduated from high school.

When I flipped my tassel and thought of love and marriage, fairy tales were still in the air and I tended to look at life, mine in particular, through that Grimm lens. I think it's rather funny now . . . at 68 . . . how close Grimm is to grim.

Is it good to hold on to that rose-colored view of life even at 18? Maybe . . . maybe not. I can't tell you for sure even fifty years later. Certainly I know by now fairy tales don't come true, the story rarely ends the way you might have imagined—or wished—as a teenager, an age when no fantasy seems too farfetched.

Before I jump to my late sixties, I need to linger a moment longer at 18 so you can get the full picture and better appreciate the story I'm about to relate. I suggest thinking of it in generic terms because I'm sure my story can apply to most of us in one way or another, although I believe I'm entitled to my own unique facts. I can't imagine anyone else sharing a story quite like this one.

First, let me set the scene.

The boy is Michael. Mikey when he was little before I knew him. Mike in high school to his friends. Michael to me, always Michael. There was something special about him—at least to me—that required his full name. Maybe it was his confidence and the ease he had with everyone in school from teachers and administrators to the upperclassmen. He never seemed the least bit intimidated or self-conscious, and self-consciousness is the very definition of most sixteen-year old boys. He excelled at everything he did whether it was sports or academics.

Everything seemed to come so effortlessly for Michael. That wasn't just my opinion, it was everyone's opinion. He could have been class president if he'd had the time to run or the inclination. He settled for sports editor of the school paper and the yearbook, a few small roles in the school plays, all county first basement three years running, and the king of his class at all the homecoming dances.

Thinking of him as Mike just didn't seem right, especially as I laid there at night in my pink, frilly bedroom gazing out at our love in the distant future—our adult love—where I saw Michael as a successful doctor or lawyer, if I borrowed my mother's dream, or a New York Yankee or movie producer, if I borrowed his. Perhaps an artist or an internationally known photographer. Maybe a senator or a news anchor. Wherever my imagination took me, it was always something spectacular for the boy who would be voted the most likely to succeed in his senior yearbook, a vote that was never in doubt.

On top of that Michael was handsome with a face that belonged on a Greek statue covered by an arresting wave of sandy blonde hair. He was interesting and easy to talk to as well. He had a way of listening to you, not just to me, but to teachers and friends, as if he thought you were the most wonderful person in the world. You couldn't write a better boyfriend even if you were allowed to make one up on paper and bring him to life. He wrote me love poems on Valentine's Day and my birthday, bought me little things for every relationship milestone—a month since our first kiss, six months after our first date, a year since, you know, the first time we did it.

Sometimes, I'd be walking down the hall and catch him leaning against the wall staring at me with a look of pleasure and pride. It's not often you can make someone that happy. Certainly it wasn't that easy for me with my mother after I met Michael . . . perhaps because she could sense where this was all leading.

Michael was humble, always deflecting compliments on his fielding and hitting, as well as his academic achievements. He was always telling me how he was the lucky one because he didn't deserve someone as good as me, although everyone else was always telling me how lucky I was. He was sincere, affectionate and kind to everyone. He didn't pick on the odd or nerdy kids like some of the other jocks. He didn't ignore the girls who hadn't blossomed yet or felt awkward around him. He went out of his way to talk with them and make them feel good about themselves.

He always seemed to know the right thing to say and do.

He was trying to teach himself the guitar so one day he could write me loves songs and he taught himself to juggle so he could entertain the little kids when he worked at the town day camp during the summer. He always kept busy, refusing to sit around at home watching television or doing nothing, which I didn't mind doing until I met Michael.

A fairy tale, right? My fairy tale . . . as it turns out . . . one I believed at the time with my whole heart. Fifteen-year old girls don't look closely at their boyfriends, they certainly don't scrutinize them the way they will the men they meet later in life. Of course, they're not expected to.

Love in general tends to filter out the darker aspects of most people, which is why I suppose they say love is blind. There is a truth to that at any age, but it's particularly true when it comes to a first love.

I didn't see that aspect—the darker truth about Michael—and I wouldn't for almost 50 years.

Michael was my first boyfriend and the only one I had throughout all of high school.

I will call myself Azu, short for azucar, which means sugar in Spanish . . . for no other reason than I like sweets and I remember the word from my high school Spanish class. I don't want to use my real name. I suppose I want to protect the innocent, which in this case is really the unaware, Michael's teammates and classmates who still believe in the unalterable past . . . our shared past . . . our long past . . . and need to visit it from time to time as they watch the future grow shorter and darker.

In a way I'm writing another fairy tale, a different kind of fairy tale, one that won't have a fairy tale ending.

Michael is his real name. I couldn't bear to change that. But the world is full of Michaels and that ought to insure his anonymity, at least from most readers. The ones who might be able to figure it out, even if I use a pseudonym . . . well, there's nothing I can do and there's certainly nothing wrong with them knowing what I know. For most of them it won't matter and for the rest it's not a truth they will have to live with for very long.

I was a freshman, the fresh meat, as some of the less couth upperclassman liked to refer to us. The tall, attractive underclasswoman sought out by a lot of upperclassman because I was well-developed, perky and unafraid. Michael was the sophomore who won my heart. He sat behind me in study hall, where we met the usual way with tugs on my ponytail, followed by funny notes and eventually kisses behind the bleachers that as a freshman I could never have imagined reaching so far past my lips.

We had three years of perfect young love . . . the kind poets write about and haunts writers for a lifetime . . . some writers, not all, certainly not me. Although I suppose this book is evidence that while it may not have haunted me, it certainly never completely left me.

Whose first love ever does?

On the anniversary of our first kiss Michael bought me a bouquet of daisies which he had read somewhere was the flower of innocence and loyalty. The last time he did that, the September before he left for college, it came with a quote from Helen Keller—"The best and most beautiful things in the world cannot be seen or even touched—they must be felt with the heart."

Michael stayed that way in my heart, even my 66-year old heart, for the next 48 years. He didn't change. He didn't age. He stayed 19, the way those we love and lose remain fixed in the moment we lose them.

That's the story. Our love—and our lives—were like a fairy tale . . . for those high school years anyway. At least I thought so. It took me fifty years to learn differently.

The story speaks to me now almost every day. It whispers things I cannot quite make out, even though the whispers grow louder when I'm unable to sleep . . . which is why I need to write it all down. Sometimes the only way to free yourself from a story is to tell it . . . to open the window and air it out. Putting your thoughts out there for everyone else is, at least for me, the best way to find the silence and stillness I need at night.

It's not healthy to keep a story like this to yourself. Michael never realized that. Perhaps his life might have turned out differently if he had.

Now that the scene is set, the narrative needs to jump 48 years ahead to a warm winter day in Florida. I've just turned 66, a natural number popularized by that old television show I was so fond of watching as a child with my parents. I haven't spoken to or seen Michael since the end of his first year of college, the day after my graduation from high school, when he came back from college to tell me a new fairy tale involving a different girl and a different ending.

That's right, he dumped me. I was crushed, certain I would never recover and had nothing to live for. You know what I'm talking about, it happens to all of us—males as well as females—we all know how deep that first cut can be. Especially if you don't see it coming and you're a day removed from high school. That kind of sudden end to love, a radical change in your imagined destiny can squeeze so tight around a young heart it becomes almost impossible to breathe.

Until the moment he said it, I was one hundred percent sure we would marry, have children, barbeque Sunday afternoons with his friends from the baseball team and their families, and die at a ripe old age gazing lovingly into each other's eyes.

There is no one more romantic than a teenage girl, even one who has just turned 18. There are two thoughts she carries to her pillow every night when it comes to her love, at least we did back then . . . Now and Forever. I even embroidered it on a pillow I once gave Michael.

I still sort of believed it for a year or two after he left. I'd get this feeling sometimes when there was a knock on the door, the telephone rang or I saw a letter in my college mail box with no return address that Michael had come to his senses . . . as if he'd lost his way for a bit—or his mind—and now realized what he really wanted was me.

Young girls don't give up their dreams easily, at least this young girl.

I eventually moved on to become a writer of those human interest stories you find in US and People magazine, occasionally in Vogue and Cosmopolitan. The kind that try to reveal someone's whole life in three or four pages. I fell in love again, a different kind of love as to be expected, an older, more mature love. The kind that doesn't always burn, but lasts. I got married, had two kids, became a grandmother, and now a snow bird.

My husband, Earl (also a made up name), a retired engineer, plays golf three days a weeks. He says he wants to get in as many days as he can before he can't. His philosophy of life has always been very simple—be kind, don't cry over spilt milk and greet every day with a smile. He likes to say happiness is a state of mind and it always beats the alternative. It was a philosophy I found easy to embrace.

Accept what you can't change and move on, change what you can . . . he's always been fond of that little bit of poster wisdom. I'd be the first to admit it ought to be a tenet of every religion.

If it makes Earl happy to play golf, it makes me happy to see him happy. Besides, I still find happiness in writing and writing is a very solitary activity. His golfing has always given me the space and time I needed to write. I wouldn't know what to do with myself if I didn't have that. I find words a good companion for my thoughts—and fears—and I enjoy painting people's lives with them. And we can use the extra income. Spoiling grandchildren can be quite expensive.

The week after I turned 66, I sat down at the computer and decided to join Facebook. I don't know why. I've been telling everyone for years I never would. I'm not a big believer in the benefits of all this instant, superficial connective technology. I watch all the young people on their smartphones in restaurants, walking down the street without looking where they're going, sitting in the cars pounding away with their thumbs and I don't understand it. I suppose the texting and e-mails give them a feeling they are actually doing something when in my opinion they are not.

Communication is storytelling. It needs to involve all the senses . . . sight, sound, touch, smell, sometimes even taste. It can't be confined to a backlit screen and a couple of digits . . . and it doesn't come through an emoji.

What's more, I hate the way these young people know everything about everyone before they ever sit down to actually talk. They know where their friends have been, what they think about world events; they even know where they had for dinner the night before. They know their shopping habits and politics. Of course, that's only if you post and I had no intention of doing any posting. I was joining Facebook for one reason and one reason only . . . to spy on my children and grandchildren—and their friends—so I would know what everyone was up to. Perhaps so I wouldn't sound behind the times when people asked if I was online. Perhaps to explore the past as well . . . there was a gold mine of human interest stories there for the Boomer generation . . . although I would never have admitted to that if anyone had asked.

CHAPTER ONE – THE INTERNET IS FOR TIME TRAVELERS

I have to admit Facebook was an eye-opener. I wound up exploring all kinds of groups and communities from semi-retired magazine writers like myself to rhubarb lovers, 60s trivia fans and Woodstock attendees. Before I knew it I was being be inundated with ads for anything I ever looked at or even thought about looking at, as if some internet god could read my mind through my fingertips.

What really surprised me was how easy it was to travel back in time . . . to find photos of the old drive-in Michael and I used to spend some of our warm summer evenings parked as far away from the snack shop as possible. It was amazing the things we could do under his father's old army blanket. I even found photos of some of our old high school football games and teachers.

Former classmates were waiting there to reveal themselves to me . . . like old books on a bookshelf eager to be re-read. The old days of bumping into a former high school classmate at a restaurant, catching up during the moments it took for the hostess to find you a table, and talking later about it with your husband in bed—don't you think she looked old, I don't know if I believed her story about the job—were over.

Now reunions were digital, real lives filtered and staged like someone selling a home, filling it with flowers and the scent of fresh baked cookies. The truth doesn't travel well over the Ethernet, certainly not on Facebook, but few people care. The internet makes us all gullible, it suspends our skepticism, just look at all the fake political news people have fallen for. In fact, I'd venture to say that few people on Facebook really want to see the truth or reveal it. They just want to be entertained for a moment or two before jumping to another friend or onto another site.

    I couldn't resist plugging in the names of a few old girlfriends and neighbors from my school days and they popped right up like it was my 13th birthday all over again. We reconnected and traveled 48 years together in a digital instant, as if our lives were a series of photos we could hand crank into a moving picture. Before long I knew all about their marriages, their careers, their children, their grandchildren, their travels, their eating habits, even their political leanings. I knew more about them now than I ever did in school.

    Certainly I only knew what they wanted me to know—what they wanted the Facebook world to see—but the photos looked real, the sentiments sounded sincere, and they all seemed to be well off . . . living busy, fun and healthy lives. I am happy and doing fine as well, I'd be the first to admit that, except they all seemed to have more energy than Earl and I had and to be doing much better financially, at least when it came to their night life and vacations. They appeared to eat out almost every night, drink enormous quantities of expensive red wine and vacation on a regular basis abroad or at luxury resorts. Caribbean cruises were a big favorite.

    Earl and I were basically snowbirds, our world confined to Florida and our home in New Jersey. We both preferred to eat at home, certainly on weekdays. He liked watching golf and reading murder mysteries, while I wrote and read my more literary books. We both enjoyed doing that to the smell of something cooking in the kitchen.

    I didn't post. I didn't have much to post about, not when it came to restaurants and travel, which I suppose caused some of my old classmates to wonder how I was really doing. I wasn't going to post photos of my children and grandchildren, not only because I valued our privacy and worried about who might be watching, but because I also remembered my grandmother's warning when I was little girl about not being boastful. Too much bragging, she used to say, brings out the evil eye.

    Not that I believed any of that, but why take any chances when the people I really wanted to see our photos and know what we were doing would see them and find out soon enough . . . in person or on the phone.

    I did respond to private messages which were basically newsy and far from intimate. We didn't speak or make plans to meet.

They were not those kind of friends back then so why would that be any different now? There wasn't a lot to reminisce about, not in terms of personal memories. When you have a daisy love—as Michael sometimes called it—starting in ninth grade in my case, you're free time is taken up with love, which inevitably comes at the expense of the other close friendships you once had in elementary school and middle school, as well as the new ones you were supposed to be making in high school.

Still, I kept watching my new/old Facebook friends celebrate birthdays and anniversaries with their husbands and grandchildren. I toured their homes and went on their vacations to the Jersey shore, the national parks, the Caribbean and Europe. I knew when and where they ate out and what they drank. For some reason, posting a martini or a bottle of wine is an important—and necessary—sign of the good life on Facebook.

My life is good . . . better than good . . . and if I had it to do all over again I would do it exactly the same way. Although it seemed a bit bland compared to everyone else's. As I said, if we eat out twice a week that's a lot, and it's usually at a local restaurant known for its comfort food and reasonable prices, as opposed to their drinks, artistic presentation, ambiance and view. I couldn't tell you the last time we went to a concert or took a long, luxurious vacation anywhere.

I started thinking about searching for Michael since all my high school memories revolved around him, but I didn't want to be his friend after all these years of silence. I wasn't hoping to resuscitate any long dead feelings or to spend a night strolling down memory lane. The bruise left by his abrupt departure had long since faded into history. Thinking about it didn't quicken my heart or make me sad. It did nothing for me at this point in my life.

I certainly didn't feel any need to measure my life against his while I lie there in bed waiting for Earl's snoring to subside so I could roll over onto my side and find sleep. It just piqued my curiosity. Writers tend to be like that, even a magazine writer focused these days on the Boomers. There can be a story under every rock, even if it's your own.

I certainly didn't want to make contact with Michael, especially since I had no idea what his life was like at the moment or had been like over the past 48 years. Like any 66-year old, I was wise enough to know the importance of avoiding situations which could possibly unsettle your or anyone else's emotional stability. Advanced age was taking care of that on its own, it didn't need any help.

All I was hoping to confirm was that Michael was alright and happy, enjoying the tail end of a good life . . . like me.

If it was a little worse than mine—you know, three wives, a stable but mediocre job requiring him to put off retirement—I suppose I would have felt a little redeemed, despite my better self. I certainly wasn't thinking along those lines, not consciously, although I think it's basic human nature to want the heartbreaker to flounder a bit without you.

That's when I discovered you didn't have to become a Facebook friend to watch someone's postings and to peer into their life. If a member didn't have the right privacy settings, if he wasn't computer savvy like my kids, who walked me through my Facebook setup, it could be like living in a house without blinds or shades.

I typed in Michael's name, Michael Greene (the last name is made up) and there he was. I didn't have to befriend him. He didn't have to know I was watching. It would be a step back in time for me only. Time travel shouldn't be this easy or quick. It should take effort and unravel slowly, revealing its surprises gradually along the way. Everything is way too instant in this age of stay-at-home connectivity.

His Facebook profile picture staring back at me was the real time trip. It was as if I was sitting in the stands again cheering him on. It was the photo of Michael playing first base in the spring of his senior year. It was the league championship, a game they won 5 to 4 in the bottom of the 7th when Michael doubled home the winning run. I remembered it well because I took the photo with a camera he had bought me on my birthday.

It was an expensive gift back in those days and he had saved quite a while to buy it.

It was a beautiful photo. It captured the intensity on his face, but the joy as well Michael always felt when he was playing the game he loved. He was the epitome of a ballplayer—lean, muscular and handsome. I don't know why baseball players are always so good looking, but they always seem to be . . . at least to me.

What really made the photo special was that Michael was lit up from behind, as if by magic, the sun embracing him like some kind of cosmic hug.

Those were the days when you had no idea how a photo would turn out. There was no screen to check at the back of the camera. You had a roll of film—in this case twelve pictures—and you pointed and shot while trying to hold the camera steady. You hoped for the best, but you never knew how it would turn out. You had to bring the film to the store to be developed. Sometimes you waited a week for it. Most of the photos came out poorly and you never knew why. In the twelve shots I took that afternoon only one was worth saving—apparently for a lifetime—and there it was on my computer screen.

Could that moment have seemed like the highlight of his life almost fifty years later? Or was it simply a trip down memory lane for Michael and his Facebook friends . . . of which there were not many.

Of course, I didn't have many either, not like my kids and some of the other classmates I'd befriended.

I would have thought I'd have been the one to keep the photo, the loving girlfriend, so I could stare at it over the next year while he was up at college and I was stuck back in high school finishing my senior year, although I had plenty of other pictures of Michael to keep me warm. I would have bet it was in the shoebox where I had put some of my Michael memories after we broke up, when my mother insisted I clean up my room.

"Get rid of the old memories," she said, "so you can make room for the new ones."

I threw a lot of the things he gave me away, the ones I couldn't went into the shoebox.

I kept it under my bed for a while and then it disappeared after I graduated and moved into my first apartment. No doubt my mother was eager to hide it away in the attic. I didn't mind when I noticed it was no longer under my bed. I had let go of fairy tales by then . . . certainly when it came to love.

I was pretty sure my mother must have given me the shoebox after I married Earl and we moved into our first house. She made me take everything that belonged to me . . . old clothes, school notebooks, stuffed animals, shoes . . . as if she was planning to take in boarders and needed the space. Looking back on it, I realize it was part of her plan to simplify her life, to get rid of the things she didn't need so she and my father could downsize, sell their house and move down to Florida.

I remembered putting some photos into the shoebox from Michael's baseball games and our homecoming dances. I remembered a couple from his prom as well. I went to his, but not to mine because he was stuck in college writing final papers—at least that's what he told me—and I wouldn't go without him.

Michael liked photos of the two of us in bathing suits—there were a lot of those—and I'm sure a few of those wound up in the shoebox. I'd started a chain of bubblegum wrappers after we began dating. I wanted to make it as tall as he was, but I stopped after about three feet. I don't remember why, probably because I didn't chew enough gum. In high school my mother stopped buying it for me since she thought gum chewing was unladylike. I'm pretty sure I didn't throw that away.

I know I put his senior baseball letter in the shoebox, the one he gave me the summer before he left for college, along with some of his love notes. I'd have needed a banker's box if I wanted to keep them all.

Earl helped me look in our attic, but we couldn't find it. I wouldn't put it past my mother to have thrown it out. After Michael dumped me, particularly the way he dumped me, she refused to mention his name and would immediately change the subject if I did.

I thought about Michael's Facebook photo—and the day it was taken—later that night in bed because I was being kept awake by Earl's snoring. He wouldn't stop no matter how many times I poked him. His soulful breathing, as he liked to call it when he wasn't denying he snored, got worse when his allergies were acting up. Sometimes they'd get so bad I'd have to go sleep on the den couch. I didn't bother moving on this night because I wasn't very tired anyway. I had too much on my mind.

After a while it came back to me. I didn't keep the photo. Michael liked it so much I gave it to him in a frame I'd bought for 99 cents at E. J. Korvettes, the biggest store in the county back then, a store that sold everything. He'd kept it all these years. I'm sure it was for himself, not because of me, although a tiny part of me hoped I might have been part of the reason.

Any spurned lover, whether first or further down the line,

wants at least one heart string of regret to quiver from time to time, even if your own feelings have been completely obliterated by distance and time. Still, I had no doubt he'd saved it for himself because it was something his wife and kids would have liked to see to appreciate just how special he was back then . . . so special even the sunlight offered up its admiration.

It was the best game of his career and his last in high school. He didn't play freshman year in college. He said he was too busy, although he told me he did join the dorm league and they took it very seriously. I don't know what he did after that. Maybe as he got older and settled into his job and family routines, he joined a men's league where he crushed the softball over the fence and became a star again.

After a while I did get up and go into my writing room to look at the photo again. He was so damn handsome back then . . . even to a 66-year old matron. I felt as if Facebook had accomplished what nothing else had been able to do . . . turn me back for a few moments into my 17-year old self.

Michael had a lot of dreams. He talked about playing first base for the New York Yankees and joining a rock band. He talked about traveling out to Hollywood after college and working in the movies. He figured he'd start off as an actor, but only for a few years because what he really wanted to do was write and direct. We all had dreams back then. I wanted to be an English professor at some New England college writing novels in my spare time.

Everything seemed possible, nothing appeared out of reach or too far-fetched, not back then. Dreaming big was part of the fun of being a teenager.

His fairy tales were always bigger than mine. They took him out into the world to exotic places like California and Europe. I'd watched a lot of sitcoms when I was younger and would have to admit I'd been seduced a bit by their typical female prospective of marriage, kids and a big house on a tree lined street in the suburbs. I wouldn't have even minded if it was in the same town where we'd grown up. There were some good colleges nearby and I could teach and write anywhere.

After graduating college I still thought teaching would be the answer, public school instead of college, but teaching jobs were scarce and I wound up writing for the local newspaper. Once I started down that path it was easy to keep following it.

Michael's Facebook page was typical I suppose of most, certainly the ones I'd looked at from my other school classmates. His profile listed the music he liked—Dylan, Blood Sweat and Tears, Van Morrison, The Moody Blues and Jefferson Airplane. I liked them as well back then. We both liked Buffalo Springfield and The Blues Project, which few of our classmates did. Of course, we were big fans of The Beach Boys and the Beatles like everyone else.

It surprised me that all the music he listed was from our high school and college years. I couldn't imagine his musical tastes hadn't changed over the years . . . like mine . . . to include jazz, bluesy torch singers and classical music.

Michael's profile said he liked red wine, eating out at fine restaurants and travel. Who didn't? Although I'd lost the itch to travel except between our condominium in Florida and our home in New Jersey. Seeing my children and grandchildren were all the sights I needed these days. I could eat ethnic food anywhere, even in Florida, and travel the world in the movies.

Somewhere along the line, I can't say exactly when, I morphed into a homebody. I suppose Earl had an influence on that. Golfers tend to be content with weekends on the links and vacations filled with 36 holes. A good golf course was about all he wanted out of a trip now . . . and the kids, he also needed the kids.

Michael said he was a big fan of the New York Yankees—that hadn't changed— but he also wrote that he liked poetry and independent art films. He listed his favorite author as Richard Yates. I hadn't read much poetry, not since college when I'd kept a copy of *Sonnets from the Portuguese* by my bed senior year. Most of the coeds back then were fans of Elizabeth Barrett Browning, her life as well as her art. I liked poetry, but poetry required time and the inclination to spend hours meditating over words and phrases, which I never seemed to have. Other than the poems I'd find in New York Magazine, I hadn't read any poetry in years.

I knew who Richard Yates was, they'd recently made a movie from one of his books, but I hadn't read anything he'd written. I found the movie depressing, but only because I crave comedies and happy endings when Earl and I go out. If I'm going to suspend my reality for a couple of hours I want to feel good at the end. Those kind of movies make it easier to fall asleep, which hasn't come all that quickly since I qualified for Medicare.

I made a note to buy one of Yates' books thinking it might offer some insight into the adult Michael.

His most recent postings were of a trip to Europe. It looked like a grand tour . . . London, Paris, Madrid and Rome. Clearly, he had money. The hotels all looked luxurious and the restaurants Michelin rated. While most of the photos were of landmarks and buildings—Michael had an interest in architecture in high school—there was one of a very serious blond with the body of thirty-five or forty-year old. I couldn't tell how old she was by her face since surgery and Botox can disguise the years, but not a body like that. A body liked that had to belong to a woman twenty-plus years our junior.

She certainly wasn't looking at him like his daughter.

She didn't have on a wedding ring. Perhaps Michael was one of those hedge fund gods who already had two or three wives and a half dozen children and had finally decided to get off the marriage merry-go-round, sticking to shooting-star romances with younger woman. A lot of younger woman are easily intoxicated with a life like that . . . five star restaurants, first class plane trips to exotic locales and front row seats at the theater.

I was never one of them, not even in my twenties.

Michael certainly wasn't like that in high school. He wasn't the least bit pretentious, not that he had a lot of money growing up. His father didn't believe in credit cards and they lived on a strict budget. He usually had a part time job during the school year and worked every summer. He was the kind of guy who was happy with pizza and a milk shake, roasting hot dogs over a campfire . . . provided we shared a sleeping bag afterward . . . and parking on Tweed Boulevard to make out under the stars.

You crave more creature comforts when you reach our age and if you have the money why not eat out and travel in style?

What if he'd never married? What if Michael couldn't find the right girl after me? Perhaps he sampled all kinds of women after we broke up and by the time he came to the conclusion I was the best fit it was too late, I was already married. Unlikely . . . he was too good looking, too likeable and too full of positive energy for that. There were plenty of girls in college—and after—who were far pretty then me, much funnier, more athletic and just as eager to fall in love.

Still, I wondered if he had any regrets. Particularly the way he dumped me. I deserved better after the four years we'd spent together, at least that was my feeling back then. Of course, it doesn't matter now.

I had a lot of self-doubt for a long time after the break-up, about myself as a person, as a girlfriend and in terms of my romantic future. Was there something wrong with me, I wondered, I couldn't see? Did I not do something I should have? I didn't have an older sister and love was not a subject my mother was comfortable talking about. I had no experience sending older boyfriends off to college, but it was certainly not like what I'd seen on TV and in the movies where the young girls sent their first loves off to war and they either returned or died. They never came back in love with someone else.

Was I doomed to be abandoned—lover by lover—and tormented by the better girls I imagined Michael and my post-Michael boyfriends sleeping with? Self-doubt coupled with regret is a recipe for disaster—at least depression—and I spent most of my free time the summer after the break-up in the basement watching soap operas and dramas so I could see at least one other woman's heart break every day.

I had let go of a lot of that heartache by the time I finished my first year of college . . . the rest of it by the end of sophomore year. Majoring in English and studying twentieth century novelists made it clear that love was everywhere and it always ended eventually, one way or another. And it always came with both pleasure and pain . . . the pain being something we all had to become familiar with because aside from its inevitability it made us, as well as love, better and stronger in the long run.

I couldn't be more content with Earl, the kids, the grandchildren and the life we made for ourselves. So why, you might be asking, was I up late thinking about Michael? Because being curious and letting your imagination run free is not the same as wishful thinking . . . or even obsessive nostalgia . . . not for a writer. It's part of the creative mindset, the endless turning over of imaginary stones in the search for inspiration and perspective.

It may seem like the same stories are being told over and over again, especially when it comes to love, but they always feel a little different when they're seen through another pair of eyes, and all eyes are different, even your own fifty years later.

I felt a story here somewhere and an article was taking shape in my mind, something I might be able to sell to a national magazine, one popular among the Baby Boomers, or perhaps turn into a book. It just needed time, as Earl like to describe my creative process, to percolate . . . the way the old coffee makers used to.

I watched Michael on Facebook and wondered if his postings were completely honest. How could anyone eat out that often and travel that much? Did he really like his life as much as he seemed to or was it a kind of branding . . . a show people seemed to put on for their Facebook friends to create the image they wanted the world to see?

What was his life really like? Had it followed a course similar to mine? Or had he reached that higher level of accomplishment foretold in our high school yearbook? What AARP member wouldn't be interested in reading a story like that—in generic terms—so they could imagine for themselves how time has treated their first love . . . the teenager they once considered their destiny?

I felt as if Facebook had opened some kind of tear in the fabric of space and time offering me an opportunity to write something that was more interesting and significant than my last two pieces, one on celebrity neighbors who had also retired to Florida, and the other on popular and affordable vacation spots for senior citizens.

What if Michael's life was really a disaster, nothing like it appeared on Facebook? What if he never married? Not all lives are about marriage and family. Not all lives are about love. Anyone who has read a lot of fiction knows that. Maybe Michael decided to devote himself to his job. You can love your work. For some people, a successful career can be enough.

Did he ever think of me and what might have been? I certainly hadn't, not in a very long time, not since college really. Perhaps a few times afterward when a hopeful relationship didn't work out. But I couldn't help it now. A writer's imagination, particularly a semi-retired one who spends two or three afternoons a week sitting around the pool listening to her contemporaries talk about their sleeping and bowel habits, can grow feverish at the thought of something new and different like this.

As far as I could tell from his Facebook page, Michael no longer worked—at least he didn't post about it—which confirmed to me he must have made millions, probably as a banker or stockbroker because I did hear some gossip from someone a long time ago about him going for his MBA. He was a hard worker, there's no doubt about that, and he had the charm necessary to attract clients with money. He was used to success, he expected it. It was attracted to him like bees to a flower.

As an amateur gardener I'm fond of bees and pollination analogies.

I can tell you from this far side of sixty that the 1970's and 1980's were wild decades. If you put your nose to the grindstone you could find yourself on the right side of history . . . financial history. By the time he looked up, ready to enjoy some of that success with the family promised to everyone on the TV shows we watched growing up, twenty years could have passed—almost without Michael realizing it—and he found it easier to go from one comely thirty-five year old to another.

Hence the photo on his Facebook page.

Time is as relentless as it silent and invisible. It will sneak up on you, particularly if you have the roar of the stock exchange floor in your ears and carry the burden of managing a growing weight of assets. Back then time seemed unimportant, almost irrelevant, a limitless resource like air and water. It's only when you reach the back end of middle age that time drops its pretense and turns loud, visible . . . and miserly.

The woman in the Facebook photo, the one from the tour of Europe was named Kim, and I had to wonder how Michael found the energy to keep up with her. Earl barely made it to 9:30 most nights. The golf catches up to him and watching television has always been his narcotic, even on days he doesn't play. No doubt Michael was in better shape. He was always the athlete back in high school and probably played tennis on a regular basis, perhaps even first base in one of those over sixty leagues.

Michael was not the kind of teenager to sit still or walk when he could run. Keeping up with him always took effort on my part.

Still, it was hard for me to imagine Michael never marrying. He was so attentive and loving in high school, so kind and considerate. He loved children, although we were barely more than children ourselves. He worked two summers at a camp, the first as a counselor and the second helping to run the sports programs. The neighborhood kids idolized him. He gave them baseballs to play with and sometimes spent time teaching them to throw and swing a bat.

I always thought he'd make a great father and there was no one I wanted more for my children.

The older Michael, this Facebook Michael, also liked to post photos of martinis and open bottles of expensive French wine sitting on tables with fancy linen, along with photos of landmarks from famous world cities, oceans and sunsets. There were photos of the Eiffel Tower, the Colosseum in Rome, the Sears Tower, the St. Louis Arch and the Grand Canyon. He didn't appear in any of the photos, nor did anyone else. They could easily have been stock photos he found in a book or on the internet. Actually, the same thing could be said for a lot of postings I saw from a lot of Facebook members.

One thing was clear, Michael had a life that was much more peripatetic and exciting than mine, which he did in high school as well. He was always on a bus somewhere to play another team. Once he even played in Yankee Stadium and another time the team spent a week in the spring playing in North Carolina. Or he was busy with deadlines for the yearbook and the school newspaper.

He didn't like to sit around his house, he said that to me on more than one occasion.

Michael was a joiner and a doer. The opposite of me. I never joined a sports team or a club, although I did write for the school paper and the yearbook, but only to be with Michael. That's the way a girlfriend was back then, especially one who starts as a freshman before she has had enough time to establish a real identity of her own.

I'd never be like that now, not if I had it to do all over again. Don't get me wrong, Michael would still become my high school sweetheart, but I would have done more things without him, dated some before pledging my loyalty . . . and I would have made more friends. I'd have been more active in my class, as opposed to being a hanger on to Michael's class and his friends. I would have certainly dated after he left for college so I could have had someone to take me to my prom.

There were a few more photos of Kim that went back six months. She was alone in all the photos, as was Ellen who came before her. She looked about the same age as Kim, but she was even more beautiful. There was a photo of Ellen behind a glass of wine sitting in front of a large fireplace that looked as if it had been taken at a ski lodge, a photo of Ellen—again wine in hand—gazing up at the night sky, and another of her sitting on the beach in a bikini sipping a big drink with an umbrella and a neon straw looking out at a Caribbean sunset. She looked well cared for and happy, although she disappeared as well when I went back another six months.

Maybe that was the shelf life of his relationships now . . . perhaps that goes back to college. I wouldn't know. Could I have been the longest relationship Michael's ever had? It was hard for me to imagine, but there are people who live like that.

Could Michael have changed that much? Stasis and change are the two constants in life, although in my opinion your basic personality remains pretty much the same from beginning to end. The people I didn't like 40 years ago I still don't like. There is no way the Michael I knew—or at least thought I knew—could have changed that much.

There were photos of martinis and wine glasses that pre-dated Ellen, as well as photos of beaches and foreign countries, although there were no other women in any of those postings. Michael had joined Facebook two years earlier and as far as I could tell he didn't travel or eat out with anyone special the entire first year. At least not anyone he wanted to post about.

I scoured all his Facebook postings and photos for a single picture of him now, but I couldn't find one. He was still the high school baseball player as far as the Facebook world was concerned. I wonder if it meant he hadn't aged well, although I could understood how he might feel. I haven't seen a photo of myself I liked in the last fifteen years. Our rooms were filled with photos of me and Earl with the grandchildren and I always look at them fondly as I walk by, but I always try to focus on Earl and the kids. I find it hard sometimes to look too closely at myself.

No one ages well in their own mind. The bathroom mirror decries any thoughts you might have to the contrary.

What you have to realize as you approach 70—if you want to be happy or at least not too unhappy—is it doesn't matter. Who cares what you look like? The only thing that really matters is how you feel. You can't control how you look, not unless you don't mind looking as if you've been surgically transformed into something you're not, something much less flexible and natural. I haven't seen a face job yet that didn't take more away than just the wrinkles and I've seen my share.

Still, I would have liked to see a photo of Michael the way he looked now with the truth of the years written on his face . . . a truth impossible to hide at our age . . . so I could move on from that happy-go-lucky 18-year old first baseman stuck in my head who I pictured traveling the world, drinking expensive wine, eating at fine restaurants and enjoying the fruits of a very successful career. I wanted to see a face similar to the weary yet contented one I saw every morning in the mirror.

Facebook can engender jealousy and dissatisfaction. I've read enough magazine articles to know that and even though I wasn't the jealous or dissatisfied type, I couldn't help thinking how nice it would be if Earl and I didn't have to worry about money and could eat out at the finest restaurants in Miami and New Jersey whenever we wanted, perhaps travel from time to time to some of the world's great cities—staying at luxurious hotels and never having to measure the cost in advance in terms of our health, life expectancy and retirement savings.

I looked again through Michael's old postings and photos, this time searching for someone his own age, an ex-wife who I was half-hoping would look a little like me. I looked for photos of children. It wasn't unusual for men back then to wait a bit longer before jumping into family life. Women like me, on the other hand, brainwashed by years of *Father Knows Best* and *The Donna Reed Show* tended to leap much quicker. None of us wanted to be eternal bridesmaids.

Of course, Facebook is not a confessional. No one has to come clean or be honest. No one is asking for forgiveness or swearing under penalty of perjury to tell the truth. Members control their own feed and decide how they should appear. Watchers like me have to fill in the blanks with our imagination, intuition and a healthy dose of skepticism.

I've always had a pretty good intuition. A writer, even a magazine writer, develops a sixth sense about what really lies below the surface of things and hides behind colorful words. Unfortunately, nothing felt clear in terms of Michael.

The gap between high school and now—48 years—felt like a complete blank.

Apparently, intuition doesn't work very well over the internet. I was betting Michael had found a beautiful wife after he got his MBA. Tall, thin and self-assured. Perhaps someone at his first job. A graduate of Smith College from a rich old American family that had come over on the Mayflower. They'd gotten married—an enormous wedding at the club—and had two beautiful children, a boy and a girl.

The perfect family, although perhaps the marriage was less than perfect, which is why there isn't any mention of her on Facebook. Indeed, Michael left his status blank as if it no longer mattered. He would never be lacking in companionship since as a man—a rich man—he could date any age woman he wanted. It gave him a pool of at least forty years, twenty years in either direction.

But what about his kids? Wouldn't he post something about them? Just a word now and then. A photo from China where his son is running the office of a large American corporation. A shout out about the new major motion picture his daughter directed and co-wrote.

Of course, some people like to keep family matters out of prying eyes . . . like me. Those people he wants to know will find out in more direct and personal ways.

Being a writer means you spend a certain amount of time—an inordinate amount of time really—wandering around inside your own imagination, particularly late at night as you lay there unable to sleep. Earl called them my flights of fancy, my what-ifs, and he laughed whenever I brought them up. What if I'd gone into teaching, instead of journalism? What if I'd gotten that high school English position I wanted? What if I had decided not to go to the party where we met?

One night as I lay there being serenading by Earl's deep sleep chorus, I played out some of those what if's . . . not wishful thinking mind you . . . just some fanciful parallel journeys. What if Earl died on the golf course? He's always telling me about some club member who keeled over after lugging his bag of clubs up the stairs to the bar.

What would I do?

I'd spend more time up north with the kids for sure. I wouldn't want another relationship, I certainly wouldn't be looking for another man. Woman friends, kids and grandchildren would be more than enough.

But what if one day I'm working in the city on an article about restaurants favored by the more mature residents of the Big Apple when he walks in? The hostess rushes up to greet him because Michael is a regular and he's stopping by for a quick lunch between appointments. He doesn't work any longer, he just consults. The firm won't let him quit. He's too valuable to let go.

We'll have lunch together and end our lives—our couples lives—the way we started it, telling each other the stories we missed over the last fifty years and laughing as we attend each of our 50th high school reunions.

His 50th was actually coming up in about six months. I knew more people in his class, the class of 68, than I did in mine.

It's not what I wanted or who I wanted, I wanted to grow old with Earl. He'll stop playing golf at some point and we can walk together on the beach holding hands and talking about how old the grandchildren are getting. I just can't help imagining the possibilities . . . the writing possibilities. That's what I do. That's the way my brain is wired. I've been doing it for forty years . . . probably longer than that.

After Michael's kids leave the nest and have their own families, his wife—Lauren in my little insomniac's story—will want to move down to Palm Beach to join some of their friends, but Michael isn't ready for that. He's too full of energy to sit around drinking all afternoon and wolfing down tiny crust-less sandwiches. I have no doubt he hated golf as well. He'd find it too slow and time consuming. It didn't offer the chess-like strategy of a game of baseball. One man against a tiny ball is not the same thing. It more muscle memory than anything else. He'll be great at it for sure, but he won't like it.

They'll get divorced. It'll all be friendly. Michael is too wise, too well-grounded and too kind for anything other than a soft landing.

But if that's the case where are the Facebook photos of his kids and grandchildren? Could they have resented him for refusing to move to Florida and kept their distance? More likely they've got the typical wealthy family concerns about privacy. They have stayed off Facebook and asked him not to post any photos.

I would never consider posting photos of my grandchildren. You put things out on the internet and who knows where they wind up. Photos of wine and the Eiffel Tower are a dime a dozen, one of Earl's favorite sayings lately. As he's gotten older, he's been speaking more and more in clichés. They always make me laugh, which is why he probably keeps adding to his repertoire.

Michael will feel awful about the divorce, but a marriage lasting as long as theirs isn't a failure, not in his opinion and not in mine. Sometimes love just runs its course . . . like ours did after his first year of college. What would be the point of Michael posting about that? Not in his present life and not for his current friends.

I always tell Earl what I am working on and thinking about. This one was no different. He's a great sounding board and has this ability to see things from a distance—to take in the whole picture. He can often find those connecting threads I sometimes miss. Everyone needs a second pair of eyes from time to time, particularly eyes that know you well.

I was sure there was be an interesting article here somewhere, one I could sell to a better magazine. You know, the 70-something adult discovering her first love on Facebook—after 50 years of silence—and painting a picture of their parallel lives, the expectations and surprises . . . the up and downs . . . that sort of thing.

I could do it anonymously, based largely on truth, but without using any actual names or places. Although the editor would probably want us to meet at the end . . . a sort of epilogue to close the story. That I could make up.

Earl thought it was a wonderful idea and he meant it. Earl was born without a jealousy gene. It's been like that since the day we met.

"What about adding other classmates to the story as well?" Earl suggested. "With his fiftieth reunion coming up and all this news about misleading Facebook postings wouldn't it be interesting to expand it to his entire class. You know, what people post and how it compares to their actual lives?"

"I could make a lot of enemies," I said and Earl laughed.

"You're the investigative reporter, doesn't it come with the territory."

"Maybe I could expand it," I said, "but it'll have to come naturally. Right now I want to start off small . . . with the old boyfriend. We all had one more or less."

I was afraid if I tried to do too much I'd become overwhelmed and never finish. It would become too jumbled—too noisy—and I wouldn't be able to hold the reader or interest any editor. Keep it simple and keep the theme clear. It's something I learned early in my career after I stopped covering zoning and school board meetings for the local paper and graduated to writing longer and puffier pieces for magazines most women read while waiting for their hair to be done, their teeth to be cleaned or their bowels to move.

"I'm sure you're right," Earl said. "It'll be more manageable than a class tell all . . . and who doesn't wonder about their high school sweetheart?"

We both laughed at that.

I told Earl I wished Michael would post more things, real things, not just restaurants and travels. His life would be easier to construct that way.

"If I want to find out about his real life . . . understand how he got where he is . . . find the parallels to mine . . . and our classmates, I'll have to contact him at some point and arrange an interview."

"I'd like to be a fly on the wall for that one," Earl said.

"But I'm not sure I really want to do that. After all these years I think I'd prefer to keep the silence between us undisturbed. I think more readers will be able to identify with it if I keep a distant perspective. Perhaps a story assembled solely from the Ethernet."

"Filled with truths and half-truths?"

"Isn't that the way people learn things these days. I'm not sure the truth is what it was when we were young. It's more a moving target."

"Interesting," Earl said.

Obviously, the idea was still in its formative stage. I didn't have a handle on it yet or even a solid theme. I just had this feeling there was something of interest there to people my age, not just to me.

Earl sat there rubbing his chin. It was his problem solving gesture. I'd seen it a thousand times back when he was working from home on one of his engineering problems. I waited for him to finish thinking it through.

"What if you make it partly a work of fiction," he said, dropping his hand down to his lap, "do some research, use real details where you can, but imagine the parts where you can't. Give it some of that dramatic license. You've always talked about writing a novel or a short story. Aren't there magazines that publish that kind of thing? Stories that could be real, but come from your imagination."

"Absolutely."

It was a great idea. I wished I had come up with it myself. I'd been writing newsy articles for so long that the idea of taking artistic license hadn't dawned on me. Michael didn't have to be completely real in my story. Fiction could be as compelling as reality. I could start with real facts, find out as much about Michael as I could, but where I had to—or wanted to—I could construct a life over 50 years based on what our generation had lived through. In the end, it couldn't be all that different from mine and most everyone else's.

I could have them meet—fictionally, of course—and craft a story that engages and satisfies the curiosity of all those 66-year olds out there who wonder from time to time what happened to their first love. It wouldn't be for one of my regular magazines . . . they want tell all's . . . but it was the perfect opportunity to branch out to something new, something more literary.

I went over to Earl and gave him a kiss.

"Now I'm really excited," I said, walking out of the room and sitting back down at the computer.

I could imagine my main character—Michael—graduating college and going out west to try Hollywood. He talked a lot about it high school and he certainly had the look they liked. The square jaw and piercing blue eyes. The waves of sandy brown hair caressing his forehead. He was six feet tall without an ounce of fat. Perhaps he had a few walk on roles I'd missed, roles he hated, like one of the surfers on the beach or an evil gang member. Perhaps Michael's enthusiasm and energy didn't translate well in the small parts he was getting.

It would be hard for him to find the kind of anger, fear and sadness that was popular in movies during the middle and late seventies.

Los Angeles had to be very expensive.

I imagined Michael needing to find something a bit more remunerative to support himself while he tried to make it. Perhaps a waiter or working as an office temp. I knew a lot of women who did that. Or maybe he changed his mind and pursued one of his other dreams. He was a good first baseman at a small high school in a suburban community, but that didn't mean he could play professionally. I know that now, back then I believed first base on the Yankees was his for the asking.

Perhaps he could have made it as a ballplayer, but didn't have the patience to endure the hungry years struggling in the minor leagues. Michael was never all the patient. He never had to be. Everything came quickly and easily to him. Who had patience in high school anyway? It's not an attribute common to most teenagers.

As an adult, I realized a long time ago that a small talent can feel more like a curse out in the real world.

My Michael would have decided to get his MBA after a few lean years in LA. There was nothing wrong with an MBA, everyone was getting them back then. The stock market was booming and even when it took its occasional fall it always bounced back.

Michael probably decided to move back East because it's where he felt most at home. Did he wonder about me when he returned? Had he heard that I'd met and married Earl a couple of years after college. I'm sure someone from the baseball team must have told him.

News like that travels fast in the suburbs.

Would I have considered going back with Michael if it was before I met Earl? Maybe . . . I don't know, we'd both changed, although certainly not if I'd already started dating Earl. Not after we'd gotten serious . . . and it didn't take long for that.

I wouldn't say Earl swept me off my feet, but I liked him immediately. He was low key and confident, not drop-dead handsome, but nice to look at. He seemed a little too serious, although he had a subtle sense of humor, and while he wasn't one for belly laughs he liked to smile and had a nice chuckle. He was as loyal as a puppy and I made him happy. I didn't have to be very intuitive to see that. He wore it on his face, I suppose, the way I once did in high school.

Loyalty is important . . . as important as love.

More importantly, he made me feel good—very good— about myself, about my dreams and about my life.

The guys I met in college didn't stick the first couple of years because I kept measuring them to Michael. After that they didn't stick because they were too full of themselves, too mannish in the sense that they wanted their women to be accessories . . . supportive, not successes on their own, but housewives. It may have been subconscious, I grant you that, but it was there . . . like any other form of subtle discrimination.

By the time I graduated college I wanted to be taken seriously, an equal to any man. I wanted a man who would go beyond the right words and actually believe it. I also knew by then what high school sweethearts were all about and where they belonged. They were a rite of passage, an introductory course in love . . . an out of control—and immature—chemical and emotional reaction. Certainly, in most cases. Certainly, in my case.

Earl was the kind of guy who saw me as a partner—an equal partner—with my success as important as his. He was the kind of guy who would stick and if it wasn't to me he'd find someone soon enough so when he asked I said yes . . . gladly. Did I think a moment about Michael? Did I wonder where he was and what he was doing? I don't recall. Perhaps for a brief instant. After all, I was in my early twenties, not far removed from those teen years. Isn't it basic human nature to look back at the recent past . . . or the distant past . . . wondering how you got here from there and thinking about the what-ifs?

Who didn't question every fork in the road back then?

I was much wiser in the ways of love and knew better than to let any high school memory get in the way. I married Earl with all my heart and never looked back. I can say that with absolute certainty.

Although now . . . fifty years later . . . Facebook makes looking back way to easy, like a new rite of passage from middle to old age.

After the Michael in my story gets his MBA, I pictured him joining a big brokerage house. Perhaps a researcher at first, but quickly moving up to analyst and then broker. He probably came close a couple of times to popping the question. But he was having way too much fun making people—and himself—rich, receiving the firm's accolades and partying with all the beautiful, single women who wouldn't take no for an answer.

Michael always did like to keep busy and have fun.

The women would all be his age for a while, but as the years passed he'd get older and they wouldn't. The ones he knew kept drifting off—marrying or moving away, keenly aware of their biological clock, burning out and returning to their hometowns—replaced by identical, but younger ones. Before Michael realized it fifteen or twenty years had passed.

That would be the never-married Michael in my imagination, the rich man about town, the heart throb of dozens of hungry, aging women, some similarly devoted to their jobs, others divorced. That Michael was more consistent with his Facebook postings . . . or lack of postings . . . although I still found this kind of life hard to believe.

Even if you're writing fiction, it helps if you can believe it.

After a couple of weeks I was getting nowhere and about ready to give up. I'd been writing non-fiction articles exclusively for so long I feared my fictional muscles had atrophied and no longer had the strength to carry a story. I thought about giving up and calling my agent to pitch an article more like all the others I'd written over the past thirty years. Perhaps expanding on an earlier article I'd done for Florida Living, this time focusing on the rock musicians who had turned into snowbirds. Everybody likes reading about their rich and famous neighbors.

I was just about to quit and save what I'd done on the computer. I even opened up my file of abandoned ideas to move it in there. It wouldn't be the first idea I was excited about for a month or two that ultimately went nowhere. It's hard to maintain the kind of enthusiasm you need when the words don't come and the idea refused to grow.

I sat there staring at the computer wondering if Michael had ever thought about me. Over the years there have always been moments when he'd come back—when our song, *Ain't No Mountain High Enough*, came on the radio, when there was a strong scent of ozone in the air after a thunderstorm, or during the first bite of a hot dog at a ballgame. There was an instant sometimes—a brief instant—when I could almost feel his hand slip into mine.

I wondered if Michael had ever searched for me on Facebook, unwilling to friend me for the same reasons I was unwilling to friend him, not wanting to disturb the 18-year old Azu who lived unchanged in his imagination. He wouldn't have learned much about me if he had tried. My daughter had helped me set up my privacy settings so no one would be able to see my profile or anything I posted—if I ever decided to post—unless they first asked to be my friend and I agreed.

Before I moved what I'd done so far into my abandoned idea folder, where nothing ever reemerged, I decided to check Michael's Facebook page one last time. I hadn't looked at it in weeks and it sort of felt like the best way to say goodbye. I couldn't find it, his Facebook page had disappeared. I didn't know people could do that, but my daughter said some people "unjoin" or change their settings, finding a level of privacy so deep they can only be found by a few specifically identified friends.

Why would anyone my age suddenly decide to do that? Few of us are that computer savvy.

Why would my fictional Michael want to make a change like that after two years?

My daughter had no idea, but she suggested I try some another site like LinkedIn and do a google search.

Ten minutes later I'd found Michael's obituary and had to pour myself a glass of scotch. Unfortunately, Earl was out on the golf course.

Michael had died two weeks earlier. It gave no reason... no lingering illness, no accident, certainly not old age, not yet anyway, which in the newspaper and magazine business usually means suicide. I didn't see how that could be possible. The Michael I knew wouldn't harm a fly and I mean that literally. He once spent a half hour chasing one out of the car rather than squashing it against the window.

How could someone like that commit the ultimate sin?

Sure, forty-eight years is a long time to hold onto the same principles. Political positions change as we get older, why not philosophies of life... and death. A 66-year old man is not nearly the same as his 18-year old self when it comes to something like that. What if he had some terminal illness? Sitting there thinking about the inevitable and feeling the pain your body—and the doctors—are putting you through might be enough to encourage anyone to want to speed things along. Me, I think I'd want to fight until my last breath, but it is one thing to say it... it's quite another to live it.

What if Michael didn't have anyone he didn't want to take leave of? What if all he had was the pain and a certain death sentence?

The obituary said that Michael was working at Morgan Stanley where he was a Senior Vice-President in charge of the Compliance

Department. It was a short obituary, but the last two lines nearly stopped my heart. It said that his wife had died after a short illness 30 years earlier and his son, for whom they had a name, Doug, had also "predeceased" him, a word that sounded incredibly cold for such a traumatic event.

Michael was survived by nobody according to the obituary . . . nobody except his mother. She had to be in her late nineties by now. She was still the 60's housewife in my mind, perhaps not the typical one standing by the stove in an apron or in front of the hall mirror fluffing up her hair, but a charter member of the club nonetheless.

Clearly, I had misjudged Michael's life. His Facebook world wasn't real . . . or if it was real it was only skin deep. Food, drink and travel posted for the world to see, concealing the true pain inside his heart.

I told Earl what had happened as soon as he walked through the door and the different story I now had in mind to write, an investigative story about how a life can start on a pedestal and wind up a suicide. I envisioned a story about the fickleness of luck and the erosion of time.

Earl thought it was would be a very interesting article, although much more difficult emotionally for me to write. Still, he undoubtedly saw the determination in my eyes and encouraged me to get started. Two days later I was in a hotel in New York City. My kids didn't even know I was back in town. I didn't want any distractions.

CHAPTER TWO – FACEBOOK LIES

I knew where to start because the obit told me. Michael's mother was still alive and it didn't take a great sleuth to discover she was living in the same house where Michael grew up. I hoped she would be willing to talk with me. This couldn't be a good time for her. No mother wants to go after her son, particularly if he did take his own life.

Having buried her grandson and daughter-in-law made it even worse.

She'd been alone for a long time. Michael's father had died in high school. She had to be incredibly resilient to have made it this far, although my memory of her back in high school didn't reinforce that. She had no friends I could recall. No strong outside relationships to help sustain her after her husband died. There were no canasta games, no lunch engagements and the phone hardly every rang. She never came out to watch any of Michael's games. In fact, she rarely left the house except for occasional nights out with Michael's father, usually business related, and weekends away when he dragged her to one of his conferences.

I didn't want to upset her any more than she was already upset. How would she handle it if I brought her back to Michael's high school years . . . to his glory years . . . and asked her to take me down what I imagined to be a long slow descent into hell? Still, I had to try. Journalism tends to be a very selfish enterprise, people get trampled on all the time in the name of truth and understanding.

Driving up to the house was weird. The world had changed, I had changed, yet the house had not.

I hadn't been to Michael's house since my senior year in high school, not since Michael returned from his first year in college and dumped me. He was kind enough not to do it in his house with his mother in her bedroom or in my house. Instead, he took me to our favorite spot, a small playground beside the elementary school where we used to go on warm nights to sit on the swings and talk about our future before making out.

I had no idea he had anything else on his mind that night. For me it was like a long intermission—him having just returned from his first year of college, me having just graduated from my senior year without him—with the main feature about to start up again, starring me as a college freshman road tripping to her sophomore boyfriend's dorm and vice versa.

"Azu, there is something we need to talk about." He said it in a voice I hadn't heard him use before on our playground or anywhere else for that matter because it sounded so serious and mature, like he'd recently discovered he had a fatal illness or I did.

I was swinging gently on my favorite swing and he was sitting on the ground in front of me, his legs crossed, the way he always did. He was as flexible as the girls that way, able to sit in a lotus position for a long time without having to get up to shift around his stuff, as we used to call it back then.

Now I thought I knew what was coming because he'd been talking about studying in Florence, Italy the first half of his sophomore year. He had taken an art appreciation course as an elective and loved it. He thought art would be a good foundation for everything, whether it was working in the movies or writing. I'd been encouraging him to do it, but not until his junior year. I wanted us to spend most weekends the fall of my freshman year waking up together like husband and wife. I offered to go to Florence to study as well in the fall of my sophomore year, although I really didn't have much interest in Florence at the time.

I was just turning 18, what did I know.

I wasn't obtuse, I could tell by his tone and look that he had something sobering on his mind. I was expecting him to tell me he had no choice . . . Italy had to be this fall because there would be no program in Florence the following year. I'd have been disappointed and a disappointed high school girlfriend back then had no choice but to bawl and wield her love like a weapon.

Italy will be there in a couple of years or after graduation— that's what I was thinking of saying—but I'll only have one freshman year. How can you say you really love me if you leave me alone my first time away? I need you to help get me through it . . . blah, blah, blah. I'd insist he take me home. There would be no making out or any of the things that usually followed, although by the next day . . . or even by the end of the night . . . I'd probably be back in his arms pretending to understand.

I remember swinging higher and looking away from him—up at the sky—as if to say I know what you're about to say and I don't want to hear it. Tell me later in the summer, tell me when we're together in a sleeping bag camping under the stars, not your first week back from college . . . not the day after my high school graduation.

It was a beautiful night, I remember that, every star was out. When I was little I used to think the stars were angels looking out for us. I looked up at them now and somehow knew they'd get us through this and we'd be alright. He would only be gone for one term and we had the whole summer to look forward to. Maybe having no distractions the first term would help me get acclimatized, make me a more mature and better girlfriend . . . and eventually a wife.

"I don't know why Italy is so important," I said without waiting for him to bring it up first.

"I'm not talking about Italy," he said. "I've decided not to go."

"That's too bad," I responded, pretending to be a little sad for him, although he still looked serious and self-conscious, not a good look for Michael, and certainly not one I was accustomed to seeing. "Why not?"

"There's too much going on in school."

I nodded, stopped swinging and stared down at him. As I said, I can be very intuitive when I try, when I stay focused and manage to silence my interior monologue. Suddenly, I felt it. I felt it as surely as if I'd grabbed hold of a hot coal. I could see it in Michael's eyes. I could hear it in his breathing . . . the eagerness behind the gravity of his voice. He wanted to get this over with as soon as possible and run off.

"You met someone else," I said. It was more a statement than a question and I didn't say it quite that calmly . . . cried it out would be a better way to describe it.

He shook his head from side to side for a moment, but then

changed directions slowly nodding up and down. He apologized like it was something that couldn't be avoided, something I'd come to learn as well my freshman in college. As if falling in love with someone new, someone from a very different place was a rite of freshman passage, like a required course in expository writing . . . as inevitable as catching the first cold that goes around the dorm.

    He wouldn't tell me her name. All he would say was she came from the Midwest—a rich family—and lived in the same dorm. Her room was directly above his. They segregated the genders by dorms back then, although Michael's school was more progressive and did it by floor. He couldn't explain why it happened, although he did tell me how. She'd kept him up one night walking the floor and he went upstairs to ask her to stop. He wasn't looking for a new relationship, it found him.

    Michael didn't use the word love, I'm sure he thought he was being kind. He just implied the feeling . . . the attraction . . . said it's hard to resist when you're so compatible and living together in the same dorm, separated every night by a few yards of cinderblock and flooring.

    Our love, our high school love, couldn't overcome that kind of attraction—a kind of magnetic love in my imagination— when we were hundreds of miles apart.

    College was a fire extinguisher for boys like Michael, I remember writing in my journal that summer, a journal I started shortly after the breakup and stopped the first week of college, a journal that disappeared long ago. I kept imagining her as a sexy older woman, like the one in The Graduate. I suppose I should have called her the love extinguisher. Maybe I did, I don't remember.

    I do remember calling her a bitch that night on the swing, although I couldn't hear my own voice since my heart was beating so loudly in my ears.

    Michael said he was going back to college in a few days, even though classes were out for the summer. She was up there working on some science project . . . she wanted to be a doctor . . . and he had found a summer job painting the dorms. He said he'd make twice as much as he'd make at the camp if he stayed home. They would be living together off campus like some young married couple. He didn't say the last part, I did when he told me where he'd be living.

I had a few choice words for Michael as well.

I'll spare you the scene. We've all gone through it. Males find it easier to let go and move on at that age . . . at any age really. I think it's the maternal instinct that makes us latch on so tightly . . . to blankets and stuffed animals, to children and pets . . . to lovers and spouses. Sometimes it's about protecting the young. At other times it's about protecting love . . . as if love were a living, breathing thing . . . just another one of our offspring.

Men may see love as something interchangeable, a letterman's pin that can be moved from one girl's chest to another or a ring that can be made to fit any finger. Women put too much effort into it to be so caviler about it.

At least that was my 18-year old thinking back then.

During the ride back to my house, Michael talked while I didn't say a word. I was about all cried out. I just looked away, staring outside the side window numb to all the comforting and familiar things passing by.

We both need to use these college years to experience things, he explained, to sample the world out there and the people in it. To grow and mature. To make sure we know who we are and what we really want. Who knows, he said, we may find each other again on the other side . . . and when we do the bond will be stronger . . . unbreakable.

A college boy's line I'm sure because he said it without any real feeling, as if one of his college buddies had suggested it as an easy way to let me down.

I'm sure Miss Summer Camp would be the first of many. That's what I finally said to him when he stopped in front of my house and I opened my door, turning to look at him for the first time since we'd left the playground.

"What happened to yhr loyalty you always talk about," I said, "and the daisy love that could never die?"

"It didn't die, I still feel you in here," he said, touching his chest. "It will always be there to sustain us as we move through life . . . it'll be our foundation for whatever comes next."

I turned in disgust at that bit of logic and slammed the car door on my childish fairy tale.

No doubt he'd rehearsed that little speech as well with his hippie college coed.

College back then was like an all you can eat buffet. It was the era of free love, a misnomer if ever there was one since love—as opposed to one night stands—is never really free . . . certainly not free of pain and consequence. We had been together for three years, four if you count his first year of college when I thought he was still devoted to me and I was still devoted to him . . . even if it was *in abstentia*.

Why did it seem to hurt me so much more than it hurt him? Was it a gender thing or a maturity thing? Could one year in college make that much of a difference?

I must say I caught a glimpse of Michael's face before he drove off and he looked more relieved than hurt. I don't know what I looked like, but I was glad my parents were already in bed. I wouldn't have known what to say to them if they were sitting there in the den watching television and I certainly wouldn't have been able to look at them. They always expected me to stop before going up to my room to tell them where I'd been and what I'd been up to. Sometimes they'd get the truth and sometimes they wouldn't. Either way, I wouldn't have been able to speak if they'd asked because I felt as if my heart was being squeezed in a vice and was bulging right up into my throat.

It felt as if it would never have room again to beat freely.

I rang the bell. Michael's mother wasn't expecting me. I'd tried calling to ask if it would be alright for me to come over to speak with her, but all I got was an answering machine. I'd left a half dozen messages, but there was not one return call. Most people might consider that an answer, but reporters, even magazine writers, rarely do.

I heard footsteps coming slowly down the stairs and I stepped back to look around again at the outside of the house. It was a colonial, bigger than the split level I grew up in about a mile away. I'd driven by my old house on the way. It had been sold a number of times since my parents moved out—they both passed away from opportunistic illnesses shortly after moving to Florida, one tobacco related and the other the result of genetic roulette—and it looked completely different. All the landscaping had been pulled out and replaced. Some sort of powder blue siding had been put up and the original windows had been replaced by bigger ones.

It did nothing for me in terms of nostalgia. I suppose because it no longer looked like my old house and I'd left that house a long time ago on my own terms. I got to say goodbye and visit it a number of times before my parents sold it. I was actually there the day they moved out, both Earl and I having come to help.

I hadn't seen Michael's house since we'd made love inside his bedroom the day before he returned to college after Easter break. It looked exactly the way I remembered it, except for being tired and worn . . . aged like the rest of us. The lawn had died in spots, turning a dirty brown, and while some bushes were dead others were wild and overgrown. The house was the same color I remembered it, white with black trim, although the paint was cracked and peeling. Surely it had to have been painted more than once over the past 50 years, although it looked as if the last time might have been a decade or two earlier.

Michael's mother was a wreck after his father died. She stayed in her bedroom even more and when I did see her she looked lost, keeping to the center of whatever room she was in as if she was afraid to get too close to the windows and the world outside. Michael had to do all the shopping and prepare most of the meals. She eventually started doing things around the house again, although Michael still had to help her pay the bills and take care of anything that needed repair. He had to arrange for someone to come in to help her after he left for college.

I offered to stop by from time to time, but he didn't think it would be a good idea.

Not only did the outside look the same, the inside did as well. It felt as if I'd stepped back into my 16-year old self and was coming over to call for Michael. The table by the door with the keys and the mail was still there, except it was covered now with old magazines. There was the same impressionist painting above it of some French street back in the nineteenth century. Michael's father had received it in payment for some work. The same snack table stood in front of the couch across from the TV, a remote on top of it instead of the TV Guide.

I could see the hallway ahead to my left that led to the basement door. I'd lost my virginity in that basement with Michael's mother upstairs. To the right were the stairs to the bedrooms. I'd spent my first overnight with a male in Michael's bedroom when his father dragged his mother . . . kicking and screaming according to Michael . . . to one of his tax conferences.

I think he did it because he knew what Michael had in mind. My parents thought I was with a girlfriend who promised to cover for me if they checked. I called them first to head off my mother's call. Those were the days when you didn't know where someone was calling from.

I could close my eyes and see Michael's room as clearly as I could see my own.

His father, when he was home, was always busy working on someone's books or studying a new tax magazine. He'd look up and grunt hello before going back to whatever it was he was doing. Michael always joked that was the warmest welcome anyone got. His mother, who insisted I call her Helen, was either sitting in the kitchen sipping tea and gazing dreamily out the window at the few trees in their backyard and the cars in the distance going by on the highway or in her bedroom fighting another headache. Sometimes when she was sitting in the kitchen I had to call her name two or three times before she'd look up.

I was looking forward to seeing Michael's mother for the first time in 48 years and finding out where my imagination—and the yearbook—had gone wrong.

She didn't answer the door, a nurse's aide did. She looked annoyed, as if she thought I might be one of those realtors trying to get the listing for the house or a door-to-door salesperson with something useless I wanted to talk her into buying. I explained who I was . . . an old friend of her son, Michael. As if that name was the magic password, she nodded, opened the door wide and invited me in.

"You were the one who left all the messages, right?"

"Yes."

"Didn't think you'd come if I didn't call back. Didn't want you to waste your time. There she is," the aide said, pointing to the wheelchair in the corner that for some reason I hadn't noticed. It was strategically placed so a ray of sun illuminated her thin, white hair, as wispy as cotton candy now. It was still dark, thick and curly in my memory.

She was looking up at the sun, but her eyes looked opaque— as hard and dry as stones— as if the window to her soul had slammed shut a long time ago.

There was drool running down her chin.

"Hi Mrs. Greene . . . Helen," I said, as cheerfully as I used to when I'd come over after school. I bent down in front of her so she could get a closer view. There was no sign of recognition. If she wasn't blind, she was either looking through me or inside herself, I had no clue.

"She doesn't talk, not much," the aide said. "Has dementia. Goes in and out . . . mostly out these days. Been like this a long time."

I stood up and walked over to the aide.

"Does she know about Michael," I whispered.

"I told her. Can't tell you she understood it, though I did see a tear. But that's not unusual . . . the tear part. She cries plenty, most of the time without even realizing it. Hasn't been back in the moment since . . . not that I blame her."

"Did you know Michael? Did he come to visit?"

"Sure did, most every month. Didn't talk much either. They'd sit there together . . . two unhappy souls if you ask me. It was none of my business so I'd go upstairs to the kitchen and wait for him to call out when he was ready to go."

I nodded and went back to Michael's mother.

"Remember me Helen, I was Michael's girlfriend in high school." I crouched down again and smiled like I still was. Just being in this house made it almost feel true again.

I looked over at the aide who shrugged. I was about to give up when Helen changed her expression to a sort of half smile and said in a surprisingly clear voice, "Azu, is that you?"

The aide came over and wiped away her drool. She shooed her away like a fly.

"It is," I said, "I'm so happy to see you."

"Where is Mikey? It's almost dinner time."

I moved closer. My knees were killing me from kneeling, but I didn't dare stand up.

"Michael isn't here."

"That's right, he had a ball game. He's a big star my Mikey."

I thought about playing along with her delusion, but decided to plunge ahead instead. I wasn't sure it was the right thing to do . . . to challenge her assumptions . . . to try to pull her away from the place where she was living at the moment, a much better place than the one I had to offer, but I had no choice if I wanted to find out more about Michael's life.

"Michael and I broke up almost fifty years ago. I haven't seen him in all that time."

She squinted at me like she was confused and I repeated it.

This time she opened her eyes wide and studied my face.

"I always liked you," she said, making another effort to smile.

"And I liked you," I said, smiling back. I liked her because she was responsible for Michael. I had no real relationship with her. She wasn't very talkative, not like my mother was with Michael, but it wasn't because she didn't like me, Michael explained that to me on more than one occasion. It was just her way.

My mother's take on it was something had happened to her when she was young, something awful that wouldn't leave her be . . . something no one could see.

I didn't think that was true, I told her, because if it were Michael would certainly tell me.

"We have no secrets," I said.

"Maybe he doesn't know," my mother countered.

I still didn't believe her, but what did I know, I wasn't even sixteen. I just figured Helen was odd, quiet and self-conscious . . . like some of the stranger kids in school.

I really did think there were no secrets between Michael and me. Of course, I didn't have any secrets to tell . . . nothing earth-shattering.

I talked more with Michael's father—which was never a problem—although he always scared me a bit. The way he looked up from whatever he was reading and stared at me over his glasses with an expression that seemed filled at the same time with both annoyance and longing. Our conversations were always brief with Michael pulling me away, either up to his room or out of the house.

I was more than willing to ignore what I couldn't understand about his parents and love everything about Michael. It seemed so simple back then. Love his house, love his room, love his family, love his friends . . . there was no picking and choosing. It was all or nothing. That's what I thought love was. Everything about him . . . everything around him . . . had to be accepted without question—on its face value—because the only one who mattered was Michael. It was his embrace I'd be living in, no one else's.

Unlike parental love, teenage love was more like a telescope than a microscope. At least it seemed that way back then.

"She was your good luck charm," Helen said, looking up as if she were talking to Michael in heaven. She looked back down at me. "I always told him that. You only get one of those in life and love has nothing to do with it."

I wondered if she were referring to Michael's father.

"I got my lucky charm," she answered, as if she were reading my mind, "or I'd have wound up like my sister."

I looked over at the aide who shrugged. I never knew she had a sister. Michael never mentioned having an aunt. I thought both his parents were only children like Michael and me.

"Then he up and died," she said. "He couldn't take it any longer . . . too bad for me."

I assumed she was talking about Michael's father, not Michael.

Her lips were quivering and her hands were shaking. She was squinting at me, her eyes growing cloudy again so I jumped in with a question.

"What happened to Michael after he graduated college?"

"Did something happen? Where's Mikey?"

With that, Helen turned her face back up to the sun and grew rigid.

The aide walked over and gently nudged me aside. "That's about as long as she's come back and I've been taking care of her now for almost five years." She moved behind the wheelchair and unlocked the wheels. "It's time for her lunch. Still a good eater and you know what they say."

"What's that?"

"They're not ready to die until they stop eating."

I nodded although I'd never heard that before. This was going to take a lot more investigative work than I had thought.

"Wait," the aide said, locking the wheels again. She went into the den where Michael's father had a desk that was always neatly organized with a place for work and a place for household bills. I peeked in, it was a mess now.

"This came a couple of weeks ago," the aide said, picking a letter off the top of one pile and handing it to me. It was already open.

"I read it to her," the aide said. "Don't know whether she heard me or not. It's from her sister."

"So Helen did have a sister," I said still in shock.

"I don't know about that," the aide said. "It's from the sister of Michael's wife."

That was probably who Helen was referring to before . . . thinking the sister of Michael's wife was her own sister.

"Do you mind if I read it?"

55

"Take it with you. I was going to throw it out anyway. She doesn't need it. Half the time she thinks I'm her sister or mother."

"What about the other half of the time?"

"She sits there waiting for her husband to come home and calls for Mikey to come downstairs for dinner."

I put the letter in my bag. I thought about asking if I could look around a bit, but I was depressed enough as it was. It's not easy traveling back—either in time or place—and finding that little remains of your teenage world and the few things left are about to disappear forever. At the moment, I felt sorrier for myself than Michael or his mother.

Selfishness may reach its peak in our teenage years, but it never really leaves us. It seemed to me as if I was the only one left to feel the loss . . . really feel it. At least that was my selfish way of thinking in the moment.

I took a deep breath and tried to shake it off. Feeling sorry for yourself is no way to go through a day. I had to think again like a journalist, as opposed to an old woman in the grips of an attack of nostalgia.

"Are there any photos around of Michael's wife and son?" I asked, as I put on my coat.

"One framed one up there in the dining room."

"Do you mind if I take a look?"

"Go ahead. I expect you know you're way around. I'm going to take Miss Helen to clean up first. You can let yourself out when you're done."

"Thank you."

I went upstairs to the dining room. There were always pictures on the breakfront when I used to spend time here. There were Michael's grandparents, his father's parents, looking as serious as ever in their wedding photo, although they hadn't aged or faded in the least over the past 50 years. There were the same photos of Michael's parents in various stages of adult life, although not one of them as kids, which I always thought a little odd back then since I used to love looking at my parents' childhood photos to search for their adult expressions.

Most of the photos were of Michael, all ones I remembered . . . Michael the baby, Michael the toddler, Michael the little leaguer and Michael the high school star. They were still there, as if this were a museum dedicated to the sixties. I looked for the photo of

Michael and me at his senior prom, but it was gone.

The only photo I didn't recognize was high on the top shelf, as if had been placed there—above eye level—because it was too painful to look at every time Michael or his mother passed by. It was a professional photo of the three of them, Michael, his wife and his son. It looked like the kind we'd take at those Sears photo shops they used to have in every store. The boy looked about four, Michael and his wife looked to be in their late thirties. I still didn't have a name for her, just for Michael's son, Doug.

They were smiling, but I found it a sad photo nonetheless. Perhaps because I knew everyone in it was dead, having died way too young, although I think it was more than that. They were smiling, but they didn't look happy. They looked as if they were posing for the camera, putting on an expression none of them really felt, encouraged by the photographer who was also tired at the end of a long day.

Perhaps they were exhausted from shopping and were hungry. Michael's easy, natural smile, the one he always wore on the ballfield and offered up effortlessly for every yearbook picture or photo I ever took of him was gone . . . replaced by one that he was straining to hold onto. His eyes were narrow, not wide open, and his lips looked thinner, as if they were withering away.

Yes, I realized it was my writer's imagination, but it's still what I saw.

His wife was beautiful with a perfect posture, although her smile looked no more genuine. Perhaps because her gaze was not directed at the camera as much as it was past the camera . . . like she was looking at something in the distance, something disturbing.

My imagination never rests.

When people have died horrible, early deaths, you can't help but look for the foreshadowing in their faces.

Doug was too young to reveal much more than his age and the fact that he appeared tired and bored.

I put the photo back and passed through the kitchen so I could say goodbye on my way out. I told the aide I would leave my card on the hall table and asked her to call me in the event Mrs. Greene said anything else about my visit or wanted to speak with me again.

I couldn't wait to get back to my hotel to read the letter, although I couldn't resist driving around town a little bit before heading back into the city. I drove passed the old high school which had added a wing and the elementary school where our playground hangout used to be. It was now a satellite campus for one of the local colleges. The playground had been replaced by picnic tables. The swings where we had spent out last moments together were gone. In their place was a group of colored recycling bins.

I was now the only one alive, the only witness remaining to the happiness—and heartbreak—that had once happened there.

When I was younger I used to think of objects and places as witnesses to my life . . . cosmic forms of consciousness that held onto their memories, as I did mine. I assumed they would always be there, even if people were not, when I felt the need to return to confirm the truth of what had happened. Unfortunately, you learn by my age that places and things disappear the same as people do—indeed often sooner than people—and when they're gone it's as if they never existed.

I don't know why, but I did want to sit one more time on that swing.

As soon as I got back to the hotel, I ordered room service and took out the letter.

The return address was on one of those small printed labels that come in the mail all the time from charitable organizations seeking donations. I have a drawer full of them. This one had a butterfly that looked as if it had been drawn by a child. The address read Sandi Lynn, 441 Big Arbor Road, Longmeadow, Massachusetts. Not a real name and address, at least I hope not since I made it up.

I suppose I should include the whole letter, instead of a few excerpts. If I were the reader and not the writer I wouldn't want it filtered, particularly by a journalist with her own personal agenda. I would have included the whole letter in any event since it wasn't very long.

It was written two weeks after Michael's death.

Dear Helen,

I was so sorry to hear that Michael had passed away. I only learned about it the other day from a friend in New York City who happened to work at Morgan Stanley as well and knew of the connection. He told me Michael would be missed and that they had a small service in his honor when they cleaned out his desk. He said there was nothing of value or significance in it or they would have sent it to you.

How sad was that? A memorial held around his desk and nothing special found inside it.

I would be able to find out more about what Michael did at Morgan Stanley. We kept our accounts there and our broker, a young man who had inherited our business after our long time broker died, would surely help.

Perhaps Michael had seen my name come across his desk over the years, although I went by my married name so he might not have recognized it. Perhaps we'd passed each other in a branch or on the sidewalk, although I'd have recognized him in an instant. Maybe he saw me and kept out of sight, feeling awkward, avoiding me for reasons he didn't think about and couldn't have explained if he had.

It all seems so unfair when I think about what happened to them. They had such bad lucky together. Fran and I used to lie in bed when we were teenagers and fantasize about our husbands and families. I don't know why mine came true and hers didn't. He was the right guy, a nice guy, I know that. There's no rhyme or reason to it. Why do some relationships seem blessed and others cursed? It seems so random sometimes.

Michael's wife's name was Fran. She must have grown up in Massachusetts. In light of their age in the photo I saw it was clear they must have met quite a few years after college, probably at work.

I reread the letter a dozen times. It offered no clue as to what happened to Fran or to Doug, but I knew from the obituary it had to be bad. They often stay silent about those sort of things in obits or at least they did years ago when the circumstances were too upsetting . . . or they were very young.

Events like these are dark clouds that can blot out the sun for a lifetime.

Michael was never good with bad luck in high school. When they didn't make the finals his junior year because their shortstop—"sure hands Brown"—made his first error of the season, Michael moped around for a week. Still, that sort of pouting is expected of teenagers. Adults, particularly mature adults, have to learn to work through it . . . to pick ourselves up and continue moving forward.

My thinking sounds so much like my mother and father sometimes it scares me.

How does someone go from being kissed by luck to being cursed by it? Is it really as random as everyone believes or is there a reason? A sort of evening out by a universe that gave Michael nothing but blessings in high school?

The church says bad luck is important. It's God's way of testing us—the hardest tests going to the strongest. Life, the priests like to say, is a thin ray of light seeping under the door from the great sunshine that awaits us in eternity.

Nice to believe if you can. I can't, I doubt Sandi or Helen could either. It's not an idea I expect gives many people, other than true believers, much solace after a couple of tragedies like that.

Could it be that certain people, harmless by themselves, are dangerous when mixed together . . . like ammonia and bleach? Perhaps Michael and I were a healthy mix, while Fran and Michael created something unstable. If there is a plan or a purpose, can one small deviation—like abandoning a perfectly matched high school sweetheart—set you on the wrong path?

Silly to think along those lines, I know, but that's what writers do. No idea is ever too outrageous.

I don't believe any of that stuff . . . although you can't live this long without knowing how much you don't know and how some people always seem to be at the wrong place at the wrong time . . . dying in strange, unnatural ways. Like someone I knew in Florida who was always breaking a limb or spraining a body part. It got to the point no one wanted to go out with her for fear of catching whatever it was she had. She died when an un-popped kernel of popcorn popped in her throat. Half the people in our development believed she must have done something terrible—in this life or a past one—while the rest put it down to carelessness and bad luck.

Michael's baseball coach in high school used to tell them all the time that luck was really skill in disguise and "the more you practiced, the luckier you got."

Not a rule I would apply to love.

They like to say in Florida—as if it takes old age to confirm it—that bad luck comes in showers, not sprinkles, a fact they always confirm while sitting around the pool trading bad news stories from up north or just down the road in the next development.

I don't believe in fate, but I do believe in luck, at least the good timing kind. Timing has always been lucky for me. When I was a young mother with my two young children in the car I missed an overturning tractor trailer by about ten seconds. I actually saw it happening in my rearview mirror. Good timing also brought me Earl. He was leaving the party just as I was arriving. We literally ran into each other at the door. He decided to stay and we've been together ever since. A minute later and we'd have passed each other like those proverbial ships in the night.

> *My sister and I drifted apart for a while after she got married. I think that happens with older marriages where the people who come together are more set in their ways. It wasn't until Fran got sick that we reconnected. I know how hard it was for Mike and Doug . . . for everyone.*

> *I wish Mike had reached out to me afterward, but he's never been the type to ask for help, nor was my sister really, even at the end. They are surely all in a better place now.*
> *If there is anything I can do, please call me.*

Fondly,
Sandi

She clearly hadn't been in touch with Michael's mother in a long time or she would have known about her dementia.

I knew I had to visit Sandi, but I wanted to have more information about Michael and his life with Fran before I did. I didn't want to appear out of the blue like some old high school girlfriend looking to make a story—and a few dollars—off their misery.

    I still didn't know much about his job, his marriage or his son, although I knew enough by now to realize his life wasn't nearly as full and happy as he made it appear on Facebook.

CHAPTER 3 – AFTER THE BREAKUP

Michael's last job was in Morgan Stanley's corporate office. It took one call to my broker to confirm that. He was a senior vice president, which seemed appropriate after all these years, even if most of those years turned out to have been at Lehman Brothers. I'm sure the bankruptcy caught him by surprise and hurt his portfolio, especially his retirement savings.

I was surprised to learn that his job at Morgan Stanley and before that at Lehman wasn't dealing with investors, managing funds or investing for the firm's account. Rather, he worked in the backroom doing compliance, making sure the various trades and investments made by others complied with all the complex laws and regulations.

It seemed like the kind of job you took to hide from the world, not the kind of job the star first baseman and homecoming king would find attractive.

I realized I had to go back much earlier if I wanted to figure out what happened. That meant his second year of college, the summer after he dumped me and we'd lost touch forever. What was college like for him those last three years? Was it harder than he let on the first year? He was the big man on campus in high school, how did that translate to a large Ivy League school like Cornell?

And what did he do immediately after college? Did he go right to business school? Did he try Hollywood first? When did he meet Fran? What happened with Doug? Was it another illness? An accident? Drugs? Was it before or after Fran died?

I felt a little odd investigating Michael, as if I were a disinterested reporter doing a human interest story like the one I'd done a few years earlier about this roommate from hell who prayed on single women. Clearly, I was anything but disinterested. I loved Michael once . . . as a teenager . . . and although the love part was long gone, there was still a small tender spot in the deep recesses of my heart for that time when we were so young and everything seemed simple and forever.

What went wrong for Michael was of personal interest, but it could—depending on what I learned—be interesting to my readers as well. Who doesn't wonder from time to time what happened to their first love and how much truth there is behind everyone's Facebook persona? Who gets to investigate and find out? No one really. I was sure Michael's story wouldn't be all that unique and be of interest to everyone.

I got a copy of Michael's college yearbook for 1972, the year he graduated. It was easy, almost everything is available on the internet these days. I studied Michael's senior photo, but I hardly recognized him. In our 1968 high school yearbook he appeared neat and clean in his black pants and button down blue shirt. His hair was short, the coaches would have it no other way, his face was clean-shaven—not that he had to work hard at it back then— and he wore his effortless, contagious smile announcing how happy he was with our little world and his place in it.

Four years later he looked like a hippie. Long hair down to his shoulders, mutton chop sideburns, a mustache that clung to his lip like some sort of living creature and a beard that was noteworthy for its unevenness, thick in some spots and almost bare in others. He wore a tie-dyed t-shirt and as near as I could tell a pair of worn jeans.

If he was making a statement so were most of the other males in his class who looked like they shopped at the same head shop and avoided the same barber . . . except, of course, for those who had ROTC under their names. There wasn't much under Michael's name—government major, English minor, member of the inter-dormitory sports council and actor.

Actor got my attention. Michael had talked about acting some day in the movies, mostly as a prelude to writing and directing, but he didn't do very much of it in high school, small roles his first two years, nothing his junior and senior year. He was too busy with sports, the yearbook and the newspaper. I wondered what plays he was in and what kind of rolls he had.

There wasn't anything else under his name, not like most of

the others. Cornell is a big school, I'd have expected him to become active in student government or perhaps the school newspaper. He always liked to write about sports. He also liked to work with kids and I'd have expected to see him participating in some community group. A number of his classmates listed groups that tutored and mentored young kids.

I couldn't find anyone named Fran in his class. There was six students named Frances, but they were all male. There were females with that name in the lower classes, but none of them looked like his type, assuming his type was me . . . long hair, long legs and dark eyes. None of them resembled, as best as I could recall, the photograph I'd seen at his mother's house.

There was a photo of the inter-dormitory sports council. Michael was at the end of the group of nine, not at the center where he always was in high school. Standing next to him was another senior, Todd Streeter. They stood close together as if they were passing quips back and forth like good friends.

I had no trouble finding an address and telephone number for Mr. Streeter. The internet is scary that way. No one can hide anymore.

Todd was a podiatrist and he was happy to talk about Michael after I told him what had happened and who I was. He had lost touch with Michael shortly after college and was "shocked and saddened" to learn of his death. It sounded like the line he relied on when his older patients passed on.

I arranged to meet him at his office the next day.

"The guy could hit," he said as soon as we sat down in his office, "and he was a real ladies man. They swarmed around him . . . he had the looks, you know what I mean . . . like the Marlboro man. Every term he had someone new. I used to call them his semester steadies. None of them ever lasted longer than that."

It was hard for me to believe those were the two distinguishing characteristics about Michael he remembered best—his hitting and his parade of girlfriends. Nothing about his intelligence and good humor. No academic accomplishments.

"Was one of the girlfriends named Fran?" I asked.

"Don't remember all of their names," he said, "any of them really."

He explained they weren't really close friends and didn't socialize very much. They basically saw each other around the dorm and at games. Sometimes they hung out together after the inter-dorm sports council meetings.

"We were all a bunch of sports wannabes, you know, good but not good enough for the college teams."

That must have been a big disappointment for Michael.

Sometimes, he said, they got high together after the meetings. Dr. Streeter told me that he didn't smoke very often because the pre-meds didn't have a lot of time for that kind of thing.

"Being pre-med was a full time job . . . more like two full time jobs."

He remembered Michael attending some of the anti-war marches and complaining like everyone else about the relevancy of some of the courses they were required to take.

"But he wasn't hardcore about it like some of the others in the dorm. You know, the ones who went to protests every weekend and took those extension courses so they could learn how to counsel the draft resisters."

"Dr. Streeter, can I ask you some personal questions about Michael?"

"Only if you call me Todd."

"Todd it is, thank you. What kinds of things did Michael like to do . . . when he wasn't in class or studying?"

"There was only one thing Mike liked to do . . . really liked to do."

"What was that?"

"Smoke pot," he said. "He was a real pothead, if you know what I mean. Half the dorm was getting stoned most nights, but he took it to another level."

Dr. Streeter stood up to close the door to his office and offered me some coffee. I accepted, not because I wanted coffee but because a good interviewer knows accepting a drink—any drink—means the interviewee is getting comfortable and more willing to talk.

"If I had it to do all over again," he said, placing a mug of coffee in front of me before taking a seat with his on the other side of the desk, "I'd have had more fun. I'd have smoked more and gone out with more girls. I studied too damn much. And I wouldn't have gone into medicine, that's for sure. That was more my parents' dream than mine. I could've made a lot more money in finance . . . and worked half as much."

I asked some more questions to bring him back to Michael. It's not uncommon during interviews about someone else. Most people prefer to talk about themselves.

Todd had no memory of Michael fooling around on the guitar. "There were some really good guitarists in our dorm. They actually formed a rock band that was pretty damn good."

I know Michael bought the guitar up there with him freshman year. He'd started late with the guitar, not like he did in baseball. He used to write me about the songs he was working on that he would surprise me with over the summer.

"What about writing," I asked. "He was an editor on the high school newspaper."

"We all were," Todd said.

He did recall Michael publishing a poem in the school literary magazine.

"I think it was junior year," he said. "The only reason I remember is because he cut it out and taped it to his door. It was up there for most of the semester."

"Do you remember what it was about?"

"I asked him once because I didn't understand it."

"What did he say?"

Todd shook his head slowly from side to side while he thought it over.

"I don't remember, not really . . . love, dreams and expectations . . . the usual college crap I suppose."

He didn't have a copy of the literary magazine, but he did remember the name—C'Art. I contacted the Cornell library the next day to see if they might have a copy of it in their archives. They did not because it was an unauthorized publication by a group of juniors who put out three issues before they gave up.

"What about acting?" I asked him. "That was listed as one of his activities under his picture in the yearbook."

I opened the yearbook and showed him the photo. Todd ran his finger over Michael's name while he thought it over.

"I only remember one play, something he did junior year. It was some Shakespeare thing they did in the woods. I think it was part of an acting course he was taking. He had a small part, a couple of lines . . . and he fell out of a tree, I remember that."

"Really?"

"It wasn't an accident, it was part of the play. It was supposed to be funny. He was supposed to play it for laughs, but most everyone gasped like they thought it was real. He looked so damn serious."

Todd looked down again at Michael's photo in the yearbook. "I don't remember him doing anything else . . . as an actor." He rested his chin on his hand and looked up at me.

"You know, we got to write our own descriptions below the pictures. You could have put down pretty much anything you wanted. As long as it wasn't a boldfaced lie or something dirty, they didn't care."

"Anything else you can remember about Michael, anything at all?"

He had to take a call about a patient first. It lasted about ten minutes. He smiled at me after he hung up. He looked down at my hand and lingered for a moment over my wedding ring.

"You sure you want to know everything," he said, reaching over to tap the desk in front of me.

"Absolutely."

"It might burst your little memory bubble."

"That's OK, burst away," I said, trying to sound friendly and charmed. It was the best way to get a man like Dr. Streeter to keep talking.

"For a while," he said, "Michael was the go-to guy in the dorm to buy grass. He had a source and he always had some to sell. It was relatively cheap back then . . . twelve dollars an ounce."

He offered me some more coffee before he refilled his cup. I politely declined. When he sat back down, he started repeating my name slowly, "Azu . . . Azu . . . Azu . . . sugar, right?"

"Yes, azucar in Spanish. I was given a Spanish name although my family comes from Ireland."

"Cute," he said, pouring two packets of sugar into his coffee.

"The more I say it the more I remember your name. Mike talked a lot about you, not just freshman year when we were all talking about our high school honeys. Mine was also an A . . . Allison. We didn't last past Christmas. She was a junior in high school and started going out with this senior jock. It turned out fine as far as I was concerned. I was working too hard for any kind of long distance relationship . . . and I was ready for a change."

He took a sip of his coffee.

"Those were incredible years though," he said, staring off into space. "I'm talking high school. That was the time to have fun. It wasn't all about med school . . . and there were all those firsts. It was the first time for pretty much everything."

"What did Michael say about me?" I asked, trying not to sound too impatient.

He cleared his throat and looked down into his coffee.

"He talked about you all through college. He compared every girl he ever went out with to you. There was always something missing . . . like this one didn't have your eyes or long legs, or wasn't smart enough, or just didn't get him the way you did. He had a million reasons why they didn't measure up to you."

The good doctor got up and stood behind his chair, leaning forward over the back of it and taking the opportunity for a quick look down at my legs. He couldn't see them through my pants, but I could have told him they weren't the same anymore. They were still long and thin, except now they looked like road maps with blue and red highways crisscrossing from north to south and east to west.

"I suppose you were his ideal. You know how we all like to romanticize everything from the old days now . . . everything that's gone? I suppose we did the same thing back then without realizing it, even though the old days were only a few years earlier."

I nodded like I understood, although I don't do that, not often. I think now is the best time of my life . . . or at least as good as any other.

"I don't mind saying it could be a little annoying sometimes. I was way over my high school honey by then. She was far from the best looking girl around, but the pool in high school was not nearly the same as college. I sort of settled for her, if you know what I mean."

I nodded again although what I really want to do was call him an "asshole," get up and leave. I couldn't do that for the sake of the story. You learn that in journalism 101—keep your reactions and opinions to yourself.

"I remember telling him more than once that if she was so damn perfect call her up and ask her out again. He always shook his head no. Not that perfect I guess. That's what I used to say. I mean who is? Nothing personal, but you get tired of listening to someone sighing over some distant memory all the time."

Why measure everyone by me when he could have had me in

an instant? All he had to do was call. During my four years of college I had lots of dates and two serious boyfriends, but none of them meant as much to me as Michael had. My mind never goes back to any of them. I can hardly remember what they looked like and what we did. I consider myself lucky to remember their names.

I'd have run back to Michael if he had called. I was still insecure and uncertain back then. It took most of college to change that.

So why didn't he? Could he have felt guilty about how he'd ended it? Did he think I'd never forgive him? I know I said that when he dropped me off after the breakup . . . I never want to see you again . . . I hate you . . . that sort of stuff, but I didn't mean it . . . or did I? I'm no longer my 18-year old self. I'm looking at it now from the point of view of a mature woman who learned quite a while ago that forgiveness is an essential part of life . . . forgiveness of yourself, as well as others.

"Why do you think he never called me?" I asked.

Dr. T. shrugged. "I don't know. Maybe it was just words and he didn't mean it. Maybe he was a coward. I didn't know him well enough and he certainly didn't confide in me."

He sat back down and took a sip of coffee, licking his lips afterward, an unconscious habit I'd noticed him do a couple of times already.

"I remember we were in this class together fall of junior year. An English class. It was the only one I took. I needed it to fulfill the distribution requirement to get my BA. Had to take at least one class in the humanities. We spent about a week on this novel by Thomas Wolfe. Can't remember the name now. It's been a long time."

"You Can't Go Home Again?"

"That's the one. It was about this guy who wrote a book about his hometown. Didn't have a lot of nice things to say and when he tried to go back they sort of drove him away. Wound up in Paris around the time of the Nazis. I don't remember what happened after that, but that was the chorus line . . . You Can't Go Home Again. Maybe that's why he didn't . . . you, the small town . . . maybe he didn't think he could go back."

"The main character does return home at the end and rediscovers it."

Dr. T shrugged.

Except the home he returns to is America, not his hometown. It was one of my favorite novels in college, probably because when I read it in the spring of my freshman year I still wanted to go back to my hometown self . . . to my high school life. Wolfe made it clear you can't do that. You can't go back to your childhood or your dreams. There is no way to escape time or live in a memory.

Todd cleared his throat. He was the kind of man who wanted a woman's full attention. He didn't want her thinking about someone or something else when she was with him. He was the kind of man I used to avoid when I was dating.

"We also read this book by Proust . . . Swann something."

"Swann's Way."

"I found that one really obtuse," Todd said. "Believe it or not, the guy locked himself away for thirty years in a cork-lined room to write it. Like he was some kind of grape fomenting."

He laughed at his little joke and I smiled in return.

"I don't remember much about it other than this cookie made him remember everything . . . in excruciating detail . . . and in the end no one was what they once were. It was really depressing. What was the name of that cookie again?"

"The Madeline."

Dr. T nodded. "I've had it," he said. "It is good, although it's more like a cake than a cookie. Ever have one?"

"Yes, they're quite good."

"But only when they're fresh," he said. "Had a stale one once that nearly broke a tooth."

Swann's Way was also a popular book for the English majors. I wrote a paper about it senior year focusing like everyone else on the ending. Proust concludes nostalgia—excessive nostalgia—is more than just a fond memory, it's a form of mental illness that arises from a person's inability to perceive and accept the changes that take place over time. People like that, according to Proust, tend to think of the past as something static and permanent. They expect it to still be there, except it isn't and they have a hard time accepting the dramatic changes. Proust says their effort to relive their youthful memories is not only doomed to failure, it's a sign of a deeper, more serious problem . . . an immaturity and unhappiness that will stay with them into old age.

Could Thomas Wolfe and Proust be responsible for

discouraging Michael from calling me? Did he take it as a warning that there was no going back? That even trying could be a sign of weakness and personal failure?

We were all so impressionable back then.

"A lot of guys talked about their old girlfriends," Todd said, interrupting my reverie, "particularly when they got drunk or stoned. I think it was because everything got so complicated in college. It seemed so much easier back in high school."

Dr. T lifted his cup up to his lips and drained what was left in it. Then he put it down and wiped his mouth with the back of hand.

"I'd have called you," he said, "if you'd been my high school honey. I've seen a photo of Alison . . . the way she looks now and . . . ." He made some sort of noise that sounded like a horse neighing, while at the same time raising his shoulders to his ears and pretending to shutter.

I hated the way he said honey and I was afraid I'd hate the word for the rest of my life. Still, I put on another smile. Women learn to do that at an early age, smile at unwelcome remarks and compliments, hoping the speaker will change the subject or be perceptive enough to move on.

I had this feeling—a feeling I hadn't had in quite some time—that Todd was going to hit on me if I didn't get out of there soon.

"What was Michael planning to do after college?"

"It's been a long time."

"Anything you can recall would be helpful."

"Didn't his father have his own business?" he asked.

"He was an accountant, but he died when we were in high school."

"Right, I remember that now. His father wanted him to become an accountant."

"Because there were always jobs for bean counters," I said, having heard that often enough from Michael during high school. "He swore he never would. Ultimately he went into banking and stocks."

Dr. T nodded like he wasn't at all surprised.

"A lot of our classmates did and they made a hell of a lot more money than any doctor I know."

"Can you recall anything? Anything he might have talked about doing? Grad school? Going out to Los Angeles?"

"Bingo," Todd said, pointing his finger at me like he had decided to pick me for his team. "He talked about going out west. For some reason Las Vegas sticks in my head. He was one of those guys who talked about taking a road trip to find themselves. You couldn't think about it if you were premed."

"What was he going to do in Las Vegas?"

"Haven't the foggiest. I think it was a stop on the way to LA."

Dr. T looked at his watch. "Gambling, girls, surfing . . . really, I have no idea."

It was hard for me to believe someone could spend four years in the same dorm with Michael and not know anything about his dreams and aspirations. Women would know everything in a week.

He looked at his watch again. "Unfortunately, I've got patients coming and a box of insurance forms to fill out. Takes me an hour or two a day. Forms instead of feet. It's a nightmare. It wasn't always like this."

I shook my head from side to side and frowned pretending to commiserate with him.

"The practice of medicine is no fun anymore . . . hasn't been for a long time, and it's not even that lucrative. I wouldn't let my kids become doctors, not that they made better choices. One tends bar at this hot spot in lower Manhattan. He's up all night, but probably makes more than I do. The other moved as far away from New York as he could get. Has some kind of catering business in Portland. I'm sure I'm his retirement plan."

"I appreciate your time, Todd."

He shook my hand. "Azu," he said my name slowly again, but without letting go of my hand. "I always liked that name. I see you're wearing a wedding ring . . . force of habit or are you still married?"

Did he think I was a widow refusing to let go? That I needed it for protection?

"Still married, closing in on forty-five years."

He sighed like he was disappointed. Maybe he'd decided someone his own age might be a refreshing change . . . or his last hope.

"I got divorced five years ago from my third."

I thanked him again as I pulled my hand away. He reached

for the door.

"I just remembered something else," he said. "Mike had trouble with this course spring of sophomore year. He was getting stoned every night and disappearing most weekends. I don't know where he was going, he didn't tell anyone, but I figured he had a girl stashed somewhere. He got an incomplete and they put him on academic probation.

"He said if he got kicked out he'd go up to Alaska and work on an oil rig. I remember telling him there was no chance of that, he'd be on his way to Vietnam the next day. We still had student deferments back then and the college would call your draft board the moment you dropped out. He said he'd never go. We all said that, but it was mostly words."

I nodded, although I wasn't very political back then. I'm still not.

"And senior year, I remember now . . . he broke his string of semester sweethearts . . . he stuck to this one girl for most of the year. She was really cute, had dark black hair straight down to her bottom and long legs. Came from money. I don't know why I remember that but I do. She was really thin, nice blue eyes."

"Fran?"

"No, named after some kind of bird."

"If you could remember her name," I said, "it would be a big help."

He rubbed his chin. "Something short and different." He thought about it some more.

"You have my card," I said, "if it comes to you."

"Wait a second, I'm really good at this kind of thing. I don't think I've ever lost a trivia game."

I stood there waiting while he looked down at my legs again. If he saw what they looked like under my pants he wouldn't bother.

"Teal . . . that's it . . . Teal. Unusual name like yours. I thought she'd been named for the color, but she said it was for the bird. Her father was a bird watcher."

He leaned against the door narrowing the exit.

"How did he die again?" he asked, when I didn't move.

"I don't know. They found him in his apartment."

"No autopsy."

"I don't know, I was saving that bit of research for the end."

"They always do an autopsy when there's an unexplained death. You can request a copy although I think you have to be a relative."

"Thanks, I'll see what I can do."

I moved closer to the door, but he stayed put. I'd have to turn sideways and slide out, press against him. There would be no way of avoiding it unless I got him to move away from the door.

"I guess I should be going," I said. "You've got your patients and your paperwork."

He didn't move.

"I always thought Mike was really smart. He was one of those guys who came to college and just let go, you know what I mean. No parents around to tell him what to do. Partying all the time, beer at first then drugs . . . all the girls he wanted. He had the look, he was like the Fonz. All he had to do was snap his fingers.

"Although it was a different story the next year. He was quieter, spent a lot more time in his room. I think all the smoking started to take a toll. The potheads tended to become very apathetic, particularly if they didn't have a plan like me. I think Mike was apprehensive about what was out there waiting for him. If you ask me, I think he was a little afraid."

"Of what?"

He shrugged. "I don't know . . . failing perhaps. Everyone had such high expectations back then for us, especially when you went to a school like Cornell. I know my mother would have had a heart attack if I didn't get into med school."

"You've been very helpful," I said. "If you can just move out of the doorway I'll get going."

He stepped aside, surprised perhaps by the firmness of my request, and I left turning to wave goodbye. "If you think of anything else, please give me a call."

Dr. T nodded and stared back at me. There was no mistaking his unhappiness. I knew it wasn't because I refused to brush up against him or because I was happily married. Being thrust so far back into the past—suddenly like that—was upsetting enough, but it has to be much worse when you add in the sudden death of an old classmate. Perhaps it made him think about how dissatisfied he was at the moment . . . overweight, alone and tired of looking at feet. Maybe it made him a little anxious and afraid. I know thinking about death always makes me anxious, facing it alone would make me more so.

What I wanted to do next was find Teal so I went back to the hotel and went through the yearbook. Not surprisingly, there was one . . . Teal Blaine . . . and she did look a little like me, the high school me.

I thought about Earl when we got married. He didn't look anything like Michael. I thought he looked a little like my father, which was probably easily explained by any Freudian psychiatrist. Although Earl did have sandy brown hair like Michael, but he kept it short so it never fell across his eyes.

Teal Blaine lived across the Hudson River in New Jersey in the tony town of Alpine. She was happy to see me once I explained what I was doing. I had to rent a car to drive out there. Her house had to be ten times the size of ours. It was the type of home that required a team of landscapers, a pool service and a handymen.

I could tell by her hands she didn't do any housework. Judging by the size of her diamond earrings and pearl necklace she didn't have to.

"I can't believe Michael is dead," she said, leading me into a lovely windowed veranda where tea and French macaroons in a variety of colors were laid out on beautiful china.

"I can't either."

"You were his high school girlfriend."

It was a statement, not a question, although I nodded anyway thinking how Michael would probably love to be on fly on the wall listening to his college and high school sweethearts comparing notes.

"He talked about you . . . Azu . . . I always liked that name. I thought it was rather unique."

"Like Teal."

She laughed like it was the funniest joke she'd heard in a long while.

"Everyone always thinks I'm named after the color. I can't tell you how many jokes I've heard over the years. You look more green than blue, you're the best looking crayon I ever saw, I've got a cousin name chartreuse. But it's not the crayon. I'm named after the bird. My father was a bird watcher. Half the time no one's heard of it. Why not Robin is the next comeback when I tell them . . . or Bluebird. I suppose it could have been worse. He could have called me Pidgeon."

    "I couldn't help smiling. I liked her. I like most every woman my age these days. It's like we're all members of the same club. We've had a lot of similar experiences over the years, not all good, certainly not at the hands of certain male bosses and colleagues, but we've all survived, arriving together at the same place in time . . . some of us with more things and less regrets than others, but with both no doubt in some proportion.

    "You know," she said, "he still carried a torch for you, even as a senior."

    "I don't believe that. It had to be just talk. Who didn't mention their first from time to time back then? It was all so recent, certainly in the span of things."

    "Sure," Teal said, nodding her agreement, "but I think it was more than that for Michael. He didn't just tell me the stories, he'd close his eyes sometimes like he was trying to go back there."

    I still found it hard to believe since that was almost three years later.

    "Mine was the captain of the football team," Teal said. "His name was Albie. We originally got together . . . if you can believe it . . . because we had the two oddest names in the school."

    We both laughed at that piece of logic. Of course, it's as good a reason as any when you're a teenager.

    "What happened to him?"

    "Last I heard he was teaching high school gym somewhere in Iowa and coaching the football team."

    "Did you break up after high school?"

    "First year of college . . . like most everyone else."

    "Ever get back together?"

    "We slept together a couple of times junior year, before Michael . . . but it wasn't there for me anymore. There was no going back at that point . . . not that far back. College was like stepping over some great divide. I needed more in a guy than the captain of the high school football team."

    I nodded, although I always thought of Michael as much more than the captain of the baseball team.

    "He needed someone more suitable," Teal added. "I was never into sports. I can't take all the blather about it. It was all he really cared about. What I liked back then was what came with it . . . all the perks as girlfriend of the star quarterback."

She poured us both some more tea.

"High school love is more a function of the time and place than the person, if you ask me," she said, putting some honey in her tea. "Who doesn't love the idea of being in love in high school? The person doesn't matter nearly as much as the label . . . boyfriend . . . and the act, of course. The hormones are screaming for it. It's much more a rite of passage than a test of compatibility.

"Albie and I didn't have a lot in common. He lived for football, talked about it year round with his buddies. He didn't have much ambition for anything else. I suppose that's why he wound up a coach. I met my husband two years after graduating college. I was working at a public relations agency and he was one of our clients."

"Would I recognize the name?"

"Not unless you were into CB radios and handles back then. It was a short craze, but very remunerative. I never worked after we got married. I like to say that our lives . . . this house . . . most everything we have was paid for by the nation's truckers. He took the first fortune and tripled it in the waterbed business. At one point we had over twenty stores. When that craze ran its course he invested in tech stocks and startups. He had the Midas touch . . . at least when it came to money."

I nodded like I completely understood, although I'd never met anyone like that. Earl and I did alright parking our money in mutual funds and riding the market up and down like everyone else. I wouldn't even know how to go about investing in a startup.

I assumed Michael did, which might explain all those Facebook photos he posted of the world and its finest restaurants.

"How about you?" Teal asked.

"In terms of investments?"

"No, in terms of Michael. Did you see him again after college?"

I shook my head slowly from side to side.

"You never met for a drink or talked a few hours on the phone?" She raised her eyebrows in disbelief.

"No, I never saw Michael again . . . or spoke to him . . . not after he dumped me the day after I graduated high school."

"I heard about that," she said.

"You did?"

"Yeah, on the swings where you used to hang out. I told him

it was a crummy thing to do, but he already knew that. He felt really bad about it. We didn't have too many regrets back then, not ones we couldn't forget or ignore," Teal said, "but that one bothered him. Even when he was stoned."

"He never called to tell me that," I said, "or to apologize. It would have been nice."

Teal shrugged. "How many guys have you known in your life who apologize for anything?"

She didn't laugh after she said that or even smile. If this story was about her I'd have probed further.

"The girl he dumped you for didn't work out. I knew who she was . . . a spoiled brat. Had a Porsche her first year, wrecked it in the spring and a week later daddy bought her a new one. I think the money made his head spin, but she got cold feet. Daddy probably threatened to cut her off."

"Money was tight for Michael after his father died."

Teal nodded. "Still was when we went out."

We sipped our tea for a while. It felt as if we needed some time to catch our breath.

"It didn't bother me when he talked about you," Teal said, breaking the silence. "I just talked about my old boyfriends. I had a lot of them before Michael. Everything was so recent back then, every wound seemed so fresh. You know what I mean. Some of them still feel that way."

She looked over at me and I nodded, although I didn't feel that way. Clearly, she had some serious problems with her marriage . . . probably a cheating husband. Men with a lot of money tend to think everything—and everyone—is for sale.

I wondered if Michael was like that.

"Would you say you and Michael got pretty serious?" I asked.

"For a while. It turned out to be more of a transition relationship, if that makes any sense . . . college to the real world . . . although I'm sure I didn't think that way at the time, certainly not in the beginning. By spring I could see he wasn't the guy for me."

"What happened?" I asked.

Teal didn't seem to be listening. She was staring out the window behind me, not as if she were looking at anything in particular, more like she was looking back at a memory.

"He came close," Teal said.

"Close to what?"

"To asking you back."

"What do you mean?"

"You don't know, do you?"

"Know what?"

"He took a road trip to visit you in college. Where did you go again?"

"Skidmore."

"Right, pretty town Saratoga Springs. We used to stop there on our way to Burlington. One of our kids went to the University of Vermont. He was obsessed with skiing. Works at a hedge fund now and never goes anywhere near the snow. At least not that I know of . . . of course. he doesn't tell me a lot about his life these days."

"Michael came to Skidmore to see me?"

"That's what he told me. Spring of sophomore year."

"My freshman year."

"I don't think it was a particularly good time for him. He was smoking a lot of dope and going home most weekends. He said his mother was having problems. He was going out with a lot of girls, but none of them stuck. Understandable when you're not around on the weekends."

"I never heard anything about that," I said.

"He couldn't get to some of his course work and had to take an incomplete. Had to make it up over the summer or he would have flunked out."

"But he didn't . . . he never came to see me."

"Actually, he did. He said he saw you walking on the green with this good looking guy. You were talking and laughing . . . looked really happy. He figured you had a new boyfriend and he didn't want to interfere. Maybe he was afraid you'd reject him, tell him to get lost. He knew you were angry about the swing."

"I wouldn't have done that."

"I know, women aren't like that, but most men don't get it."

"I never saw him." I said still in shock.

"Maybe he never planned on speaking to you. Maybe all he wanted was see you, remind himself of old times . . . although it's hard to imagine longing for old times like that when you're barely twenty. He said you looked happy so he turned around and headed back to school."

"I can't believe it," I said. "He drove almost three hours for that?"

"Longer, he took a bus."

I didn't have a serious boyfriend my freshman year. I went out, but nothing lasted very long. I had a lot of male friends, but I was always that type of girl. I got along really well with boys even in elementary school. I was never self-conscious about it like a lot of my friends. I still do . . . perhaps that's why Earl and I get along so well. He's the type of man who needs friends more than lovers. Golf is proof of that. I think being best friends is more important at our age than being lovers . . . probably at any age.

How is I didn't spot Michael as I walked across the green on my way to class? Isn't there some force in the universe that's supposed to call out to you and turn your head when someone you love . . . or loved . . . is standing nearby? How did I not sense it? How could he have traveled all the way from Cornell to Skidmore and lost his nerve? That was so unlike Michael.

"If you ask me," Teal said, "guys don't get over things as easily as they pretend to . . . some guys anyway . . . guys like Michael . . . you know, the thinking type who spend a lot of time living up here." Teal tapped her temple. "That's one reason I broke it off and refused to follow him out west. He was always overthinking things, always looking way too closely for the dark clouds. I think that's what made him so unpredictable."

"Unpredictable?"

"He'd have these dark moods sometimes when he didn't want to leave his room. He seemed to be really struggle at times."

"With what?"

Teal shrugged. "Himself? The world? The way he saw it or it saw him. I don't know. I guess the bottom line is I began to have doubts about him after a while. I heard my father whispering in my head. He was always telling me when I was young that if I was unsure about something, if I had the slightest doubt, I shouldn't do it.

"I know it sounds cold, but we were graduating and going out into the world . . . college was ending. It was time to get serious and I could feel it in my gut . . . the doubt."

I took a deep breath. I was still thinking about Michael watching me walk across the green. I couldn't have been more surprised if Michael had faked his death and popped out from behind the curtain to claim this sixty-plus matron and take her back to the 1960s.

"I didn't meet Michael until the beginning of senior year," Teal continued without any prompting. "He was quiet which is what attracted me to him at first. I was sick of all the loud seniors who thought they were God's gift to women. They were all going to be doctors, lawyers and rich businessmen. Michael didn't know what he wanted to do. I found that refreshing at the time.

"Graduation seemed way off and I still thought I wanted something different. I knew money was important, but I always had it. My family was pretty well off. I guess I was nearing the end of my rebellious stage, but I wasn't there yet. You'd be surprised at some of the guys I went out with. My parents certainly were."

"Tell me about your husband, what does he do now?" I asked. It's not that I was interested, but I had to change the subject for a moment. I needed to stop picturing that day at Skidmore, which didn't exist until a few moments ago.

"Him," she chuckled, "that's easy. He's a serial fiancé. He finds younger woman to propose to and dumps them before they get him to the altar. The kind of guy who makes all kinds of promises and raises everyone's expectations, but in the end always disappoints you. He's on his fourth or fifth engagement since our divorce. They get younger and younger while he gets older and older, and believe me he looks his age . . . more than his age. This latest one is in her late twenties."

"When did you divorce?" I asked, nosy now.

"After our two sons graduated college and joined him on the world stage. Both following in his footsteps. It's all about money . . . twenty-four-seven. One girl is the same as another. They'll never settle down . . . not for long anyway. They're real love is gambling. Now that's a love they'll never betray."

I cleared my throat and wrote it down. You never know what might make a good article. Why not a story about the children— and the marriages—of the baby boomers who made obscene amounts of money. The old story about money being unable to buy happiness. Of course, it's been told many times over the past century or two.

Tell me more about your time with Michael?" I asked. "How did you two meet?"

"It was the first weekend of senior year at one of those welcome back frat parties."

"He was in a frat?"

"Oh, yeah, all the guys were in frats, except for the nerds. It was a head frat, you know what I mean?"

I nodded.

"He was sitting there smoking a joint . . . a big fat one . . . taking it all in like he was watching a movie. He had really good stuff. I'll tell you a secret," Teal leaned forward and looked around as if we were in a restaurant and she wanted to make sure no one was eavesdropping. "He was a dealer back then, not big time, but he had a following. He'd been doing it more or less since sophomore year. He was stoned half the time I was with him. There was this thing about the stoners back then."

She paused as if she were waiting to see if I was interested.

"What's that?" I asked.

I'd been in college through those pot years as well and did my share, but my friends were weekend warriors when it came to getting high, keeping their noses to the grindstone during the week. I got stoned less and less after the first year. It used to make me feel paranoid sometimes so I stuck mostly to beer and wine.

"They were so laid back . . . so unmotivated. It's hard to imagine how they got through college. It's like we'd get stoned, have sex and that was it. That was all there was to life. Except maybe for the pizza afterward. Although I couldn't get him out of the room sometimes and had to go pick it up myself."

I nodded as if I had a similar experience although I didn't know anyone like that in college. Michael certainly wasn't anything like that in high school

"Do you still get high?" Teal asked me.

"I haven't in years."

"Because I have some good stuff if you'd like. My dentist gets it for me."

I politely declined.

"I don't do it often, but sometimes it takes the edge off. It doesn't take as much time as alcohol to kick in and I always feel a lot better afterward."

Teal picked up one of the cookies and took a small bite. Then she looked down at it as if she found it disappointing.

"Did you guys smoke in high school?" she asked.

"Once."

Michael got a joint from someone on the baseball team. He

said it would be great for sex . . . it was and it wasn't. Physically it was great, but I kept thinking his father would barge in at any moment and forbid me from ever seeing Michael again, as if I were corrupting him instead of the other way around. And when I had an orgasm it felt as if I were falling down an enormous black hole, one I might never be able to climb out of again. I suppose it was my first paranoid experience. The others in college were not as bad, but they didn't leave me as euphoric as it did most of my classmates.

Michael laughed when I told him how I felt, but he never got another joint so we didn't try again.

In college, it was never about the sex, not for me. It was always with a group of friends. We'd sit around smoking and listening to music, maybe the Beatles or the Moody Blues. Whatever we put on always sounded like the best music ever recorded. Then we'd get the munchies and head out for burgers or pizza.

It was hard for me to imagine Michael as a pothead or worse, a dealer, even though I knew money was tight after his father died. He'd gotten some money by way of a grant and a loan, but he still had to work in the food hall his first year. The students who dealt in Skidmore were scuzzy and spacy, undoubtedly smoking away their profits.

It was hard for me to imagine Michael lying around in a marijuana stupor . . . without ambitions and dreams.

Perhaps it was hard for him—harder than I could have imagined—falling off the high school pedestal . . . struggling to find the same kind of success and love in college.

"I'll tell you something else," Teal said, interrupting my reverie, "he was the best in bed I've ever had. Maybe it was the pot, but I think it was more than that. He knew his way around the territory, if you know what I mean. I suppose he had a lot of experience thanks to you. He said you guys started in tenth grade."

I nodded, although I was in ninth.

"Much earlier than I did it with Albie. Of course, even that kind of chemistry loses its heat after a while. It's certainly not the same now, hasn't been for quite a while. I don't care, not really. I'd rather go to sleep after a big night out and just be held . . . or lie there side by side. That's more than enough these days. Don't you agree?"

I nodded again, although I felt myself blush thinking about what she'd said earlier. Michael and I were so young. We didn't know what we were doing. We learned together. I suppose it always seemed so good in high school because it was forbidden and new. We were propelled forward by some kind of maddening chemical reaction. It was effortless, almost unconscious. Who had time to ask and learn if we were doing it right? We learned unwittingly, I suppose, despite ourselves.

"How long did you go out with Michael?" I asked.

"Most of senior year, I broke it off about three weeks before graduation. I could see the handwriting on the wall. He wasn't going anywhere . . . at least he didn't have any idea where. I decided sometime in the spring I wanted the good life after all, you know, a big house and nice vacations. Things I had growing up. College wasn't forever . . . any more than high school. Michael couldn't make up his mind. One day he was going to write a screenplay and make a movie, the next he was going to teach. Half the time he was too stoned to care."

"He was thinking of teaching?"

"Not like a public school teacher. He wanted to be a college professor writing novels on the side, although that plan didn't last more than a month. By the time we broke up he was talking about going out west to LA to become an actor, stopping first in Las Vegas to make a fortune playing cards. He played a lot of poker at the frat and won pretty regularly."

"Did he talk about playing baseball?"

Teal laughed. "What guy didn't back then? He played for the frat in the dorm league. First base. I went to a couple of games. He was pretty good, but far from the best player on the team. There was this big guy Hank, played for the football team, batted fourth and hit these mammoth homeruns with a flick of his wrist."

"What did Michael finally decide to do after graduation?" I asked. "Did you keep in touch?"

"For a short while. He called me a couple of times from the road . . . that was when long distance calls still cost money."

I remembered how much I spent after Michael went away to college. When my father saw the first phone bill he blew his stack and limited me to five minutes during the week and an hour on Sunday when it didn't cost as much. It didn't matter because we still wrote letters back then and letter writing seemed so much more meaningful. You had time to think about what you wanted to say and how you wanted to say it. I wrote Michael something most every night and mailed the letters twice a week. He didn't write back nearly as often, but I understood . . . college was all new and so much harder.

I put his letters in the shoebox under my bed. I'd have liked to read them for the article to get the perspective of a 17-year old in love again. I wish I knew where it was or if my mother had tossed it instead of giving it back to me when Earl and I bought our house. I wish she were alive to ask.

"I took this job in New York City at a public relations firm. My father knew one of the partners. It didn't pay much, but there were a lot of perks . . . concert tickets, dinners and shows. A lot of opportunities, if you know what I mean."

Teal gazed again out behind me with the same distant look in her eyes. After waiting a bit I cleared my throat.

"Sorry, I was just thinking."

"About the job?" I asked.

"About Michael. Maybe I could've made it work. He was a good guy. Kind, not full of himself, a little lost, but a lot of us were back then." She looked down at her hands. Her nails had recently been done. They were a light cream color, classy and very sixtyish.

"You know," she said, "he did ask me to go with him, more than once, and I did think about. I didn't like the idea of spending three months in Las Vegas watching him play poker. Maybe if he had a job out there waiting for him and a place to live. I didn't want to play the starving girlfriend. We had all these recruiters coming to campus, but Mike refused to interview with any of them. He said he wanted to be spontaneous . . . like he was expecting someone to spot him on the street and offer him a leading role in a movie."

Michael did have that kind of luck in high school. One day they were shooting an ad for some science journal in our high school chemistry lab when the director saw Michael walking down the hall. He put him in the photo standing next to this irradiating device they were advertising and paid him twenty-five dollars, a fortune back then.

Teal sighed.

"I haven't really thought about any of this in over forty years," she said. "I don't see the point in thinking about what was or what could have been. All spilled milk if you ask me. There's enough to worry about in the here and now."

I nodded, although as a writer I probably think more about the past than I should. Last summer I spent most of a rainy afternoon imagining my life as a hundred-piece puzzle—not yet completed of course—trying to figure what pieces of the past I'd include and how they'd fit together to make the whole picture. Isn't that sort of what historians do? Of course, a life is never as simple as a puzzle because the pieces rarely all fit together . . . or even a mathematical equation, another one of my silly ideas, where the total—the present—is supposed to equal the sum of the past.

"The real reason I suppose I didn't go," Teal said, leaning forward again as if she were about to reveal another secret, "was that I was also a little nervous about what might happen to Mike down the road."

"Why? What do you mean?"

"Did he ever have one of his episodes in high school?"

"Episodes? I don't know what you're talking about."

"You know, a panic attack, some sort of insane bout of paranoia . . . something like that."

"No . . . never."

Teal shrugged.

"Maybe it was all the drugs. He started doing more than just pot. I don't know exactly what or when. I didn't ask and I didn't want to know. It wasn't my thing," she said. "I didn't mind drinking and getting high, but that's where I drew the line. I wasn't taking any chances with that LSD stuff, just like I wasn't sticking out my thumb and hitchhiking out west like he was talking about. I've never been nearly as colorful as my name. You remember what they said back then . . . the heavier stuff would lead you right to heroin."

"Did Michael use heroin?"

"No, absolutely not. I'd have known that. But he did start talking about speed and opiated hash . . . and LSD. I remember telling him I didn't like the sound of opium."

I'm sure all those drugs, even an excess of grass, could have an effect on a person's personality. I suppose it could be permanent if someone is fragile in a way you can't see . . . a personality defect deep below the surface, hidden away even in high school.

I tried to think of something about the Michael I loved back then which appeared out of the ordinary, some sign Michael was more fragile than I thought, but I couldn't think of anything. There were times he stayed home from school, not because he was sick, but because he said he had to help out his mother. There were other times when I called that Michael couldn't meet me for reasons which didn't make all that much sense.

What's so unusual about that? He had more responsibilities at home than I had . . . and there was his mother. She wasn't like any of the others.

"There was this one night in March, about six weeks before I broke up with him," Teal said, "when he came knocking at my door at two in the morning. Scared the hell out of me. He said he'd been up late working on a paper, but his eyes . . . I'll never forget his eyes . . . they looked swollen, like he'd been crying, and they were a lot more red than blue. They looked like hot coals.

"He looked up and down the hall before coming in as if he thought he was being followed. Then he shut my door, made sure it was locked and turned off the light. I thought he wanted to get in bed with me. I was OK with that, but he didn't. He wanted to talk. He had this book with him. He was taking this course on Russian Literature and said he found some disturbing messages hidden inside it, messages the author had placed there no one else had noticed before. He kept whispering like there might be people outside with their ears pressed to the door."

Teal lowered her head and covered her eyes with her hand for a moment while she looked back there.

"The book was notes about something."

"Notes from the Underground?"

"That's it. He said he'd discovered some of the notes were really warnings."

"What kind of warnings?"

"He wouldn't tell me. If he did he said they'd come after me as well. I don't mind telling you I was a little scared. I'd never been around anyone freaking out like that. I figured it was something he'd taken, one of those bad trips you hear about."

"Do you remember anything he said specifically?" I remembered reading *Notes from the Underground* my junior year. There were sentences on almost every page that made me stop and think. It was a depressing book, but a lot of the Russian Literature we read back then was. Still, it contained so many kernels of truth . . . or at least it seemed that way at the time. I wondered what I'd think if I reread it now.

"I don't remember. Frankly, I wasn't listening all that closely. Something dark and dangerous was lurking out there he said, something only the author could see. I forget his name."

"Dostoyevsky."

Teal nodded while she sighed. "I think Mike was afraid they'd come after him because now he could see it too."

"See what? Who would come after him?"

"I don't know, but I don't think he meant people. I think he was talking about something different . . . something more ghostly."

"Do you remember anything else?" I asked.

"He said something about balloons."

"Balloons?"

Teal nodded.

"Maybe he was joking," I said.

The Michael I knew was a great joker. He could tell you a comet was heading toward the earth and say it with such a straight face you'd look up for it.

"He was dead serious. You had to see his eyes. He was talking a mile a minute and it wasn't easy to follow. He kept peeking out the window like someone was out there. He went on like that for an hour."

"What happened?"

"He eventually fell asleep. I took him to the campus infirmary the next morning. I insisted . . . told I'd never open the door to him again if he didn't go."

"What did they say?"

"I don't know. They kept him a couple of days and he was back to himself when he got out. He said it was bad acid. That's when I started to realize I couldn't take any chances. Once the egg shell cracks," she said, "it only gets worse."

"People are not eggs," I said, "they can heal."

"Yes, maybe . . . but it's not so easy when it comes to something like this, particularly when it starts at such a young age. Why take that kind of chance at twenty-two?"

I couldn't blame her, although if he called me I'd have rushed right over to help him. It had been less than three years since he'd broken up with me and he still occupied a sizeable space in my heart . . . small yes and getting smaller, but still there. I could always feel it after the end of another relationship when sleep became too elusive. No college boyfriend had yet to completely fill all the spaces in my heart and not for lack of trying.

Some things books and words don't have answers for . . . only time does.

Deep down inside I think I still believed we would wind up together again. I saw Michael as the popular, successful college senior getting ready to do whatever he wanted, wherever he wanted. The college senior who had gone out with a lot of coeds and finally realized none of them measured up to me. Three years might seem like a long time to carry a torch, even one that was burning out, but it's really a minute when it comes to the heart.

That was the remnant of my fairy tale, what was still left of it . . . at least subconsciously. At least it was there until my senior year when I realized Michael had graduated and gone into the world without ever reaching out to me, without ever calling or writing. At that point I knew he had completely banished me from his heart, filling my old space with someone or something else so I was determined to do the same. I found someone senior year and even though it didn't last past graduation it felt like something special and it went a long way to eliminating any lingering feelings.

I learned what I should have learned a few years earlier . . . the heart is a very resilient organ with plenty of room for new loves to replace old loves . . . and old loves are like favorite books—enjoyed and learned from—then returned to the shelf to gather dust.

Forty-five years is like a minute when it comes to love. It doesn't seem real sometimes when I think about how quickly Earl and I got here from that first night at the party.

"Did it ever happen again?" I asked.

"He swore he would lay off everything except grass and he seemed OK for a while, but then it happened again a couple of weeks later . . . although not nearly as bad."

"How do you mean?"

"We were at a party high on cheap wine and pot. He seemed pretty content sitting there beside me on the couch when I suddenly felt him tense up . . . like every muscle in his body was making a fist. I asked him what was wrong, but he didn't respond. He just stared out the window like he could see something looking in. Of course, there was nothing out there but trees.

"What's wrong? I must have asked him three or four times before he whispered they were there again. It was another paranoid moment, different than the first time . . . shorter . . . less intense. Nothing about the book this time. Fifteen minutes later he seemed better and we left."

"That's awful," I said. "He probably shouldn't have been smoking,"

Teal nodded. "He wouldn't quit and he wouldn't go back to the infirmary."

I wiped my eyes which had grown moist without my realizing it.

"Another time we were walking across the green when he looked up and stared at something. I looked up. There was nothing there. He said it was too dangerous for me to be near him and walked away."

I wrote it down slowly . . . trying to understand how drugs could do something like that to someone. I'd read about the risks over the years, but never experienced it.

"Anything like that ever happened to Mike in high school?" Teal asked.

"No, never."

"It had to be the drugs. I remember reading about the flashbacks people were getting from bad LSD trips."

We sat there staring at each other.

"How about to any of your college friends," she asked after a while, "did they ever have bad trips like that?"

I shrugged. "The crowd I hung around with smoked some pot, but mostly we drank wine. Ripple, Mateus, Blue Nun. I took speed once because I had to stay up late to do a paper. I couldn't sleep for two days."

We both sighed as we looked down into our empty tea cups, Teal probably looking back on those disturbing moments with Michael while I stared further back at high school and all the wonderful moments we had together . . . searching for a single dark cloud. Other than his father's death and his mother's strange ways, I couldn't come up with anything.

Did I look hard closely at Michael back then? Probably not.

Could I have changed anything? What if I had called Michael a year or two later to say hello and to see how he was doing? Girls didn't do things like that back then, although they do it now. What if I had noticed him that day on campus? We didn't have to get back together, but perhaps reconnecting as friends would have made a difference. It doesn't take much for a destination to change, especially on a long journey. A slight turn in any direction . . . a few degrees either way is all it takes . . . fifty years later and you'll find yourself in an entirely different spot.

I probed Teal for more information, but she had very little else to offer. She couldn't think of any other college friends of Michael I might talk to. She said they were like "two peas in a pod" with lots of acquaintances, but very few friends.

"I don't have any friends from college," Teal said, sounding a bit embarrassed to admit it, "which is why I suppose we were such a good fit senior year."

Teal looked down at her manicure. Her hands were more wrinkled than her face.

"I lost touch with everyone I knew in high school too. My good friends," she said, "are from the club . . . divorcees like me."

I thanked Teal for her time and went back to the hotel to do some more internet research.

Apparently, it was not uncommon for "mental illnesses" to appear in people for the first time in their early twenties, even where there has never been any evidence of it before, particularly if they experimented with mind-altering drugs. Some people are indeed like eggshells, one article said, susceptible to cracking under the influence of something out of the ordinary, whether it's a terrible accident, excessive drinking or psychedelic drugs. It happened a lot in the 1970s and it still happens today.

Some drug trips, I read, can cause a psychosis which will pass in a few days in most cases. However sometimes—for some people with a predisposition, a family history or just plain bad luck—the schizophrenia and psychosis triggered by one bad episode can mark the beginning of a lifelong battle.

I'm not saying Michael developed some kind of mental illness, I had no way of knowing that, but it was clear he had experimented with a lot of drugs and in the end he didn't have the kind of college experience he had expected . . . indeed, we had all expected.

I know it's egotistical to think you could make a difference in a person's life, particularly at such a young age, but I couldn't help believing it would never have happened if I'd been around during his college years. I'd have tried to stop him from doing drugs, at least to the extent Teal said he did. I had nothing to feel guilty about, I knew that, but I still wished I had known what was happening so I could have at least made the effort.

What could he have been thinking as he stood there on the Skidmore campus and saw the freshman me laughing as I strolled by with one of my classmates. He had to be in the grip of some strong, unsettling emotion to have taken a bus all that way and then quietly turn around the moment I walked by.

I figured it was time to visit his wife's sister in Massachusetts.

CHAPTER FOUR – THE PROPOSAL

Sandi was very gracious. Older people who've had losses like she did, losses that come way too early in life, often find a way to talk about them. Time may not heal all wounds, but it does help put them into perspective, as well as words.

She nodded approvingly when I told her some of the themes I was considering for my article, like how suicide rates are rising even among the elderly, despite the psychological well-being the experts tout we can expect later in life, and how no one tells the truth on Facebook, particularly to people from the past who knew us when our expectations were so much higher. Certainly most everyone had a high school love and wonders at one time or another how their live has turned out, even if it's only for a moment in response to an old song or a sudden smell.

"Of course, you want them to be happy," she said "although it wouldn't be so terrible if their lives turned out a little less happy than your own . . . just a little."

We both laughed after Sandi said that.

I think that's probably the basic premise of Facebook for most people . . . look happier and busier than anyone could hope for. Post a life that's beautiful and lacks for nothing. Be the hero of your own story. No need to be too truthful or truthful at all. Hide the cracks behind words and pictures that make people smile . . . and feel a little jealous.

Sandi lived in a lovely old home in Longmeadow that had been in her family for eighty years. She was Fran's younger sister and showed me a family photo taken recently on her 60th birthday.

"What a lovely family," I said and I wasn't being polite. She had four kids and they each had two kids, and they all looked like Kennedy's—athletic, blonde hair and ruddy complexions.

"My husband threw me one of those fake surprise parties. Everyone thought it was a surprise, but I knew all about it. I helped him plan it. I just pretended to be surprised. Actually, you're the first one I've told."

"I promise not to put it in the article."

Her husband, Mitch, owned a chain of coffee shops. He was up to twenty.

"He opened the first one a month after he had his first Starbucks."

Sandi's hair was black, obviously dyed, and she had a beautiful white smile. Another miracle of modern dentistry. She was slim, well dressed with a simple gold necklace and diamond earrings.

She offered me wine instead of coffee which I readily accepted.

"It's as if my life turned out the opposite of Fran's."

Mine seemed to turn out the opposite of Michael's as well, I thought as I nodded, keeping my lips snapped shut like the clasp of an old purse.

Most women can talk easily about personal feelings and quickly feel like friends. I've had meaningful conversations with women at the checkout line in a department store. It always amazes Earl. Men can stand on line for an hour and refuse to look at each other, let alone start a conversation, and if they do it's about sports or how much they hate shopping.

Sandi was easy to talk to and quickly felt like a friend.

She asked me what Michael was like in high school and I told her. She looked rather surprised to hear it. She told me about Fran's high school experience and hers as well, especially their boyfriends.

"Mine was Richie. He was the academic type. Ran track for a year, but didn't much care for it. Just wanted a letter. He got fifteen hundreds on his SAT and if they had a letterman's sweater for that he'd have worn it every day to school. Became a dentist. When I heard I had to laugh. He was so squeamish when it came to dissecting the frog in biology. I never saw him as the kind of guy who could spend his life with his hands in other people's mouths."

"Did you continue going out in college?" I asked.

"First year, our colleges were only an hour apart, but I met someone in the spring. He did as well. We talked about it the summer we graduated. We've crossed paths over the years at reunions. No sparks, but good memories. He married after me, has two kids and four grandchildren. He's put on quite a few pounds. He jokes that he has to have a piece of chocolate before every patient so they don't mind his breath."

"How about Fran's high school boyfriend."

Sandi picked up her wine and leaned back. "That's a different story."

"In what way?"

"She had a bunch of them, but senior year was a wild one. The complete opposite of Richie. His name was Steve. Drove one of those muscle cars you could hear coming a mile away. Didn't do care about school. Managed to graduate, but didn't go to college.

"My parents couldn't stand him. None of her friends could either. They broke up pretty quickly after Fran went away to college. He started working at the pipe factory. I heard he became a cop a couple of towns over and did OK for himself.

"Fran had this rebellious streak when it came to men."

"Besides Steve?"

"All of her boyfriends in high school were different, the opposite of anyone her friends or my parents would have ever expected. One came to pick her up on a motorcycle and my father wouldn't let her out of the house.

"By the time Fran came back from college that first Thanksgiving she had a new boyfriend. A hippie with sideburns down to his chin. My father didn't like him either, but my mother thought he was a big step up."

"What did your father do?"

"A lawyer."

"Michael wasn't a hippie when they met . . . was he?"

"No way. They met way after college. No one was a hippie at that point."

"How old were they when they married."

"They were both thirty-four. That was pretty late back then."

I nodded. It was.

"I was married at twenty-six," Sandi said.

"I was twenty-five."

"So how was Michael different?" I asked.

"Fran was an English major in college. She studied

nineteenth century English novels and wrote poetry. She wouldn't have dated a business major, not even if he looked like Mark Spitz and had more money than God. It was a matter of principle for her. Then she took a job after graduation working at an advertising agency writing copy. All of a sudden she was dressing like she belonged in Vogue and going out with these ad executives and clients. She called them her captains of industry. They were the kind of men who flashed their Rolexes and bank balances along with their smiles.

"I figured she was headed for a rich, corporate bigwig, someone my father would definitely have approved of. Both my parents were frantic for her to get married and give them grandchildren, but she was having way too much fun and turned down every proposal . . . and believe me she had quite a few. But that kind of thing doesn't last forever. Eventually she stopped being the "it" girl, which is more or less when she met Michael."

"And Michael wasn't like that . . . driven to make a fortune as a stock broker?" I asked because that's how I pictured Michael after he exhausted his Hollywood dream. At least it seemed consistent with his Facebook postings.

"What makes you think Michael was a stocker broker?" Fran said. "You really did lose touch with him, didn't you?"

I nodded, explaining that I hadn't heard a word from Michael or really anything about him for almost fifty years, not until I came across him on Facebook.

"And he looked like he was living the high life," she said. It was more a statement than a question.

I nodded again.

"Everyone on Facebook tries to appear that way," Sandi said. "Weren't you one of his Facebook friends?"

"No, Michael and I didn't talk much after my sister died . . . not at all after Doug," Fran swallowed hard, "overdosed."

I couldn't help but shutter. It had to be the worst fear of any parent whether it was back in the days of heroin and LSD or crack and today's opioids.

We both took a moment to sip some wine and slow our hearts.

"What was Michael doing when your sister met him?"

"He was a bank teller . . . the head teller at a Chase branch in midtown Manhattan . . . and still living with his mother."

"At thirty-four?"

Sandi nodded slowly.

"How could that be?" I wondered out loud. I found it hard to believe. It was as if he was still living back in our past. "Why?"

Sandi got up, went into the kitchen and came back with some cheese and crackers. She poured us both some more wine.

"Fran said his mother wasn't well. She didn't talk much about it because he didn't, but apparently it had been like that a long time. She had emotional issues . . . and I suppose it was a lot cheaper living at home. He couldn't have been making all that much as a bank teller."

Fran took a moment to cut herself a piece of cheese, put it on a cracker and eat it. Then she washed it down with some wine and I mean washed it down. There was no sipping at this point.

"Apparently Michael had some money at one point which he got through his father's will, some kind of trust he couldn't touch until he turned twenty-one. Did you know about that?"

"No. Michael never mentioned it. He didn't talk about his father much after his death."

He didn't talk much about his mother either. When we were together he talked about us or baseball. I never really thought about how secretive he was concerning his family back then. I had other more pressing things to think about, like what we'd be doing over the weekend and where we could find someplace to be alone.

"He got it after he graduated college. He was going to use it to get started in LA. Fran said it wasn't a lot, but enough to stake him for a while. Unfortunately, he lost it."

"How?"

"Gambling in Las Vegas. He stopped there first. He wound up in LA renting a room above a grocery and doing temp office work. He told Fran he auditioned for everything . . . movies, television, commercials."

"Did he get any work?"

"I'm not sure, all I heard about was one MTV video. My sister showed it to me once. He was in this background party scene. He looked very self-conscious, sneaking looks up at the camera as if he were trying to hide from it."

"He never seemed the least bit self-conscious in high school."

Sandi shrugged.

"Which wasn't long before that," I added, as if trying to

convince myself as well it couldn't be true.

"Maybe in actual years," she said, "but it was almost a quarter of our lives back then."

She had a point . . . those four years of college felt like a time of momentous change.

"He stayed in LA about four years, worked for a while as a tour guide at one of the big studios, then as a PA on a couple of movies before returning home and moving in with his mother. I'm not sure if it was all about the money, I'm sure his mother must have begged him to stay. He didn't talk about it . . . or her . . . not when we were together. I don't know how much he said to Fran, but it didn't seem she knew all that much either."

Michael's mother was alone for a long time in that house which couldn't have been easy for her. She didn't have any friends, none I ever saw or heard about. Her life revolved around Michael and his father . . . and her room. She never seemed all the comfortable in her skin, although I was too focused on Michael to care or wonder about it, especially since Michael was nothing like her.

The more I looked back on it, the more I remembered how quiet Michael could get sometimes—relatively speaking—when we were at his house, even when we were there alone. Perhaps it didn't offer him the same worry-free sanctuary mine offered me.

"That means he moved back home around nineteen seventy-six," I said. "The year I got married."

Sandi nodded. "Michael knew about it."

"How do you know? Did Fran tell you that?"

"No, she didn't know anything about it. Michael mentioned it to my husband when they were coming back from his bachelor dinner. It was just the two of them. He had a little bit too much to drink and swore him to secrecy. He would only tell me if I swore not to tell Fran. I wouldn't have anyway. It's not the kind of thing you tell your sister . . . particularly after she just gets married."

"What did he say?"

"When he heard you were getting married Michael said it helped make up his mind."

"About what?"

"That it was time to come home. He told Mitch he came home to try to stop you . . . and win you back."

I started choking on my own saliva. Sandi jumped up and

returned with a glass of water.

"He said that?" I finally got out the words after clearing my throat half a dozen times.

"His exact words. It didn't bother my husband all that much. He still had a crush on his old high school girlfriend, he said, so what. She dumped him in college and he spent the next ten years looking for that same feeling again. Not the same girl, he said, but the same burn. Mitch said it was hard for some people to let go, which might explain why Michael waited so long . . . why they both waited so long. Maybe they were both holding out for the same rush they got that first time in high school . . . even though it's impossible. It's not the kind of love you really need as you get older . . . you know, that kind that lasts, instead of just burning. But it takes some maturity to figure that out. Maybe they were a bit stunted back then. Anyway, that was Mitch's take on it."

"But that's not the way it happened," I said. "Michael dumped me, I didn't dump him."

"What's the difference," Sandi said. "So he regretted his mistake and didn't have the nerve to admit it until it was too late. Men can be stubborn that way."

"I spent two years pining over him."

Sandi nodded like she knew the feeling. "I had a friend in college who used to call them the nonsensical longings. She was a psych major . . . said every teenage girl gets them. College girls too. Sometimes it feels like it's impossible to let go of the dream, you know, the fairy tale we watched on TV back then. Fortunately, women don't get stuck . . . obsessed really . . . the way men do because we know the truth."

"What's that?" I asked.

"Someone else will come along . . . we can be happy with any number of men. The looks and the sex don't matter all that much . . . not as much as they think . . . not in the long run. Not compared to what we really need. Give me a stable, kind man who is willing to listen and change his mind . . . who can see things sometimes through someone else's eyes instead of just his own . . . or is willing to make the effort. That's all I ever really needed."

I didn't have to respond because I knew it was true, every woman does. The sex with Earl was never as good as it was with Michael, nor was he as good looking, but I didn't care about that because Earl made me feel safe and loved. He encouraged me to take chances and brought out the best in me. He never made me feel overshadowed . . . or just a shadow . . . like some of the other guys did in college and afterward.

My love for him was different than my feeling for Michael back in high school. It was deeper and more satisfying, as much in my head as in my heart. It was not the kind that could ever be dismissed in an instant on the playground.

"What did Michael do to try to stop you from getting married?" Sandi asked, picking up her wine and sitting back like she was expecting a good story.

"Nothing," I said, "absolutely nothing. I never heard from him. I never saw him. I didn't even know he was back in town. He made no effort to get in touch with me, let alone change my mind. Not that I would have . . . or he would have been able to. I wasn't the same girl I was in high school."

Sandi nodded. "Most woman know when it's time to move on. Most men have to be hit over the head a couple of times before they figure it out."

"Did Michael tell your husband he did something?"

Sandi nodded. "He said he spent a month hanging around this playground you guys used to go to in high school. He was sure you'd show up one day to sit on your swing to think it over. He planned to be there when you did. I thought maybe you did."

"I never went back there . . . not once after he dumped me, not until the other day when I was visiting Michael's mother. It wasn't there any longer, just a bunch of picnic tables and recycling bins."

I won't deny I had to wipe away a tear at this point, but it wasn't a tear for me, it was a tear for Michael. Did he think I'd magically appear and fall back into his arms? Was he stuck in his high school glory days?

"Well, he never left," Sandi said, "not his mother, not the playground, not his old life as far as I understood it . . . not until he met Fran."

I was in a state of shock really, which I tried my best to conceal. How is it I never heard he was living back home? I visited my parents all the time, but they never mentioned anything. My mother must have known. It's a small community and if someone's kid moved back home the news would get around. Someone must have seen him in the supermarket and put two and two together.

Of course, if my mother did hear about it she probably wouldn't have told me. She'd have found it odd and unsettling. Maybe she'd heard about the drugs in college as well and was afraid I might call him, if only to see how he was doing and offer my help. Maybe even leave Earl and become a divorced woman. Clearly, if that were the case she didn't know me well enough because even I'd called Michael, I would have never left Earl and Earl would have understood.

"The wedding was very nice," Sandi said. I suppose she could see the shock on my face and wanted to help me get the interview back on track. "It was mostly our friends and family. Michael's mother was there, although she was quiet and left early. She had a driver who brought her and took her home."

"She never drove when we in high school. Michael's father did all the driving until Michael got old enough."

Sandi covered her mouth a moment while she thought more about it.

"Michael was a good guy. He could be very funny at times . . . when he was in the right mood. He had this dry sense of humor, which I'm sure was a big part of the attraction for my sister. And the fact that he was drop dead gorgeous, there was no denying that. It was like he was too bright to look at sometimes, as if he belonged up on a billboard advertising cigarettes . . . like the Marlboro man."

Sandi's head bopped up and down when she said that.

I know excessive beauty can sometimes feel like a curse for a woman, particularly if she wants to be taken seriously in the business world. I wonder if being too handsome could have its drawbacks as well . . . perhaps that's all people see sometimes.

"He could be very quiet at times . . . withdrawn really. You could be talking to him and he would barely respond. It was as if he was far away, staring out the window at someplace in the back of his mind. In his own world I suppose. Fran said she found it endearing . . . his getting lost in thought like that. She called it the little boy in him.

"Mitch thought it was strange he didn't invite one friend to the wedding. Of course, he'd just returned from all those years living in LA."

The Michael I knew was never withdrawn . . . certainly not

when we were together.

"Anyway, they went to Barbados for the honeymoon and moved into Fran's apartment in the city. He quit the bank and started working at an insurance company in the underwriting department. Back room sort of stuff. My sister encouraged him to enroll in the MBA program at Fordham. He was smart, there was no doubt about that. He started working on it part time."

I tried to write it all down even though I was recording the interview.

"But he dropped out after a year. Said it was boring. Decided he wanted to be a writer instead and started doing that in his spare time. Fran said he was working on a novel about a guy who discovers he had an aunt he never knew existed . . . his mother's sister . . . who spent twenty-five years in a mental institution."

"Did you ever read it?"

Sandi shook her head no. "Fran did, at least parts of it."

"What did she say?"

"She said it was dark and there was some truth it."

"Like what?"

"The part about the aunt."

"Michael had an aunt?"

"That's what she said. His mother's older sister."

"I never heard a word about her when we were in high school."

"Apparently she spent most of her life in a mental institution."

"What was wrong with her?"

Sandi shrugged. "According to the novel, at least the way Fran explained it, she had some sort of psychosis . . . delusions that popped up from time to time. This was before all the drugs we have now for that sort of thing."

"What kind of delusions?" I asked, certain an experience like that must have had a serious effect on Michael's mother, explaining perhaps why Helen was so quiet and such a homebody . . . perhaps why she always kept away from the other mothers. Maybe that was the way she grew up, her own mother keeping them all at home— without friends—intent on keeping her older daughter and her problems out of sight, far away from the gossiping neighbors.

"I don't know," Sandi said. "She went into some public institution for treatment when she was young . . . late teens or early twenties . . . and never came out. According to Fran, they gave her a lobotomy and she turned into a vegetable."

"And Michael knew all about her, even in high school?"

"I don't know when he found out."

"Do you know if the manuscript is still around?"

I'd have loved to get my hands on it, read what I didn't know about Michael's family—the big secret I had missed—and get some idea of how it might have affected them . . . and him.

"Fran said he got a dozen rejection letters from agents and then tore it up one night."

"How sad," I said, "after all that work."

I knew very well what it was like to write something and be disappointed. I have boxes full of rejected stories. I've had magazine editors send my articles back with words that were barely civil. Still, I never threw them away. They go into my rejection box or should I say boxes since I have three by now. You never know when you might have another idea—or a new perspective—and want to rewrite something. Also, times change. What was once rejected as tired and old can somehow seem new again a decade later.

"He could get like that sometimes," Sandi said.

"Like what?"

"Fran called it impulsive and moody. I'm sure he was fighting some of his own demons. Sometimes she called him her lone wolf . . . in a loving way. Sometimes she wouldn't talk about it."

I didn't feel right probing any deeper into their marriage. It wasn't the type of article I had in mind. I was thinking of something more superficial . . . like a timeline tracing the life of a first love from the early highs of high school to the lows that brought him to take his own life. A narrative that might help put that journey into perspective. A history that would help the baby boomers understand how someone our age got from there to here. The truth revealed in a time line, by a linear progression. I wasn't looking to psychoanalyze Michael . . . or his marriage. I wasn't qualified to do that.

"You haven't told me how they met," I said, forcing myself to move on.

"How did anyone meet back then . . . before the internet . . . at a party. That's how I met my husband," Sandi said.

"Me too," I added.

"Someone from the ad agency was having a party. She said Michael was sitting by himself smoking a joint. She said he was the best looking guy there, the best looking guy she'd seen in a long time. My sister was never bashful so she walked over, sat down beside him and decided it was time.

"She needed to fall in love again. She hadn't for a while. Not since this older married man who kept promising to leave his wife, but never did. I'm sure she felt like she was running out of time. You know, the biological clock and all that. She told me they sat together for the whole party, but she couldn't remember anything they talked about because the whole time she kept staring at his hair, the way it fell across his forehead, wanting to push it up out of his eyes."

"I used to do the same thing in high school."

"They were married three months later."

"Quick."

"Even by today's standards," Sandi said. "But they were both pushing thirty-five . . . that was old back then."

Sandi got up, walked into the dining room and came back with a photo of Fran. She was beautiful, much prettier than me. I was happy about that.

"This was taken a few years after college," she said, putting it down on the coffee table.

We both stared at it in silence for a while.

"She was in love," Sandi said. "She called me the next morning to tell me. It didn't mean that much to me since she'd said the same thing a hundred times before. She was always falling in love. It was never that easy for me. She was more like my mother that way . . . always making friends. I took more after my father."

She gently rubbing some dust off Fran's photo.

"She must have had a half dozen boyfriends in high school and I lost track of how many in college. She went out with med students and law students, artist types and jocks. After she started working it was mostly rich successful men, but no one ever stuck. She was beautiful and lively and could get pretty much anyone she set her sights on."

Sandi sighed. It was one of those long sighs. If this were a movie, the camera would have moved from the photo to Sandi and then focused on the sadness in her eyes.

"At least when she was younger," she added. "When you reach a certain age, thirty was the magic number back then, at least it seemed like that . . . it became harder and harder to find a guy to fall in love with . . . the right guy. A lot of the good ones were taken and there were younger girls just as beautiful to compete with."

I found myself nodding without even realizing it.

"He found a better job at Lehman Brothers once Fran got pregnant. He was doing backroom stuff. Michael was bright and good with numbers. He did well and was there a long time. When they went bankrupt he moved to Morgan Stanley which I think became part of Chase. Still doing compliance. That's where he was working when . . . when he died."

"Suicide?"

Sandi thought it over.

"I don't know, we'd lost touch, but the poor guy buried his wife and child." Sandi shuttered. "How does one get passed that?"

She sat there staring down at her hands, people I interview often do that when they're thinking about sad and troubling things . . . like death. I stared blankly out the window.

Death seems unavoidable at my age. It's everywhere in Florida. That feeling of immortality I had in my twenties and thirties, even my forties, is long gone. I wish I could have it back.

"Did you know about his spells?" Sandi asked.

"I heard about them from his college girlfriend. He never had them in high school, I never saw them. She told me he got into some heavy drugs and had a panic attack after a bad trip."

"I don't know anything about that, but he'd get into these states. Fran called them depressions, but I thought they were more than that. He'd stay in his room and wouldn't come out for the longest time."

Like his mother, I thought.

"I suppose he was a bit of a manic depressive. Now they call it bipolar. It seems to be everywhere these days."

When I didn't respond, she continued. "He did a good job hiding it, certainly at work. Eventually he became head of compliance which Mitch said was a pretty big position. He made a lot of money so that was never an issue."

Enough I suppose for all those fancy dinners and travels he

posted on Facebook. Maybe it was all true . . . although it was hard to believe given Sandi's description of Michael. Of course, it didn't matter, real or not real the postings were clearly intended to make his life appear happy and satisfying when it appeared to be anything but that.

Sandi moved to the edge of the couch, closer to her sister's photograph.

"It's like he . . . they . . . were cursed," Sandi said. "It wasn't long after he got the big promotion that Fran got the diagnosis."

She told me about Fran's breast cancer. Doug was barely five.

"It was more aggressive than the doctors thought."

Sandi poured herself some more wine. "I'll tell you one thing . . . watching your sister die like that, a young woman with a young child . . . well, that burned out any feeling I had for the church. I haven't stepped inside one since. Not even on Christmas."

I didn't respond. I consider myself a spiritual person in the sense that I believe there has to be more to us . . . to life . . . than our bodies, but I didn't believe in some bearded old man—or woman—sitting up there in the clouds watching over us. I believe in Mother Nature and the Cosmos. I'd never had a tragedy like Sandi's so I wouldn't presume to put myself into her shoes.

"How did Michael handle it?" I asked.

"He was very supportive. He did and said all the right things. He was the same way with his mother. She had a lot of health issues . . . the kind you can't always see. He was a good man when it came stepping up like that. His demons were his own. Whatever they were, he kept them to himself."

With Michael dead now, I supposed there was no way of ever finding out what those demons were.

Sandi wiped her eyes, stood up and returned Fran's photo back to the dining room. She returned with a picture of Doug.

"He's fourteen in this photo."

He looked more like Michael, the Michael I remembered, except his smile was crooked, almost like a sneer, and he had a grey pallor as if he hadn't been outside in a year.

"He was already taking drugs when this was taken," she said.

"At fourteen?"

Sandi nodded.

"Did Michael know?"

"No one did. Michael was working long hours and had

stopped the childcare by then."

Sandi stared down at the photo before wiping away some more tears and putting Doug back.

"It's hard for me to look at them for very long," she said after she returned.

"How old was he when he overdosed?"

"It was his sixteenth birthday, a combination of pills and alcohol. His friends got him so drunk they had to call an ambulance. Unfortunately, they waited too long."

Sandi took out a tissue and wiped her eyes. I did as well.

"I know I shouldn't have blamed Michael. It was hard on him . . . raising Doug without Fran. He was working all the time, too long and hard to have much of a life for himself. He was as unhappy as Doug. The two of them alone were not a good combination."

Sandi took a deep breath and let it out slowly.

"We sort of stopped talking after a while. Him and I, not Doug. I stayed in touch with Doug as best as I could, but I never saw it coming. Mitch says I shouldn't blame myself, but I do . . . in part. I should have made more of an effort. Talking on the phone occasionally was not nearly enough."

It's a refrain I've heard often enough when doing interviews . . . I should have made more of an effort. There's not much you can say in response to that.

"How's Michael's mother doing with all this?" Sandi asked.

"She's got dementia."

"I sent her that letter as soon as I heard about Michael."

"The aide said she read it to her, but who knows what got through."

"I hardly knew her. I don't think I ever saw her again after the wedding."

"Did Michael go out after Fran?" I asked.

"Not when Doug was young. I don't know what happened as he got older or after Doug died. I didn't ask."

I told her again about his Facebook postings and she shrugged.

"He had to do something with his money. Maybe he spent it all on those women and restaurants and killed himself because he was broke . . . or maybe he found out it wasn't enough to silence the demons."

She said it like a character in a novel . . . like she was talking to a friend and speculating on the reason a friend of a friend had taken his life. She said without much feeling.

How could it be that I still had such compassion for Michael—sadness really—and I hadn't seen or heard from him in almost 50 years?

There was really nothing more to ask Sandi. My heart was breaking for everyone. I was living such a normal, happy life, having had no idea about—or giving much thought to—Michael and his life. He was a fond memory frozen in my mind at 18—the way a young soldier might who joined the army after high school and died in action. Perfectly normal I know, but now I did know and I couldn't believe how awful it had turned out for him considering how perfectly it started.

I just assumed Michael must have found a happy life similar to mine.

I collapsed back at the hotel room and slept for 10 hours before calling Earl and telling him everything I'd learned. I've always been able to unburden myself to Earl. He's one of those guys who listens without passing judgment and accepts that things can go wrong and often do. He's always telling the kids the important thing to do is to keep moving forward . . . one step at a time, one foot ahead of the other, putting as much distance between you and the pain as possible.

He could hear the anxiety in my voice when I told him about my visit to Teal and Sandi and he said all the right things. He has always been like an emotional sponge in a way, absorbing my anxiety and sadness and leaving me feeling a little dryer and lighter. Whatever it is on my mind never bothers him as much as it bothers me. Few things do.

He offered to fly up and keep me company, but I felt better having spoken to him and told him I wanted to finish this on my own.

"It shouldn't be much longer," I said.

I told Earl how Michael had traveled to see me in college, spotted me walking across the green, but stayed out of sight. I also told him how Michael had spent days sitting in the playground before we got married hoping I might appear.

"He must have been going through a very tough time," Earl said, "with Los Angeles not working out and the problems with his mother. Those kind of things always make you long for happier times. I'm sure he felt as if he'd made a terrible mistake letting you go, but it was more a reflection of how he felt about himself and his life at the moment . . . certainly compared to high school."

That's one of the things I loved about Earl. He didn't attribute bad motives to everyone and everything. He always made an effort to see things through the eyes of others.

"I feel really badly for him," Earl added.

He meant it too. He reminded me it was almost 50 years ago and there was nothing I could do now to make Michael feel better. If there was something, I'm sure he'd have told me to try. Earl never had the least doubt about my love, nor should he. And he didn't dwell on things or overanalyze them. He was quick to let go of painful or awkward moments, not that he didn't feel them or appreciate their significance, he just didn't believe in letting them hold him down.

What Earl felt was always distilled through a lens of acceptance and patience. He knew things would pass. He was uncommonly calm and even tempered . . . never too weighed down with regrets or perpetual yearnings. He wasn't looking to conquer the world. He only wanted to be happy and content with his life. He enjoyed routines. Earl liked to joke that consistency and boredom were all he needed out of life, particularly as he got older. That's why he liked golf so much, he said. Once you learn not to let the bad shots upset you, it's like a long afternoon strolling through the park. I would always joke in response that I tried my best to add to his consistency and boredom, and he'd respond with a smile and a kiss saying I most certainly did.

I knew after we hung up he'd sigh compassionately and then go back to looking through one of his golf magazines and eating the pizza he'd brought home for dinner. He wouldn't let the bad thoughts and feelings linger, not the way I did, not just for Michael and the sadness of his life or for the passing of time, but for the opportunities lost to reach out to help him.

You have to love a man like that. A man who finds the humor—and contentment—in just about anything. Particularly if you have a writer's personality, always thinking too much and agonizing over everything, even the things beyond your control.

I envied his equanimity. Unfortunately, it always seemed to be beyond my grasp.

I sat there wishing I had gone to the playground before the wedding—I don't recall if I ever thought about it—not to change anything in my life, but to offer Michael some kind of closure . . . and perhaps help set him free to find a better, happier ending.

A bit egocentric, I know.

Still, I could couldn't help wondering how he could hold onto a teenage love for so long—four years after college—and feel as if he were being held hostage by a decision made years earlier, a decision countless teenagers and early adults have been making for thousands of years? Some poets tell us it happens all the time, that there are lots of people who are too sensitive, too fragile, and too deeply analytical to move on, at least not as easily as the rest of us do. People who don't see the past as something inert and unchanging, but expect it might change in revisiting it. Of course, I'm not one of them. I'm the mature matron of 66, the wife of over 40 years, the mother and grandmother and the freelance journalist who says no, the past is done, it's over. It's gone and needs to be filed away . . . and if you can't let go of it, it's because it clings to some other serious emotional issues.

I still couldn't believe Michael's death was suicide, even if he had some of those serious emotional issues. It seemed to me that if you make it to your sixties those kinds of emotions should be loosening, not tightening, their grip.

CHAPTER FIVE – LIFE GOES ON

    Sandi had mentioned a nosy neighbor Michael moved next to after Fran died, after he sold their house in New Jersey and moved back to the city. I figured nosy Nancy, as she called her, was the next person I had to interview.
    Sandi didn't have her number, but she did find her last name which was all I needed.
    When I looked up Michael and Fran's old address in New Jersey, I was surprised to see they lived barely twenty minutes away from me. I wondered if we ever unknowingly crossed paths, perhaps at the local mall, at a restaurant or a couple of rows apart at the movie theater. Michael and Fran could have been sitting in a car ahead of Earl and me at a red light without any of us knowing.
    He must have taken the Path train to the city and back home every day. I often took the Path train depending on what I was working on. It's quite possible we sat at different ends of the same car, perhaps even a few seats apart. If you're reading or your mind is on something else, you could be ten feet from your best friend without noticing.
    The apartment Michael purchased after Fran died was in a coop in Washington Heights. Nancy, his nosy neighbor, still lived there. She was happy for the company, she told me that as soon as I arrived, having retired a few years back from her job as head copyeditor for New Yorker magazine because of severe arthritis in her hands.
    "Couldn't grip a red pencil anymore," she said, sipping the cappuccino she'd asked me to bring her from Starbucks.
    She'd never heard of me as a journalist, but I'd never had

anything in the New Yorker. She didn't strike me as the Cosmo or People type.

The apartment was small and we sat down at the kitchen table. The window besides us looked out on a brick wall.

She asked about my career. She kept a poker face when I mentioned some of the magazines and newspapers, mostly local, I'd written for. When she heard I'd never had an article in the New Yorker—and never even submitted anything for consideration—she offered to put me in touch with the right people.

"They might be interested in an article like this," she said, insisting I let her copyedit it before I submitted it, even if it wasn't to the New Yorker.

"One article in the New Yorker," she said, "and it'll go right on top of your obituary."

The idea didn't thrill me—working on my obituary like it was a college application or resume—but I smiled and nodded nevertheless.

"Working there as long as I did is quite an accomplishment," she said, lowering her voice, perhaps so it wouldn't sound like bragging. "No one had ever served as long as head copyeditor as I did. No one's come close."

"That is an accomplishment."

"They gave me a big party when I left and this," she said, jumping up and rushing into her bedroom.

She came back with a gold watch with the New Yorker logo on its face.

"It's real gold," she said.

"I can see that. It's beautiful."

"I don't wear it outside . . . only around the house. This is not the kind of neighborhood for something like this. They'll rip it right off your arm."

Nancy put the watch back and returned to the kitchen table. She made a fist and patted her heart. "Michael was the love of my life," she said, although she had to be at least fifteen years older than him. If Michael was in his mid-forties when he moved in next door, she had to have been close to sixty.

She hadn't heard about his death until I called and she knew what it meant when I told her in response to her question that the obituary didn't give a cause of death.

"The poor man," she kept repeating every time she took a sip of her cappuccino.

"I didn't have time for a husband," she said. "I was a career girl. You had to be if you wanted to move up at the New Yorker. I was the head copyeditor by the time I was forty. The first woman to hold that position. The magazine was founded in nineteen twenty-five, did you know that?"

"I didn't."

"It's known around the world for its rigorous fact checking and copyediting."

"That I know, it has quite a reputation," I said, glancing down at my own watch. "But tell me more about Michael. What was he like when he moved next door?"

"He was moving back to the city from New Jersey. It was after his wife died. You know about her, right?"

I nodded.

"Poor girl. It was a death sentence back then . . . you know, breast cancer. If it were today, she'd probably still be here. It's a different world now. They can use your own immune system to fight it. They have all kinds of designer drugs, personalized medicines targeted to the DNA in your tumor. We wrote an article about it before I retired. The author was a well-known cancer researcher. He predicted we'd be able to grow our own organs in twenty years. They'll take some of your DNA and grow you a new liver on a pig or in a lab. It'll be very simple . . . like replacing a light bulb."

"That would be nice."

"I'm sure I won't be around to see it."

"Me neither," I said, although I wasn't sure I wanted to be. I wouldn't mind if they could take my brain and put it in some sort of android body, but I didn't relish the idea of being replaced piece by piece.

"So what was Michael like when he moved in?"

She held tight to her cappuccino as she lifted it slowly to her lips. Her hands were shaking a bit. She put it back down just as slowly.

"A broken man . . . what could you expect. Doug was even worse. Both basket cases. I did what I could. I'm not much of a cook, but I'd bring over dinner sometimes and keep an eye on Doug when Michael was working late, if the babysitter had to leave. She had a family of her own.

"Doug had to be about eight when they first moved in. I've never been very good at judging the ages of children. He had this look even back then, I don't know how to describe it. It wasn't just sad, it was also angry . . . defiant. I didn't have to have a lot of experience with children to know he'd be trouble."

"Losing your mother can't be easy," I said.

"No, it can't, but there was more to it. I can't say what their marriage was like, I didn't see it, but the way Michael talked sometimes . . . well, if you asked me, he wasn't madly in love and neither was she. Of course, a lot of marriages become like that after a while and they last perfectly well. My parents were a good example. No real love there. Children can sense it. It affects them . . . I can assure you of that."

She paused again, slowly raising the cup to her lips without once taking her eyes off me. I held onto my understanding and sympathetic expression as long as I could before looking back down at my notes.

"It was hard for Michael to be left alone with a little child like that. And he had no help . . . other than me and the people he paid. Of course, he had his own issues . . . his own bouts of sadness. Sometimes children can weight you down, if you know what I mean."

I generally liked older woman, but in Nancy's case I was prepared to make an exception.

"Doug had a lot of problems that had nothing to do with losing his mother."

And you know that how? I thought.

"They called it hyperactive when I was young. The kind who could never sit still. Now it's ADD . . . attention deficit disorder. The boy couldn't focus on anything for more than a minute. Kids like that get angry, I saw it all the time at the office."

"You had children at the magazine?"

"No, of course not, but I'd hear about it from co-workers. They talked about their children *ad nauseum*. And there were plenty of articles I copyedited over the years about child rearing. You might consider writing one of those, they always sell."

"Good idea," I said, pretending to write it down.

"Let me tell you, Doug had a short fuse. Michael had his hands full."

"Where was he working while he lived here?"

"At some brokerage house . . . Lehman Brothers I think, although I'm not one hundred percent sure. They're all the same to me. Didn't try to sell me anything or ask to manage my money. I gave him credit for that. Not that I had a lot. I don't think he liked it very much."

"What makes you say that?"

"Never talked about it. Never came home with a smile. If you ask me, he'd sort of given up on life by the time he got to me . . . understandable after a loss like that. His expectations were way too low for someone his age. Do you know what I mean?"

I gave her a quick nod. "What did he do with Doug?"

"Had him in private school, always had someone come in after to watch him and give him dinner. The women never lasted more than six months."

She took off the lid of her cappuccino and peered down into it. She appeared disappointed. I cleared my throat and she looked back up.

"Michael came home late most of the time and he was always exhausted. He was lucky to have me around to pitch in when I could. The man could sit around on weekends doing nothing . . . pulling down the shade and locking himself away . . . like the daylight might burn his eyes. I'm sure he had work to do, but it wasn't healthy, if you know what I mean. I'd knock on the door sometimes to keep him company . . . had to."

I stopped writing and looked up. I must have raised an eyebrow without realizing it.

"Don't misunderstand me," she said, "we weren't intimate or anything like that. I was beyond that by then. He just needed someone to talk to . . . a woman's point of view. Sometimes he just needed to get out of his room and have some conversation. A woman can sense that kind of thing."

"How long did he live here?"

"Just about three years. He got some sort of promotion and decided to move to a bigger apartment in Riverdale. It was a nicer place to raise kids, that's for sure. It wasn't filled with those kind of people . . . you know, drug dealers and welfare bums who refused to work a day in their lives. This was a very different kind of neighborhood when I first moved in. It was really nice. A woman could walk home at night without looking over her shoulder."

If I didn't hate her before, I did now. Some people carry their prejudices to the grave, no matter how many of "those kind of people" they've met—and liked—along the way.

"I visited him there once. It was near a subway stop or I wouldn't have gone, although it was the end of the line. It was a nice apartment . . . much bigger with a lot of sunlight. I remember looking out his kitchen window and staring at the Hudson River and the Palisades behind it. It was almost like staring at infinity. Now that's a line you could use."

"I'll write it down," I said.

"He had Doug in a special school by then or maybe it was a special class, I forget which. It wasn't that he was stupid. He was actually pretty smart and he could really draw. Had a good eye. He was just one of those sullen kids. There's no other word for it. People don't use that word much anymore. Sullen . . . morose is another word that's fallen out of favor. You get sensitive to things like that when you're a copyeditor. Some words come and go, but there was no getting around it . . . he was gloomy and resentful, not very talkative . . . somber, troubled . . . in other words, sullen."

"What about Michael?"

"Still had his looks, although you could see the lines beginning to deepen and the grey coming in. Didn't stand up as straight as he had when we first met, I can tell you that much. He wasn't happy at work or at home . . . poor man."

"He told you that?"

She leaned over the table almost knocking over her empty Starbucks cup.

"Wasn't a big talker, I'm sure you remember that from high school, but I've always been very intuitive about these kind of things. You have to be when you work at a place like the New Yorker with all those literary types. They like to hear themselves talk, but they try to keep what they're really thinking to themselves, if you know what I mean?"

I nodded.

"I know Michael had other dreams, who didn't. Do you think I wanted to be a copyeditor my whole life? I could write better than half the writers I edited."

She picked up her cup again and stared down into it. She looked a bit sullen to me and the thought of it made me bite down on my lower lip so as not to smile.

"What dreams did Michael talk about?"

She covered her mouth while she thought it over. "I remember he once said he wanted to write a movie. Said he had some good ideas, but so did everyone back then. Of course, I didn't say that to him."

"Do you remember any of the ideas?"

She shook her head no. "He didn't go into detail."

She watched me write down some notes and waited until I was finished to continue.

"There were a few strange things about Michael you should know," she said.

"Like what?"

"He had no friends for one thing, at least none I ever saw or heard him talk about. I had a lot of friends from the magazine. They were always coming over for tea. Most of them have moved away by now . . . or died. That's what happens when you reach my age."

When I didn't ask, she volunteered it.

"Eighty-three."

"Well," I said, "you don't look it."

"That's also what happens when you spend most of your life in a room without windows."

I didn't know how to respond to that so I asked her what other strange things she'd noticed.

"He never went out . . . except for work. No parties, no movies and I did offer to babysit. The only woman I ever heard him mention was Sandi."

"His wife's sister."

"And his mother, of course. He was a dutiful son."

"She's still alive," I told her.

"This must be hard for her."

"She has dementia."

"She's lucky if you ask me," Nancy said.

I turned away and looked out at the brick wall so she wouldn't see my expression. This time she was the one to clear her throat to call me back.

"Michael was a loner. I guess you might call him a recluse. Always kept the window shades down, even during the day, said he didn't like people looking in. If you ask me, it was the opposite . . . he didn't like looking out." Nancy shrugged. "Some people are like that . . . afraid of what they might see, you know, trying to keep the world at a distance. It's very sad if you ask me."

I could only hope I wouldn't become as opinionated and judgmental when I reached her age. I knew Earl wouldn't be. Hopefully, he won't let it happen to me.

"Was he like that in high school?" Nancy asked.

"No, the opposite. Michael was very outgoing. He was popular, a great athlete and the prom king."

"Really," Nancy said, sitting back in the chair, her mouth falling open as if it was beyond her ability to believe it.

"It's true."

"Hard to imagine losing a wife could change you that much," Nancy said. "Something else must have happened . . . something before that."

"I don't know."

It was part of the reason I was doing this, I explained. I didn't tell her about the drugs he did in college. I didn't want to hear her pronounce judgment. "Did Michael ever see anyone while he was living here or take any medication you know of?" I asked.

"You mean like a psychiatrist?"

I nodded.

"I don't think so. I'd have noticed. As I said, I'm very intuitive about that kind of thing."

At this point I'd had enough. Nosy Nancy was a waste of time.

"Thank you for your time," I said, standing up to leave.

"I guess I'll have to wait for the article to come out to learn the answer," Nancy said, as if there was an answer.

These kind of things rarely have answers or identifiable causes.

She stood up slowly with effort, hiding her shaking hands behind her back as she walked me to the door.

"Sometimes I could hear Michael talking to himself late at night. The walls here are not all that thick. I couldn't make out what he was saying, but he sounded . . . ."

"Angry?"

"Scared."

Nancy sighed as she closed her eyes and stared back at that memory.

"I asked him about it one time . . . said he talked a lot in his sleep, although it didn't sound like that to me."

I told Nancy I would try to send her a copy of the article to copyedit and perhaps to pass along to someone at the New Yorker, if it hadn't already been sold by my agent, although I had no intention of doing that.

She started to close the door then stopped abruptly.

"Wait," she said, "I can't believe I almost forgot this. It'll be perfect for your story."

She rushed into the bedroom. I heard her rummaging around somewhere. I peaked in and saw her on her hands and knees digging into the back of the closet. She came out with a small manila envelope with the return address on it for the New Yorker.

"Michael left this behind. Not the envelope, the stuff inside. He left the door unlocked after he moved out and I walked through the apartment. He could be a little preoccupied at times and I wanted to make sure he hadn't forgotten anything."

She looked past me, as if she were looking into his old apartment through the locked door across the hall.

"There's something sad about an empty apartment, especially that first day. There's life there one minute, it's filled with people living and breathing, doing everyday things, and the next moment it's empty . . . just a few balls of dust carried back and forth by some invisible current. I read that somewhere," she added, "in case you were wondering. Anyway, it sat vacant for a long time before new people moved in. Had to be three or four months. They weren't very friendly . . . a young couple too busy for anyone but themselves. They didn't stay long. It's been a revolving door since Michael and Doug left."

"What's in the envelope?" I asked, trying not to sound too impatient.

"I found these photos in his bedroom closet. They were on the shelf above the clothes rack in a manila folder. I put them in this envelope figuring he'd want me to mail it to him. I always figured they were his wife, Fran. I couldn't be sure because he didn't keep her photo out in the apartment which I also thought was a little odd, although I'm sure it would have been hard for either of them to see it all the time.

"He showed me a photo of her once after I asked. The photos I found looked a little like her, but I couldn't remember. Anyway, that's what I assumed. I called him that very evening to tell what I'd found. I offered to mail it to him, but he wasn't interested. I suppose he had plenty of others, although I had to wonder why these were kept in a separate folder on top of the closet . . . like he was hiding them away. I was tempted to ask him why, but I don't like to be too nosy. I suppose that's why I copyedited articles, instead of writing them."

Nancy stood there a moment as if in a daze.

"He told me to toss them. But I wasn't going to do that." We both looked down at the envelope in her hand, as if to confirm she hadn't. "You know the way these things go. Maybe not tomorrow or even next year, but there would come a time he'd regret it and want them back. Probably call me to see if I still had them . . . although he never did. Didn't even ask about them when I went visit him in the new apartment."

"You kept them anyway," I said, sounding almost accusatory.

"People change their minds all the time, particularly men. I think that cliché is all wrong, men change their minds a lot more often than women do. I stuck it at the back of my closet in this odds and ends box I keep on the floor. I haven't looked at them since the call, but I looked at them just a moment ago . . . in the closet . . . and it's strange."

"What's strange?"

"I don't think they're photos of his wife."

"Who is it then?" I asked.

"I think they're photos of you. I can tell by the eyes," she said, drawing an imaginary line around her own eyes.

"They must be old high school pictures."

"No," Nancy said, "they're not."

"You must be wrong," I said, extending my hand to take the envelope.

"You tell me" she said, sounding happy to prove me wrong.

There were six photos . . . all of me. None of them were from high school. The first photo was of me in college walking across the green with a classmate. I had no memory of the moment or the day, but I recognized the guy, Jon. He was a friend I made in my creative writing seminar, except that was my junior year. Teal said Michael had come to visit me—and seen me walking across the green—my freshman year.

Perhaps she got the year wrong, although she sounded so sure. Could he have done it more than once?

The next photo had to be about six years later. I remembered buying that outfit after Earl and I got married. It was for a job interview I was having for a freelance position at Vogue. It cost more than we could afford, but I loved how it made me look . . . literary, yet down to earth—my feet on the ground, my spirit soaring up to the heavens. I had a very big imagination back then, much bigger than I do now.

Anyway, I'm standing in front of the Vogue building brushing something off my blouse. I'm not looking at the camera because I have no idea anyone is taking my picture.

Could Michael have been working nearby and spotted me. Perhaps he carried a camera with him. There were people who did that back then in case they came across something newsworthy. Papers paid for photos like that and would give you your own byline. Perhaps he took it out when he was surprised to find me standing there.

I looked apprehensive, anything but cute. I know I felt like a woman back then—a married woman—but I looked so young.

Could Michael have stalked me from time to time? Perhaps he had these periodic relapses of nostalgia . . . nostalgia being was one of the ways he had of dealing with his unease in the present, the problems with his mother and his lower expectations. If I was being stalked wouldn't I have had some inkling about it? Isn't there some bell that's supposed to ring in your head when someone is watching you, someone who shouldn't be watching?

Did he drop in on his high school baseball buddies the same way? There were no photos of them in the envelope, no photos of anyone other than me.

Perhaps seeing me brought him back to those wonderful high school years and gave him a boost of energy and self-confidence. Maybe he needed to feel that way again even for a few moments. There is no real harm done watching someone from time to time at a distance . . . at least to the watched . . . I can't imagine it's very healthy for the watcher.

It was very strange to think of your first love popping in and out of your life like that, unbeknownst to you.

How long did he do this, I wondered?

The third photo was a few years later. I'm still living in the city, except now I'm pregnant carrying home groceries. That clearly was no accident. He had to know where I lived. Perhaps he knew my routine. Did he take a single photo every time he came to see me or were there more?

The last three photos weren't that clear, although there was no denying it was me. I was in the suburbs now, we had moved to our first house and he had to take the photos from further away. There were no crowds on the streets to hide behind. He must have had some difficulty holding the camera steady and adjusting the lens.

Everything wasn't auto-focus and automatic everything back then.

I was in a playground in one. I had two kids, one in a stroller and one on the swing. In the other two I was walking down the street in town doing some errands, the kids undoubtedly back home with Earl. He had to have met Fran by now. Perhaps he was about get married. Did he stop after that? Was this the last time, a watcher's way of saying goodbye?

Unfortunately, the last photo suggested otherwise. It was also unclear, but I had to be in my early forties . . . at least judging by my clothes and the car.

How often did Michael spy on me? Once every five years or was it more often? Did it stop for a while after he married and had his son? Did it start up again after Fran died . . . like some sort of relapse? Did he want to make sure I was growing older . . . and stouter . . . weighed down by life just like him?

Maybe he'd finally lost interest which is why he didn't want Nancy to send him the photographs?

Or perhaps there were more. Could he have continued doing it right up until his death?

I felt sick to my stomach at the thought of it.

"Am I right?" Nancy said. "They're all you, aren't they?"

I nodded.

"A bit strange, don't you think?"

I continued nodding while I put them into the envelope and handed them back.

"No, you keep them. It might be some help in your story." Nancy sounding happy to have finally made a real contribution to my article.

"Thanks," I said, leaving as fast as I could.

I couldn't bring myself to tell Earl that night when we spoke on the telephone. I planned to, but I wanted to take the night to process this information on my own. I wanted to try to understand how this could have happened—for how long and for what reason—and how I never noticed it or ever had any idea.

I suppose it's totally understandable. How could anyone expect anything like this to happen?

The vast majority of first loves—the ones we don't marry or who don't die in a war—usually live parallel lives with marriages, careers and children. Maybe they do a little better or a little worse, but the degree hardly matters. One day you bump into them on the street or in a restaurant, or meet them 25 years later at the high school reunion and they look older . . . like you . . . and are happy . . . like you.

They look fine, they act fine and they are fine . . . like you.

You are a pleasant memory to him and he is a pleasant memory to you. As you stand there at the reunion, drinks in hand, your spouses across the room talking with the classmates you did keep in touch with over the years, there's a moment of silence—more like more like a moment of stillness—when time reaches back to touch the 16-year old you, pushing that feeling of youth and budding love forward again for an instant as if it caught in the wake of a ship. Then puff, the moment disappears, the present comes back into focus and you each say something nice to the other about how well they've aged and how great it's been to see them. You exchange air kisses and walk off.

In all likelihood it will be the last time you ever see each other.

I couldn't remember reading one book, and I considered myself well read, or any newspaper or magazine articles—not even some third-hand story about a friend of a friend—where something like this has ever happened. Apparently, it exceeded the vivid imaginations of the great fiction writers and the Florida gossips.

I had no luck with Michael's next apartment in Riverdale. It was a nice building, but very insulated. No one seemed to know anything about Michael and Doug or if they did they weren't talking. It was one of the reasons Earl and I left the city. We wanted neighbors to befriend, neighbors who we could call on at any hour and count on in a pinch.

When I told Earl about the photographs the next day, he paused for a moment to take it in, staying silent for longer than normal, but when he finally did started speaking he was as empathetic and understanding as always.

"It reminds me," he said, "of that play you're so fond of."

"Which one?"

"Long's Day Journey into Night."

"Eugene O'Neil," I said, the comparison having escaped me until Earl brought it up. "You're absolutely right. I don't know why I didn't think of it."

Earl had the gift of distillation, the ability to see the big picture and break it down into simple and understandable pieces. He'd have made a great reporter.

"He must have been terribly unhappy during those moments," Earl said.

I nodded into the phone.

"What was that line from the play?" he asked. "The one you used to quote it all the time . . . how the past can dominate the present for some people . . . and seem like their future."

"The past is the present, isn't it? It's the future too."

"That's it. It's a good line, I've always liked it."

"Me too."

"Although I'm not sure I agree with it," Earl said. "Not entirely, maybe for some people. For someone like Michael, who needed to revisit the past from time to time without interfering with the present, your life or anyone else's. Who couldn't let go of it."

I could almost hear Earl thinking over the telephone.

"Since it started before he got married," he said, "It had to be something he'd been dealing with for a long time . . . probably going back to high school."

It made sense, but if it was something from our high school days, I told Earl, I had no idea what it could be. Perhaps it had something to do with his mother and her problems . . . or the aunt he'd never met? Perhaps it was nothing more than depression, a deep, debilitating depression that he climbed out of by finding high school years again . . . through the camera.

People who are gone for whatever reason and for however long can still impact us . . . every novel I've ever read makes that clear. Feelings and memories don't disappear simply because the people do. Most are able to free themselves from the past—and the people—and move on, but what if you can't? What if it's holding tight to your subconscious and won't let go?

"Speaking of the past," Earl said, the Golf Channel on in the background, "you got something interesting in the mail today."

"From who?"

My heart was in my throat because for a moment I was afraid it was a suicide letter Michael had left it in an envelope addressed to me that someone at work had found in his desk and dropped in the mail. It was a strange thought, but no stranger I suppose than having him spy on me from time to time to take my picture.

"Believe it or not it's from Michael's high school class reunion committee, not yours . . . his. It's the class of sixty-eight. They're having a reunion in June and they've invited you."

"Maybe they're inviting the class before and the class after," I said. "A lot of schools do that these days."

"I don't think so. It doesn't say anything about that on the printed invitation. It just says the class of sixty-eight. There's a handwritten note from the president of the class."

"Jen Clark,"

"Yes, she expresses her condolences about Michael."

"Why to me? I haven't seen him in fifty years."

"It's a normal thing to say. I'm sure she has no idea you guys didn't keep in touch. Anyway, the committee wants to invite you as an honorary sixty-eighter since you spent so much time hanging out with them in school."

I hung out with Michael and his classmates much more than I did with anyone in my grade. I suppose that's why I had so few friends my senior year after Michael and his class had graduated.

"I'm not attending," I said, "you can RSVP no for me."

"Don't be in such a hurry. Think it over. It might be good for your article. These were Michael's classmates as well as yours. They may know something you don't."

I didn't respond.

"Of course, it's up to you," Earl said. "But at least keep the option open for now. See what else you learn before you decide. It should probably be a last minute, game-time decision."

"Fine," I said, knowing he was right, "although I can't imagine what could make me change my mind."

After we hung up, I took out one of those little bottles of vodka from the tiny hotel refrigerator and drank it.

I kept wondering whether this was a concerted effort by the past to mess with my present or just a series of unfortunate coincidences. I knew it had to be the latter, but I've become a little more fatalistic with age—or at least more willing to admit everything I don't know—so I couldn't say I was one hundred percent sure.

CHAPTER SIX – BASEBALL IS FOREVER

Michael's best friends in high school—after me—were on the baseball team. They were always discussing the next season or the next game over lunch, or walking down the halls talking about their swings, sometimes when he was walking hand in hand with me. They were always punching shoulders, slapping butts, swearing they'd be friends for life, raising their boys together in the same neighborhood, and coaching their little league teams.

Two in particular, Max, a lefty pitcher, and Griff, the team catcher, hung out with Michael almost every moment we weren't together. Neither one had a steady girlfriend through high school like Michael, although they always had girlfriends and dates whenever we doubled. They both went to state schools on baseball scholarships. Max became a social studies teacher and Griff went into construction.

I decided to interview them as well on the off chance that baseball was indeed forever.

Max invited me to meet him in his classroom after school. He was teaching at our old high school which I found ironic since he wasn't much of student back then. He always gave the teachers fits. He could never sit still or pay attention, and was always making jokes about everything whether it was a royal beheading or the Civil War.

"Surprised," he said when I walked into his classroom after school, standing up in his teacher's outfit—khaki pants, a button down shirt and a red tie.

"Absolutely," I said, "you look exactly like a teacher and nothing like a baseball player."

We both laughed. I always liked Max because he didn't take himself too seriously. He didn't take much besides baseball seriously back in high school.

"Who'd have ever thunk it?" he said, walking around the desk to give me a big hug.

He'd put on weight—all in his stomach—and lost most of his hair. He looked content, like a man who may not have gotten everything he wanted, but who did get most everything he needed. He'd already told me over the phone that he'd been married for 42 years to a woman he'd met in college, had three daughters, all married, and five grandchildren. His wife was a kindergarten teacher.

Neither one of them were ready to retire.

"We wouldn't know what to do with ourselves. Can you imagine me back then saying I'd love being a teacher?"

We both laughed as he pulled over two student chairs so we could sit across from each other. It felt good to be with Max again, almost 50 years later, and to see him happy. I'd have been ecstatic if this had turned out to be Michael's life. He didn't have to set the world on fire any more than I had to . . . he just needed to find his place in it like Max and I.

"I was heartbroken when I heard about Mike," he said. "I'd heard about his wife and son, but that was a while ago. I had no idea what was going on with him, not really. We'd lost touch. I think Griff was the only one who still spoke to him.

"I should have made more of an effort to stay in touch," Max said. "Maybe there was something I could have done."

"I could say the same thing."

"It's different for you," Max said. "No one could have expected you to keep in touch . . . an old girlfriend . . . but I was a friend."

"What could you have done?"

Max shrugged. "The last time I talked to him was on our fiftieth birthday."

"I forgot you guys shared the same birthday. Did he call you?"

"No, I always called him. Up until our fiftieth we always tried to talk on our birthday, not every year, but most of them. For some reason fifty was the last time. I don't know why. I think he moved and his old number didn't work. Once we missed a couple of years it sort of broke the streak. Before I knew it ten years had passed."

"Do you remember what you talked about on that last call?"

"Funny, I do," he said. "Probably because I've been thinking about it since you called."

"Do you mind if I record this?"

Max shook his head no and waited for me to turn on the recorder.

"He filled me in on his son. It was the first I'd heard about it. None of the other guys on the team knew about it, not even Griff."

"I guess baseball isn't forever," I said.

"Baseball is forever . . . relationship aren't. You know that as well as anyone."

I took a breath and plunged on with my questions.

"Can I ask a little about you for background purposes?"

"Sure."

"Did you play baseball in college?"

"All four years. I was the number two starter my last two years. Played in a couple of leagues afterward. Last one was an over thirty-five league. Slow pitch softball. The game gets in your blood."

"Did you keep in touch with Michael during college?"

"That first year yes, we all kept in touch."

When I didn't ask another question right away, he continued. "Mike told me about his plans to break up with you."

"When."

"Just before summer vacation."

"He'd met someone," I said.

"In the spring. I never met her. Her name was Georgia or Georgina. I forget which."

"Georgia?" I laughed because it took me fifty years to learn her name . . . for some reason I found that funny. "She sounds like a real peach."

Max smiled. "She wasn't from down south. She came from a rich family in Gross Pointe, Michigan. Her father was like number two at Chrysler. He told me she changed her jeans at least twice a day."

"Why?"

"Because they would stretch out and lose their crease. He said she dressed like a fashion model. I never met her, but I saw a picture. She looked a little like you if you ask me . . . long hair, long legs . . . you had a prettier face."

"You thought I was pretty, huh?"

"The whole baseball team had a crush on you."

"Look at me now," I said with a smile.

I had no problem with what I looked like or my self-image, as long as I didn't spend too much time staring into the bathroom mirror. That always disabused me of any other mental image of myself I tried to carry around.

"Beautifully aged . . . like a bottle of fine wine."

"Boy," I said, "have you changed."

"My wife taught me to talk nice or be quiet."

We both laughed.

"Go on," I said.

"First, she was going to come down to New York for the summer. Her parents had an apartment in Manhattan, but then she changed her mind and decided to stay up at school and work with some professor so Michael got a job up there painting dorms. Then her parents convinced her to come back to Michigan for the summer and study abroad in the fall . . . in Paris. That was right after he broke up with you. It all happened so quickly. It was over before it really started.

"He stayed up there anyway painting dorms. Said it was hot as hell. Quit at the end of July or maybe he finished, I don't remember. Came back home in August to help out his mother."

"I was home in August. How did I not know that?"

Max shrugged.

"How is it I never saw him?"

"He stayed home most of the time with his mother. Said there was a lot to do around the house."

"Why didn't he call me?"

"He didn't talk about it, but I'm sure he thought about it."

"How do you know?"

"Still had your picture in his room. I think he figured it would be unfair to you . . . after what he'd done. You were starting college in less than a month, three hours away from him. I suppose he felt you needed your freedom."

"That doesn't sound like Michael," I said, reverting a moment to my 17-year old mindset.

"He was changing," Max said as he nodded his agreement. "I don't know if it was college or something else."

"How do you mean?"

"I don't know how to explain it."

"Try."

"He didn't go out for the freshman baseball team for one and the coach really wanted him to . . . and he'd really gotten into smoking grass. I mean we were all doing it freshman year, beer, grass, pizza, it was a weekend ritual. But he was doing it most every day. He was in a suite with this junior who came from San Diego and went into Mexico every break to buy a ton of it. He sold it on campus, but it was free for the guys in the suite.

"Maybe I would've smoked more if I had the opportunity. I don't know. We had a pretty tough baseball coach. I wasn't allowed to drink any beer for two days before a game. If he found out you did, you were off the team."

"You think it was the marijuana?"

"I don't know, but whenever we talked he seemed more serious. He didn't sound like himself. He didn't have the same confidence."

Someone knocked on the door and opened it without waiting for a response. It was another teacher.

"Sorry Max, didn't know you were in with someone. Don't forget the department meeting in the morning."

Max nodded and waved.

"That might have been another reason he didn't call you in August. I think he was a little afraid of being rejected."

"By me . . . no way . . . not back then."

"Even after what he'd done and the way he'd done it? He told me you were really upset and said you never wanted to speak to him again."

"That's the kind of thing you said back then after your boyfriend dumped you."

"Did you mean it?"

"How can I remember that far back? I was hurt and angry. I might have wanted him to suffer for a while."

"The more I think about it," Max said "the biggest reason he didn't call you might have been his mother. I think the dorm painting gig ran through the middle of August, but he had to come home early to help her. She had a tough time that first year with Mike away. He didn't talk much about it, but she completely stopped leaving the house. One of my mother's friends told her that.

"My mother had this friend who was a nurse in the emergency room. She told her Mike's mother came in unconscious one day having drank too much and taken some sleeping pills, and they had to pump her stomach. She said Max stood there without saying a word. He never told any of us about it and I never brought it up with him."

"How awful to have gone through that alone," I said.

"His mother didn't want him to go back to school . . . that much he told me. She wanted him to take a job and live at home. Mike said he didn't want to turn into his father."

Max moved his chair in closer. "You know, she had a nervous breakdown sophomore year and Mike had to come home almost every weekend."

"I never heard a word about that either. How did you find out?"

"My mother's friend again. It turned out she lived a couple of houses down from Mike's mother and saw Mike there. Couldn't do a lot of his course work and almost flunked out. Had to go to summer school to make it up."

"I wish I'd known."

"Not much you or anyone else could have done about it."

I nodded, but I'd have come home a couple of those weekends to help . . . if he'd asked or called.

"Still spent his summers up at school . . . as long as he could. Obviously, it wasn't easy when he was home. He said he liked painting the dorms. Said the money was good and he liked the quiet."

Every summer I used to come back from college and take some boring office job my father would find for me, hoping to run into Michael.

"How about after college?" I asked. "Did he go to your wedding? Did you go to his?"

"He came to mine. It was about a year after he moved back from LA. He came with this older woman. Really striking, like that older woman in The Graduate, what was her name?"

"Anne Bancroft?"

"Mrs. Robinson . . . reminded me of her, but he spent most of the night hanging out with the guys from the team while she sat there at the table smoking and drinking. He came over to me at the end of the night, clearly a little drunk, and asked about you. I told him I hadn't spoken to you in years, but I'd heard you'd gotten married. He said he knew that. I asked him if he was serious with his date. He looked over at her and covered his mouth. I thought maybe he was going to throw up. No way, he said. He'd just met her a few days ago. I found that really odd . . . bringing someone you just met to a wedding."

"Did you see him after that? Go to his wedding?"

"He told me during one of our birthday calls he was getting married somewhere in Massachusetts to a girl he'd met six weeks earlier at a party. He said he wasn't inviting anyone because it was small and far away. He didn't sound all that enthusiastic about it. Said they were like two drowning swimmers clinging to the same life raft."

"He said that?"

"More or less. I took it to mean they were getting old and wanted to start a family before it was too late. They were both in their thirties, which was late back then. Rita and I already had three kids . . . all the guys from the team had families. He said she looked like a model and you know how Mike looked. That would have been one fine combination."

"After that?"

Max shook his head slowly from side to side. "Just the calls on our birthday."

"Baseball team reunions?"

"We had them all the time . . . mostly we'd meet for drinks, sometimes a Yankee game, but he never showed. Griff always invited him and he always said he'd be there, but he never came."

"How does a life turn out so differently than anyone could have imagined?" I wondered out loud. Eighteen is young, but aren't we largely formed by then, at least personality-wise. Was there something there about Michael none of us noticed? I suppose I was hoping Max, the mature educator, might have an answer.

"He was the last person I'd have thought would kill himself," Max said. "We were all so sure back then we'd wind up traveling through life together. Marrying our high school and college sweethearts, moving back home, going to each other's houses every weekend for barbeques. Taking our kids to little league games together, teaching them how to hit and field, watching them play high school ball together.

"We were all so sure you guys would wind up together. You were like the all-American couple . . . perfectly matched . . . meant to be."

"Apparently not."

I told Max about my family and my work as a journalist, and he told me he was working on a novel and had been for almost twenty years. It was a mystery that started with the murder of a popular high school history teacher.

"Better than watching sitcoms and roaming the internet," he said.

"What does your wife do when you're writing?"

"She's a voracious reader. She goes through one or two books a week."

I thanked Max for his time and promised to send him my article if I ever finished it.

"Come to the reunion," he said as he walked me out of the school.

"I don't know."

"You were as much a member of our class as Mike and me. You were there for every dance and every class picnic."

"On Michael's arm."

"Everyone liked you Azu . . . not just Michael. People feel really badly about what happened. They're in shock. I think your being there will help . . . it will certainly help the guys. They'll get a kick out of seeing you."

"I'll think about it."

"It might help you figure this all out. Maybe there's a message there somewhere, something we need to hear, something we can learn."

I nodded.

"It can't hurt."

"I realize that," I said, knowing I probably wouldn't be going to my fiftieth reunion next year, not because I had anything to hide or anyone I wanted to avoid, I just didn't have the same feeling about my own class, not like I did about Michael and his friends . . . my best friends as well during ninth, tenth and eleventh grade.

My next stop was Griff.

Griff lived in New York City. He was the catcher on the team which mean he controlled all the action. He knew what pitch was coming and he positioned the fielders based on what he called. I haven't watched much baseball since marrying Earl. Except for golf and the football playoffs, he wasn't much of a TV sports watcher. What I knew about baseball came from high school because Michael explained it to me. He considered the catcher, the pitcher and the cleanup hitter the three most important players on the team. Michael batted cleanup and every once in a while would come in late in a game as the relief pitcher.

I suppose I shouldn't have been all that surprised to find Griff had wound up in a similar position . . . the construction manager in charge of coordinating large scale building projects. He rattled off all the buildings he'd worked on and it sounded like a who's who of the New York City skyline.

He was always pretty serious in high school. Michael said he had to be because calling pitches was serious business. He explained how Griff would go to the games of their opponents to scout their hitters so he could have some idea about their weaknesses. Some players couldn't hit the curveball or the high heat, others had a definite preference for the low, inside pitch.

"You have to stay away from their comfort zone," Michael would tell me.

Griff also had to make a game time decision based on the warm-ups about which pitches were working best for their pitcher and which pitches to avoid. For some reason, which I couldn't understand, sometimes the breaking ball just wouldn't break and the fast ball refused to flutter . . . as if they had moods and minds of their own.

I never saw the fastball flutter, but I got the drift.

Griff had a big organizational job on the team.

He hadn't changed much. Griff was just as serious as he was in high school. He had his secretary bring me into his office and sit me down on the chair across from the desk. No kiss, no hug, not even a smile, just a wave and a nod like a priest offering me a benediction. He didn't seem nearly as happy to see me as Max did.

Perhaps he saw me as the harbinger of death, here to remind him how the old baseball team was breaking apart forever.

I looked at him and he looked at me, both of us no doubt taking the measure of what time had done.

Griff used to have long hair, not down to his collar, the coach wouldn't have allowed that, but certainly long by athletic standards back then. He was bald now, about 50 pounds heavier and round shouldered, as if he'd spent the first half of his career carrying more than just responsibility on his back. His eyes were different, not so much older as tired . . . not the lack of sleep kind of tired, but something deeper, more pervasive. Where his eyes were once in constant motion, darting around all the time like he had to know everything happening around him, they were now very still. It was as if they found looking at things now, including me, exhausting.

I didn't have to be very intuitive to know something was wrong. He didn't waste any time confirming it.

"I'm retiring at the end of the month," he said, his voice hoarse and also tired sounding.

"Is that good?"

"It's not by choice," he said. "No one else knows this . . . none of the guys on the team . . . but I have lung cancer."

"I'm so sorry."

"I smoked until last year. Everyone smoked when I started in construction. They worked jackhammers with cigarettes dangling from their mouths. The doctor says it's operable."

"That's good."

"Probably operable. They don't say anything for sure . . . about as wishy washy a bunch as I ever met. I guess I'll find out soon enough."

We both sat quietly for a few moments to let the room absorb the news.

Griff asked me about my life. I told him about Earl, the kids and the grandkids. He knew what I did because he'd seen an article in People magazine about thirty years ago.

"My first wife had a subscription and I used to read it in the crapper," he said. It was his first smile.

He told me about his life . . . two wives, six kids, eight dogs.

"Not all at once," he said, "two at a time. I like big dogs, rocks, setters, but my second wife liked'em tiny. We had two toy Yorkies, cute guys, but I must have stepped on one or the other at least twice a week. We got divorced about five years ago, she kept the dogs. I've got a companion now. It's a lot cheaper."

"Tell me about your interactions with Michael?" I asked.

"Since when?"

"Start at the beginning."

"I met Mike in elementary school . . . in little league. Played together for eight years. Helluva a good ballplayer . . . and a good guy."

"That's it?" I asked.

Griff shrugged.

"He was one of my best friends. We hung out together when he wasn't with you."

"Where did you hang out?"

"The usual places . . . the pizza shop, the batting cage. At the Triangle Pub when we got old enough to use fake IDs."

"Did you ever notice anything out of the ordinary about Michael back then? Anything a little strange?"

"Strange, like how?"

"I don't know," I said. "I'm trying to find a reason for all this . . . for his life and death."

"He was like all the other guys on the team as far as I could tell," Griff said, "except for his mother . . . she was a strange one, you knew that?"

I nodded.

"She never came to any of the games and he never had us over to his house."

"Did you know he had an aunt . . . that his mother had a sister?" I asked.

"I didn't know if she did or didn't. It's not the kind of thing we talked about."

"What did you talk about?"

Griff laughed.

"What do you think? Girls and baseball . . . not always in that order. We didn't get too personal back then. Everything wasn't so touchy feely like it is now."

Griff looked down at his hands for a moment before reaching over to pick up a cold cup of coffee. "Want anything?" he asked.

"No, I'm fine."

"Looks like I'm drinking coffee, right?" he said. "I mean it is coffee, but I put a shot of bourbon in it. Started doing that after the diagnosis. I love bourbon. I figure I might as well drink as much of it as I can if I'm not, you know, long for the world."

"I'm sure you'll be fine. They're so much better at this now."

He shrugged and gave me a weak smile.

I don't know why I said that, I had no basis to believe it,

although people say it all the time in Florida. I think it's because they're suspicious . . . if you don't say something like that then you may be guaranteeing a bad outcome.

"Did Mike ever tell you about that road trip he and I took junior year of college?"

"I never spoke to Michael again after we broke up."

"Really?"

I nodded. "Do you find that surprising?"

"Yeah, sometimes he'd talk about you like he'd seen you just the other day."

"In college?"

"In college, after college. He told me he saw you about five years ago."

"He didn't."

"He said he did."

"Maybe he saw me," I said, "but I didn't see him."

Griff looked confused.

"He certainly knew all about you, where you lived, what you were doing. Basic stuff like that. He was always telling me you were doing alright so I just figured you guys must have stayed in touch."

I know it should have given me the willies, but it didn't. It just made me sad.

I asked Griff to start with the road trip and work his way forward to their last conversation.

"He came to visit me in the dorm. It was early in the spring and the baseball team was going down to Florida to train. I played all four years. We were never very good, but we had some rich alums who foot the bill. We were driving down in a caravan of cars and I squeezed Michael in with me. The coach was a real space cadet and didn't realize it."

"How was he?"

"Quiet, I don't know, maybe a little sad. He'd just broken up with someone. I had as well so it worked out fine."

"Anything in particular stand out?"

Griff shook his head slowly from side to side before changing it to up and down. He took his time answering

"He talked a little about his mother. He rarely talked about her. Said she was having some problem."

"What kind?"

"I guess we called it a nervous breakdown back then. Said he'd been going home a lot of weekends to help out. Said he hated going back . . . sitting there in the kitchen by himself."

"You know, she's still alive."

"Holy shit, she must be pushing a hundred."

"She's got full blown dementia."

"He told me she once tried to kill herself."

"He told you that on the Florida trip?"

"I'm not sure. It could have been before that or it could have after we graduated. I don't trust time anymore. It's too damn deceptive. The years get all messed up. It's hard to tell one from the other. It's like trying to look back after climbing a tall mountain."

"You've certainly become the philosopher in your old age."

Griff laughed and I laughed along with him.

"Did Michael say how she tried to kill herself?"

"Gas in the oven . . . I think that's what he said."

That could be a second attempt, I wrote in my notepad, if Griff and Max were both remembering correctly.

"What else did you talk about on the Florida trip?"

"I don't know, the usual stuff . . . girls and baseball. He said he saw you one of the weekends he was down visiting his mother. Said he went to buy some groceries and saw you coming out of the A and P."

"Why he didn't come over and say hello?"

Griff shrugged.

"Why do you think?"

Griff placed his hands flat on the desk and tried to stretch his back by arching backward. It made him wince.

"I think he was embarrassed about what was happening."

"With his mother?"

"Yeah . . . and the fact that he hadn't been doing very well in school . . . or playing baseball. Maybe because he was smoking so much pot. Brought some with him for the ride. Had a lot on his mind I suppose."

Griff stretched his back again. Then he stood up.

"Can't sit for hours like I used."

"I know the feeling," I said. "Although for me it's always my knees."

Griff walked behind his chair and leaned over it.

"Maybe he wanted you to remember him the way he was in high school when we used to call him Mr. Perfect. You remember that?"

"You guys did, I didn't. It would have been ridiculous for him to feel like that."

"Easy to say now. We were barely twenty . . . what did we know from ridiculous."

How is it I didn't sense him nearby or hear a word about any of his difficulties? My mother must have heard about it—it was a small community—although if she did she wouldn't have said anything to me.

Why didn't I ever make an effort to find out what was happening with Michael? I know I was curious, I suppose because I was still hurt and angry. By the time I let go too much time had passed. At least that was my thinking as I sat there in Griff's office. Of course, there was no way for me to remember what I was really thinking fifty years ago.

"Anything else happen on that trip?" I asked.

"Not much . . . we both scored. You remember what spring break in Florida was like."

"I don't, I never went."

"You were always a goody two-shoes."

"Hardly, I was sleeping with Michael in ninth grade."

"Well, except for that. Boy, were we ever jealous of Mike back then. My first time wasn't until my freshman year of college."

Griff said they lost touch for a while after the Florida trip, although he did hear that Mike had gotten into some heavier drugs, and he did speak with him after graduation.

"Told me he was headed out to Las Vegas and LA."

"Did he say why?"

"To find himself I suppose. We didn't talk for quite a few years after that, not until he returned from LA and started working at the bank. The guys would get together for beer nights once or twice a year. He'd always tell me he was coming, but he never did."

"Why do you think he didn't show?"

"I hadn't thought much about it until you called. I don't know why, I figured it was his business. Maybe it was because of his mother. That had to be a killer in terms of his personal life. Things change, life throws you a few high fastballs, some you can't catch up with and before you know it you're out."

"Out?"

"Trapped."

I nodded. A mixed metaphor, but I got the point.

"My first wife, Sherri, smart woman, tried to spend every dollar I made as fast as she could. Once bought a vase, a glass thing about three feet tall from China for five thousand dollars which broke a month later when the dog knocked it over. When it came to jewelry there was no stopping her. It's like she considered diamonds an essential food group."

I smiled, Griff didn't.

"Anyway, she used to say Mike grew up backwards."

"What did she mean?"

"She said it was bad to be put up on a pedestal in high school. You know, the best looking, the best athlete, the smartest . . . the cutest girlfriend."

I looked down at my notepad.

"I see you blushing," he said. "Hey, you're still not bad."

"I'll take that as a compliment," I said.

"That's the way I meant it."

"So what did your ex-wife mean?"

"She said falling so far so fast when you're young can really screw you up. She thought it would be a lot better to start at ground level and climb up on the pedestal when you're in your thirties and forties . . . when your old enough to know that falling off is inevitable and it won't make a damn difference to the rest of your life. Anyway, that was her theory."

"My husband calls it the big fish in the small pond syndrome," I said. "Some people have a hard time handling the sudden transition to little fish in the big ocean."

Griff nodded as he stretched one more time before sitting back down in his chair.

"I guess I'm the lucky one," he said. "No one's ever put me up on a pedestal, not in high school and not after . . . certainly not my wives and kids."

"I'm sure your kids did when they were young."

"At that age it wouldn't have mattered if I were an ax-murderer. I'm talking about when they got older."

I didn't want to go into Griff's relationships with his six kids. I imagined that could be an article by itself so I asked him about his other contacts with Michael over the years.

"I eventually stopped calling him every time the guys on the team got together. Maybe we'd talk every two or three years on the phone. Catching up . . . that kind of thing. He told me when his wife took sick. That was terrible . . . and then when she died. And his son with the drugs.

"It's like he used up all the good luck in high school that God had allotted for him and all he had left were the catastrophes."

"Do you believe that?"

"Nah, not really. Just bad luck, plain and simple . . . maybe a few bad decisions along the way to help it along."

Griff looked down at his hands as he rubbed them along the desk.

"You know," he said without looking up, "you came up in just about every conversation."

"After all these years?"

"Yep. We always talked a little high school and the baseball team . . . and you. He'd always be the one to bring you up."

I took a deep breath and held it in for a moment before letting it out.

"That's why I thought you guys were still friends," he said. "Last time we talked he told me you were one of those snowbirds. Said he saw you down in Florida."

"It's too strange," I said, "because we never spoke again after we broke up, and I never saw him again, not in New York, not in New Jersey . . . and not in Florida."

"Yeah, you said that, but it sounds weird considering the way he talked. Why would he make stuff like that up?"

"He wasn't making it up," I said.

"What do you mean?"

I told Griff about the photos I'd gotten from Nancy and what Teal had told me. "What if he was visiting me in his own way to see me at a distance? It wouldn't be hard to find out where I lived and what I was doing. Maybe it was his way of taking a trip down memory lane."

Griff sucked in the air like he was inhaling an imaginary cigarette, then he let it out slowly. "Doesn't make any sense to me," he said. "What would be the point of that?"

I had no response to that and all I could do was shrug.

"And it's a little creepy if you ask me," Griff added before coughing into his fist. He had a real smoker's cough.

"That was my initial reaction," I said. "Now I just feel sort of sad about it."

"The whole thing blows my mind," Griff said, "considering the way he was in high school. We all envied him."

"Tell me about your last call with Michael?" I asked.

"It had to be about two years ago, maybe a little longer. I hadn't heard from him in a while so I called to see how he was doing. He didn't pick up. He never did. I'd always leave a message and wait for him to call me back. He did most of the time, not always, and I didn't press it when he didn't. If he didn't call back, I'd wait another year and try again.

"Anyway, he did call back this time . . . a couple of days later. He sounded pretty good. Said work was fine. He was working in the backroom at Morgan Stanley checking the trades. Doesn't sound like much, but it's really important and I'm sure they paid him well. He told me he would have to retire in a couple of years . . . they had a mandatory retirement age. I thought it sounded ridiculous when he said it, but now I think it's a good idea. It's better than being forced to retire by the big C."

Griff took a moment to take a deep breath after saying that. "Sorry," he said.

"No problem."

"I don't like feeling sorry for myself and I don't want anyone feeling sorry for me."

"I'm not," I said, "because I'm sure you'll find a way to beat it. The way you used to find the weakness in every batter's swing."

Griff chuckled. "I wish it were that easy."

"What else did Michael say in that last call?"

"Said he'd been on vacation."

"Did he tell you if he went anywhere?"

"I don't remember. I don't think so. Said he'd been off the whole month. Apparently, he had to take off four weeks in a row at least once every two years. Some kind of SEC regulation. Did say he spent a lot of money."

"On what?"

"I don't remember . . . restaurants . . . things. Maybe he was trying to spend it all before, you know, he left for good."

"There are quicker ways to spend your money," I said.

"Tell me about it. A couple of divorces can drain the bank

account pretty quick."

"What else did you talk about?"

Griff rubbed his chin. "That's when he told me he had to be in Florida for some conference and would probably stop by to see you again . . . he said it like it was the most ordinary thing in the world." Griff raised his hand and covered his mouth for a moment. "Now that I think about it, I don't think he said again. I think he said one more time . . . he was stopping by to see you one more time. I remember thinking that sounded strange, like maybe you were sick or something, but Mike didn't like a lot of questions and I didn't ask what he meant. Maybe he was thinking about doing it a few years ago. Damn, I should have said something."

"I suspect anyone who takes their own life starts thinking about it a long time before they do it," I said.

"Maybe he started thinking about it after his mother tried it," Griff said, "or back in college when he was doing all those drugs."

"God, I hope not," I said, slumping back against the chair.

"Did you get the fiftieth reunion invitation?" Griff asked.

"I did."

"You going?"

"I don't know, maybe."

"Come on," Griff said, "you're like an honorary member of our class. Most of the guys from the team will be there. We're going to do something to remember Mike."

"What?"

"Don't know yet. The other classmates as well . . . the ones who have passed on."

"How many are there?"

"I'm not sure. I think about fifty."

"Sounds pretty high for a class of two-sixty" I said.

"Vietnam, drugs," Griff looked down at his chest, "smoking."

"We have lived through some tumultuous times."

"That's for sure."

Griff got up to escort me to the door. This time he gave me a goodbye kiss on the cheek.

"Good luck with the surgery."

"Don't worry," he said, "I'm planning to go down swinging."

"I'm not worried."

"I'll see you at the reunion."

"Maybe."

I turned to go when I felt Griff's hand on my shoulder.
"Do you know how he did it?" he asked.
"No."
"I'd be interested."
"Why?"

"Just curious," he said, but he said it like he was thinking he might find himself in a similar circumstance if the cancer got really bad. Griff was not one in high school to dwell on a loss, but he wasn't the type either to tilt against windmills.

CHAPTER SEVEN – GOING HOME

I needed some Earl desperately and I flew back to Florida. I could do research just as well at home as I could from up in New York.

I showed Earl the photos Nosy Nancy had given me. He studied them for a long time.

"I'd almost forgotten you were this young," he said with a smile.

"Thanks a lot."

"I suspect there are a lot more," he said. "I bet he did come down to Florida like he told Griff . . . to see you and say goodbye."

I didn't know how to respond to that. The thought broke my heart.

"I know," Earl said, as if reading my mind. He reached over to rub my leg. "He clearly didn't want you to know . . . or freak you out. It's hard to imagine after all these years, but I think it has more to do with his growing up years than it did with what happened to his wife and son."

He looked down again at the photos.

"These photos are well before that. It had to be something that goes back to his childhood, maybe something with his mother . . . something he was hiding in high school . . . even from you."

It made sense theoretically, but I couldn't agree.

"I knew him too well in high school for Michael to hide anything like that," I said.

"But how well did you know yourself? How closely did you look? You were young, expecting the fairy tale, looking at most everything through rose-colored glasses. I bet you never shined that intuitive flashlight of yours in his direction."

It would turn out Earl was much more intuitive than I was

when it came to Michael and my past.

"I wish there was a way I could talk to him now," I said.

"There are always things we wish we had said or done when people we love . . . or once loved . . . leave us."

"It's so much odder after fifty years of silence," I said.

"Absolutely, although I'm not sure how much the years mean in a circumstance like this. The time inside us is very different from the time outside. It's not as linear, it's more like a collage."

"Maybe you should be writing this article," I said.

Earl's reasoning, his simple way of seeing things, sometimes astounded me.

"I'd rather be playing golf."

"Do you talk about time on the golf course?"

"T-times."

We both laughed.

"I suspect it didn't feel like fifty years to him," Earl said, "any more than it feels like fifty years to us."

I nodded, although I was still feeling uncertain and lost. My investigation couldn't provide any answers and my original theme—that Facebook postings rarely reflect the truth about a person's life—no longer felt worthwhile. There was much more here . . . about how hard it is to see into another person's heart, especially when we are young . . . about the signs we miss either because we're not looking or are too blinded by love . . . and about how a life can change dramatically and without warning.

"I know you'll find the handle," Earl said, knowing what I was thinking since we'd been talking a lot about it since my return.

Handle is the word I always use for the overriding theme of an article.

"You'll find an explanation," Earl said, trying to reassure me the way he always does. "It will be a nice tribute. It will help all of you understand what happened."

"I think it'll take a book to do that," I said.

Earl thought it over for a moment. Earl was a cautious, thoughtful man, a man of few words, but his words were always meaningful and kind. I couldn't have gone through this life with anyone else. He wouldn't have been my choice in high school, but who knows what they really need at sixteen?

"I think that's a wonderful idea," he said. "You've always wanted to write a book and this sounds like something even I'd want to read."

I smiled. I was thinking out loud, but I think Earl was right.

"But you know what that means," he added.

"What?"

"It means you have to attend the fiftieth reunion."

"Why?"

"Because everyone who knew you and Michael back then will be there. These are the people who can truly appreciate your shared past and see it through the same fifty year lens. They may have some insights and if not they'll give you some ideas. I don't see how you can complete your research without going."

"I really wasn't planning on going," I said, nodding at the same time.

"No one is going to make you," he said with a big grin, "but if you're doing a book, I think it would be interesting . . . and worthwhile. You can skip yours next year, but if you are going to write about Michael, you should go to his."

Strong words for Earl who generally liked to avoid sounding too judgmental or insistent.

My head was filling up with ideas, too many ideas for one magazine article. I'd always wanted to write a novel. I'd been talking about it since I met Earl. I could change the names and places, but still make it real. It would be ironic, I thought, if it took Michael's death after fifty years of silence to push me into it?

"OK," I said, "but only if you go with me."

Earl smiled. "I'll gladly go if you want me to, but I suspect when it comes down to it you'll feel better leaving me up in the hotel room."

I disagreed, although Earl was better at knowing what was in my heart sometimes than I was.

The reunion wasn't for almost three months, but I made our reservations at the hotel. We'd be back up in New Jersey by then anyway so it would be an easy drive. Until we returned home, I planned to do my research from right here in Florida—by phone and by internet— protected by the routines and the life I cherished more now than ever.

It turns out that every unexplained death in New York City requires an autopsy and I was able to order a copy online by requesting it on behalf of Michael's mother. I know it was wrong—and a violation of the law—but investigative journalists, and I tried to fancy myself as one, sometimes have to bend the rules.

I didn't expect to find any surprises and if I was changing all the names what harm would it be.

It took four weeks to arrive.

There were some surprises, like the fact that Michael had undetected lung cancer for quite some time, which "he was likely unaware of" and which "did not contribute to his death, nor was it likely to." Apparently, it was the type of cancer that someone could walk around with for a lifetime without it ever making its presence known. Perhaps that's why so many doctors worry about too many screenings, afraid they may wind up over-diagnosing and over-treating an illness which if left alone would never become symptomatic before the patient dies of some other cause. I read that some people could live with cancers in their bodies for their whole lives without realizing it and without it interfering with their health in any meaningful way.

Could Michael have had the beginnings of it in high school? His father was a big smoker and I'm sure he had a lot of second-hand exposure as a child. And what about all that pot smoking in college? How much do we really know about what goes on in our own bodies over a lifetime? I'm sure it's much less than we'd like to believe.

The report also said he was in the early stages of Parkinson's. He was aware of that, the coroner concluded, because he found traces of Levodropa in his body, a drug commonly prescribed to treat it. There was an anti-depressant found, Seroquel, a drug used to treat depression, as well bipolar disorders and schizophrenia. Michael was also taking propranolol which treats high blood pressure and tremors. The coroner also found a high level of caffeine and alcohol, although not at a level, he wrote, that might be indicative of someone intending to kill himself with alcohol and pills.

Not like his mother had supposedly tried.

Michael had other physical problems . . . a thickening of his arteries, a narrowing of his joints, not unusual for a man in his mid-sixties, although more than the coroner would normally have expected to find. The deterioration of joints were probably the result, the report stated, of "the deceased having played a lot of organized sports in his youth."

None of those problems were the cause of death.

The cause of death was surprising. I would have thought it would be a drug overdose or some improper combination of sleeping pills, anti-depressants and alcohol. Even a shot of some household pipe cleaner or another corrosive acid. But the cause of death was fluid in the lungs. In other words, Michael had drowned in his bathtub.

I couldn't imagine Michael intentionally doing that or anyone else for that matter. People drown in bath tubs for any number of reasons. The coroner recognized that stating he could not confirm based on his autopsy whether it was an intentional act or accidental. He said the drugs in his system, combined with the alcohol and the hour could have caused him to fall asleep or pass out in the bath. He could have submerged intentionally as well and let himself drown. There was no way of knowing for sure.

The thought of him accidentally drowning upset me even more. If it wasn't intentional, Michael deserved a better way to go . . . of course, we all did.

I couldn't help remembering all those times we went swimming—in the ocean, in one of the nearby mountain lakes, even at the local pool. Michael was a great swimmer. His long arms and strong legs propelled him effortlessly and smoothly through the water. There was no keeping up with him, not for me, and not for his teammates.

The next thing I did was call my broker at Morgan Stanley and tell him what I was doing. He gave me an introduction to the new head of the Compliance Department, Jeff Cone, who allowed me to interview him over the telephone.

He started off by telling me that Michael was the best Compliance Director they'd ever had, if not the best in the industry. That was nice to hear.

"He had an incredible memory," Jeff said, "and there are so many picayune rules and regulations, it's almost impossible to keep them straight. He had a quick eye and a real feel for it. Mike could spot an infraction in an instant. It was uncanny sometimes, almost like he could see things no one else could."

"He was incredibly bright when I knew him," I said.

Work seemed to be a haven for him. He was well respected, ran a tight ship, and never disappointed anyone. That was the Michael I remembered.

Jeff was less forthcoming when it came to Michael's personal side.

"He didn't talk much about himself . . . about what was going on in his personal life . . . not like the rest of us did, you know, complaining about things at home or talking about our crazy weekends. We all knew about his wife and kid, which I'm sure explained why he kept his relationships at work very business-like. He'd talk sports like the other guys, that sort of thing, but nothing personal. Didn't know if he was dating or what he did at night or on weekends . . . he never talked about it."

They were all shocked by his death, Jeff said, particularly since he was scheduled to retire at the end of the summer.

"The firm has a mandatory retirement age for compliance, sixty-five."

"Michael was over sixty-five," I said.

"They gave him a couple of extensions. He was good and he didn't want to leave. I suppose he didn't have much else to do, I mean outside of work. He ran out of extensions, they wouldn't give him more than two."

Michael had to be depressed about that. Could that have been the final straw? If Michael didn't have any other hobbies or interests he was screwed, particularly if he didn't have a companion . . . other than his mother.

"Do you have any idea if Michael have any hobbies or interests, something he talked about doing in his retirement? Traveling? Writing? Anything?"

Jeff took a moment to think about it. I heard him give instructions to someone who must have walked into his office with a question. His remarks were technical and I had no idea what he was telling him to do. I couldn't imagine Earl ever being happy in compliance.

"He liked photography. He was always reading about cameras and checking the stores for the latest models. Whenever he went somewhere on vacation he'd bring in photos of buildings and scenic stuff and put them around the office. We have to take six weeks' vacation in compliance . . . four of them consecutively . . . company rules."

"Where did he go?"

"Mostly around the country. Europe once. He really liked to take photos of landmarks and buildings. Said he thought he'd have made a good architect. We worked together for fifteen years and that was about as personal as he got."

"Can you think of anything else? Anything he might have enjoyed or ever talked about doing?"

"No . . . well, yes. He once came in on a Monday morning very excited . . . for him anyway. This was a while ago, probably not long after I started. He mentioned going to this great art exhibit."

"Do you remember what it was?"

"It was not the kind of art I liked or even heard of before." Jeff breathed loudly into the phone while he thought it over. "It was a kind of diorama. Like the ones we used to make in shoeboxes when we were in elementary school, except he called them shadow boxes. They were done by a guy with the same name as one of the Ivy League schools. Give me a second, it'll come to me. You have to have a mind for trivia if you're going to make it in the compliance."

Jeff serenaded me with some more breathing.

"Cornell, that's it. The artist's name was Cornell. Joseph Cornell. Funny I remember it after all these years. Mike was really excited. Thought he could do something like that . . . said he might try his hand at making one."

"Did you ever see one he made?"

"No, I'm sure it was all talk. He never mentioned it again. He wasn't the kind of guy who volunteered too much information . . . or invited too many questions."

I thanked Jeff for his time and looked up Joseph Cornell. He was actually born in the Hudson Valley at the very beginning of the twentieth century, not too far from the town where Michael and I grew up. His father was from a socially prominent New York family, but died when Joseph was 14 leaving them destitute.

It sounded familiar, although when Michael's father died he was almost 17, and while money became tight he didn't leave them destitute.

Joseph Cornell's life was never the same afterward. He had to take care of his mother and sickly younger brother. He never married and lived like a recluse. He started making shadow boxes out of odds and ends around the house and things he found around the neighborhood. He used old photos and objects he bought in bookshops and thrift stores.

His shadow boxes found their way to an art gallery in Manhattan and took off. One critic said his boxes relied on the "Surrealist use of irrational juxtaposition and on the evocation of nostalgia for their appeal."

The word nostalgia hit home.

In the end, Cornell wound up living alone in a house in Queens.

I wondered if Michael had researched him after seeing the exhibit of his shadow boxes. I searched the internet and found that there was a big exhibit at the Met in 1970, another at Cooper Union in 1972 and a retrospective at the MOMA in 1980. It had to be after that at a smaller exhibition I couldn't find online. Perhaps at another gallery. I wondered if it was Cornell's life or his art that drew Michael to him. Probably a combination of both.

I also wondered if Michael did attempt to make any shadow boxes. If he had they'd probably be in his apartment. I doubted anyone had cleaned out his apartment, a cooperative in the Upper East Side, and if Michael's death was intentional it was likely he pre-paid his maintenance charges to make it easier for his mother. Although he was also a banker of sorts and just as likely to have any recurring charges taken every month directly from his checking account.

I called his mother and this time the aide answered. When I told her I was interested in seeing Michael's apartment she sounded relieved.

"They've been sending letters and calling non-stop," the aide said.

"Who?"

"The coop people. They want her to clean out the apartment and sell it. She can't do any of that I keep telling them, even if she wanted to, but if you could do it for her I'm sure she'd appreciate it. I don't know who else to ask."

"How can I do that?"

Apparently home care aides know a thing or two about the law or perhaps their agencies do. She told me to get myself appointed as her guardian to replace Michael. Then I could do whatever needed to be done.

"No one else is interested in doing it," she said. "I can get her to sign whatever you need signed. All I have to do is stick a pen in there and guide her hand."

I told her I would be happy to help.

Michael had the power of attorney as her guardian, but that expired along with him. The agency referred me to an attorney who did this kind of thing and since he could find no other living relatives, he had no trouble going to court and arranging for me to be appointed as guardian for Helen and executrix for Michael's estate.

I hadn't seen or spoken to Michael in fifty years, but I was an old high school friend to the court and now responsible for disposing of his life and taking care of his mother.

Earl thought it was wonderful to have an old friend like me step up to the plate, an analogy that made me wince. The word friend hardly seemed appropriate. Unfortunately, there was no one else around to do it.

I was charged with disposing of everything of Michael's so that the money could be put in trust for his mother, and then to make some sort of will for her to dispose of the assets once she passed on.

By the time the paperwork was in place, Earl and I had already closed up our Florida snowbird retreat and made our way back to New Jersey for the April showers. The first thing I had to do was empty out Michael's apartment so the realtors could start showing it.

Rather than commute back and forth to New Jersey, Earl suggested I spend a couple of days in the city getting things organized.

"Stay at a hotel," he said. "I'm sure you can charge it to the estate."

I told Earl I'd prefer to save money by staying at Michael's apartment. "I'll get more done a lot quicker that way," I said.

It made him shudder, but he didn't try to discourage me.

Since I didn't know Michael anymore, not really, I didn't imagine I'd feel that strange about it . . . like it was haunted or anything like that.

I first visited Michael's mother again who was overjoyed to see me, except she still saw the high school me and thanked me for helping Michael while he recovered from his baseball injury. In her mind, Michael was playing college ball and recovering from a broken leg he got sliding into home.

"I don't know why he has to stay in college if he can't play," she said.

"Probably team rules," I responded.

I promised to visit again soon and drove back to the city.

The apartment was on 95th and Park Avenue in a beautiful old building that looked as if it hadn't changed in a hundred years, except for becoming a cooperative in the 1980's and modernizing its lobby.

The doorman had my name and once I showed my driver's license he gave me the key. It was one of those buildings with two apartments to a floor so it was very quiet when I got up there. The doorman had told me that the people in the apartment across the hall, a middle age couple without kids, kept to themselves, worked long hours and never returned until very late.

"But it's not unusual," he said. "People in this building keep to themselves, if you know what I mean. A nod and a good morning . . . that's about it. No one gets too chummy."

I suppose rich, doorman buildings can be like that, particularly the ones without children.

I must say that my heart was racing as I stuck the key into the door. If I had welcomed Michael back into my life after his death, this felt as if he were now welcoming me back into his. It seemed like an enormous invasion of privacy entering into someone's apartment, particularly when they are not there . . . even if they're never coming back.

There may be things people—especially solitary people—leave lying around that they would never want anyone to see.

Well, I thought to myself as I turned the key and opened the door, at least he'll never know.

The apartment opened into a large foyer which was a mess. There were boxes everywhere filled with all kinds of odds and ends, snippets of ribbons and yarn, small toys and dolls, wooden letters and numbers, tiny cars and furniture, colored paper, magazines and miniature plastic food. It was as if Michael were planning to open an old-fashion curio shop.

It was cluttered, not to the extent of a hoarder, but clearly Michael was someone who collected things. Things few other people would be interested in. Things he might find in an old bookstore and thrift shop . . . like Joseph Cornell . . . and once he put his purchases down it looked like they stayed there until he needed something.

It was a large Park Avenue apartment with high ceilings and wainscoting. It felt like a step back in time, not to high school, but to a hundred years earlier when the light at night came from gas lamps and the heat from a fireplace.

It had to feel a little haunted living here alone.

The kitchen was to the right and the back of the foyer. It was small and almost devoid of food—the cupboards were bare—suggesting that Michael did indeed eat out most of the time. The refrigerator had some food in it, some milk and cheese, along with the typical collection of condiments, mostly spoiled, and I had to empty it, scrub in clean, and drop everything down the incinerator chute. I was amazed it was still used to dispose of garbage. At the far back end of the kitchen was a small maid's room that was completely empty, not a stick of furniture, just a lot of dust balls fleeing from my every step.

At the front of the foyer—also to the right—was the entrance to the dining room.

The dining room table, a heavy antique with thick carved legs and inlayed wood on top looked as if it had come with the apartment a hundred years earlier, a piece too heavy to move more than once. It was covered with more bric-a brac, some things still in the bags they were put in when Michael purchased them.

I'm sure he knew what was in every bag.

The dining room opened up into the living room which was the size of Earl and my entire first apartment. The furniture was relatively new, but oddly reminiscent of the 60's furniture in his mother's house. The walls were bare. There wasn't a photo or picture anywhere. So much for Michael's interest in photography. What drew my attention was the living room coffee table, silver base and glass top, on which there were a half dozen art books, some opened as if Michael had been looking through them a few minutes earlier.

I sat down to look through them. Many of the pages had holes where small photos of art had been neatly cut out. On a tray beside the books was a collection of scissors laid out in size order, some very small, the kind you might use for cuticles or a moustache. There were scraps of paper scattered on the floor around the table like snowflakes.

I sat there for a while trying to imagine what Michael was thinking as he sat here flipping through a thousand years of art deciding which picture to cut out. I went through each of the books looking for pages with missing paintings. There was no pattern that I could discern.

I suppose it was partly curiosity, but it was also partly procrastination. I was avoiding Michael's bedroom, the master bedroom. I was afraid of what I might find there, especially in the bathroom, perhaps his body outlined in chalk, everything exactly the way it was when they found him. I had intended to save it until the end, but I decided to get it over with before checking out the other two bedrooms.

Fortunately, there was no sign of his death. The doorman on duty had called the police when Michael hadn't been seen in a few days.

"We knew he was home," the doorman told me when he gave me the key, "because we keep track of the comings and goings of our residents and their guests. You never know when it could be important."

He showed me the day book which checked everyone in and out. He showed me the check by my name. I was now listed under resident.

"He was checked in, but not out. After two days, we knew something was up. He always left at seven thirty sharp for work and he usually took his dinner out so we knew it couldn't be good."

He looked at the front door and the elevator to make sure no one was coming.

"I hope it was an accident or a heart attack. Can't be good for the building if he killed himself. I must say he was a strange bird, no one would argue with that, although he always gave us a nice gift on Christmas and he was never very demanding, not like some of the other residents who think we're servants. You can't imagine some of the things they ask us to do."

I nodded like I could, although I couldn't. I'd never lived in a doorman building. Earl and I lived in a third floor walk-up until we had our first child and saved enough to buy a house, the New Jersey house we still live in.

Once the police found him and took the body, the doorman told me, the super had the cleaning people empty the tub, wipe it clean and straighten out the bathroom.

"Better for the building," he said.

I suppose they were trying to make it easier for the family

when they came in to clean out his things, thinking no doubt that he had one and that his death was just another one of those drug overdoses plaguing the country in recent years.

There was nothing unusual about Michael's bedroom, except for the fact that his bed was unmade. When we were growing up his father always insisted he make his bed. He said an unmade bed was a sign of sickness. I was never in the house when it wasn't made. When we were alone and messed it up, we always remade it before we left.

Michael had a closet full of blue and black suits, nothing brown. His shirts were all laundered and hung by color, white or blue, and he had lots of ties, mostly red. There were more ties in Michael's closet than Earl had owned over his entire working life. There were no jeans, no t-shirts, no jerseys and no sweatshirts, none of the clothes I remembered Michael loving so much in high school.

Clearly, he was more neat and organized when it came to his clothes than anything else in the apartment. I'm sure the big brokerage houses have very strict standards.

There were still no photos anywhere in the bedroom and no pictures on the wall. It hardly looked lived in. There was no warmth to the décor. It didn't feel like a room with a history, no evidence anywhere of sad and happy moments, no lingering memories of illness and recovery. It didn't feel comfortable and safe the way most master bedrooms do . . . a place where people can go to escape their troubles and return to their dreams.

It could have been a hotel room.

I went back to the grand hall, as I had come to think of the foyer, to check out the other two bedrooms.

The first one, nearest Michael's bedroom, was a shrine of sorts to his life. That's where all the photos were, either on the walls, or in frames on the credenza. There was no bed, just a couch, a small table and some chairs. It was a place for someone— for Michael—to sit on those nights when he needed to take in his life in a glance.

It was in chronological order starting with photos of his parents. There was his mother, younger than when I knew her with a big smile and a bright look in her eyes. She never looked that happy when we were going out and she certainly did not in the photos that followed with his Michael as a young boy. In those later photos, the shadow never left her face.

There were solitary pictures of Michael as a toddler and a little boy. He grew tall and strong and an instant later he appeared in his first little league uniform. He looked the typical boy, always in motion . . . a motion filled with energy and purpose. Twelve inches later he arrived in high school where the baseball uniform looked more professional and the poses more practiced.

There were more photos of the two of us than I could remember taking. There were pictures of me at the beach, in the stands watching him play which I assume was taken by one of his teammates, and pictures of me sitting on Michael's bed pretending to do homework. I remembered that moment well. Immediately after the photo, Michael pulled back the cover and undressed me. There was even a picture of me on our swing, the swing I sat on the last time we were together, as well as some photos of us at dances and picnics.

I suppose I must have had similar copies of most of those moments at one time or another, the same photo taken a second earlier or a second later. They've all disappeared, some torn up and thrown away by me in the months after the breakup, others no doubt tossed by my mother while I was in college . . . the rest having disappeared sometime after I got engaged to Earl.

There weren't a lot of photos from college. There was one of Teal, I recognized her from the yearbook, not our interview, and a couple of frat pictures, the type where the whole frat sits outside on a warm spring day and everyone raises their bottle of beer . . . or in Michael's case his fat joint.

There was a photo in Las Vegas where Michael is standing in front of a poker table at some tournament. He was smiling, not quite the easy smile I remembered, but something more tentative. Perhaps he was ahead at the moment—barely—and still had hopes of winning a fortune and using it to conquer Hollywood.

There were some photos from Los Angeles. I'd been there often enough to recognize Santa Monica and Westwood. The pictures were mostly of buildings, but there was one of a woman who had the same long hair and long legs I was known for. It was the look Michael liked in high school and apparently continued to crave, except she had a big round face, as opposed to my narrow one, the kind of face a child might draw with a crayon.

It was a little creepy standing there as if in a museum of

Michael's life watching it unfold. The only thing missing were captions.

I was almost afraid to turn and look at the rest of the room.

Fran and Doug had a whole wall devoted to them. She was beautiful, far more beautiful than me, but she didn't seem all that relaxed in any of the photographs. She looked tense, watchful, as if she had to remain vigilant at all times, even in front of the camera. Doug was indeed a striking combination of the two of them . . . deep blue eyes that were big and expressive, a perfectly shaped nose and full lips . . . except his lips did look frozen in a perpetual sulk.

There were the usual photos of them in the park and at the beach, dressed up for a night out, even one with Michael's mother who appeared a bit disoriented. There was nothing that could be construed as a last photo. They just stopped, the rest of the wall—about three feet—blank to the corner, both Fran and Doug disappearing as if into the emptiness of eternity.

It was when I turned to the last wall that I got dizzy and had to sit down.

It was a wall devoted to me, not photos from high school, but after that from college to a fairly recent one of me in Florida. While the photos from high school were all familiar, even if dimly lit in the deepest recesses of my memory, these photos were not. None of them were posed. You can always tell when someone is completely unaware they are being stared at through the lens of a camera.

The photos captured me—at a distance—from every stage of my life, starting with the day Michael came to visit me my freshman year at Skidmore, saw me walking with another guy, and turned around . . . to a day I vaguely remembered in Florida a couple of years earlier when I went shopping for a new sundress, one big enough to cover my ever expanding hips and stomach.

If only he had come up to me to say hello . . . or I had spotted him.

There was a photo taken of me sitting on the steps of Colby Hall laughing and holding hands with Fred. I knew it was my junior year because that's when I dated Fred, a grad student instructor in math who was not much older than me. The romance didn't last very long, the chemistry wasn't there, although we remained friends until he left the next year for an assistant professor position at a small college in the Midwest.

I don't remember the moment as much as I do the day. It was the first warm day of spring and the first time I got to wear my jean shorts, cut from an old pair of jeans, and my new Daisy Mae scoop blouse that revealed a lot more than I'd ever reveal now.

When I think about it, the chemistry might have been off because Fred was probably gay. Back then some people tried to deny it, both men and women, more than some I bet. Maybe Fred was hoping that by entering into a more traditional relationship he could follow a more traditional path. He was a very sweet guy, a great listener, and quick to get whatever it was I was inarticulately trying to say.

I don't know how that possibility didn't occur to me until now.

You tend to think of your younger self as being just as smart and aware as your present self, but it's not true . . . not even close.

The next photo was Spring Fling weekend when the school trucked in sand and we all pretended to be sunbathing on the beach. There I was in a bikini on a blanket with a few of my college friends. I was sipping a big drink with a funny looking straw and looking out in the distance, as if I were staring into the same infinity offered by a real beach. Michael must have gotten pretty close, unless he had a telephoto lens, because it was a clear, full photo. If I had looked to the right at exactly that moment, instead of staring straight ahead, I might have seen him hiding behind the camera a dozen feet away.

The next group of photos was the married me. We were living in our first apartment on the upper west side and there I was coming out of the store with a bag of groceries. I still looked like a young girl, not all the much different than the way I looked in high school. There were other photos of me walking around the west side. I was alone in all of them. There wasn't a single photo on the wall that included Earl. Perhaps that helped with Michael's fantasy . . . or his nostalgic trip back in time . . . if that's what this was all about.

I often wondered during those early years whether I'd bump into Michael one day and what it would be like, but it never happened. I'd certainly stopped thinking about it by the time he took the photo of me pregnant, sitting on the top step of our building looking out at the sea of people flowing by.

His camera followed me out to New Jersey. There was a photo of me pushing a carriage in town. He had to be sitting in a car with a powerful telephoto lens. Could he have been wearing a disguise as I passed by him on the street?

I suppose I should be relieved that Michael was only a photo stalker and not any more than that, the thought of which did give me the chills while at the same time breaking my heart. Perhaps if I had seen him once and we'd started talking—become friends again—it would have been different for him. I'd have done that in an instant if it would have helped.

I know Earl would not have had a problem with it. Earl would have been just as happy to help and be his friend as well. He still spoke to his old junior high girlfriend from time to time—his first kiss—and we'd gone out together a couple of times, her and her husband, me and Earl. They'd given up their home up north and were full time Floridians.

There were photos of me in my early journalist years covering zoning board meetings and school board elections. There was even a photo of me leaving the Path train. Michael would have had to know something about my schedule to be waiting there. Unless he'd been waiting for days for me to pass by.

There were photos of me from every stage of my life. It was eerie watching my youth slip away, my hair grow short and grey, and my waist thicken. In the span of a few feet on a Park Avenue apartment wall I turned from a young woman and wife into a dowdy and frumpy grandmother . . . the same one I used to see when my mother was alive.

Although if I looked hard enough and squinted a bit, I could almost see the young girl still there inside me. I can still see it sometimes in the mirror, as well as on the faces of other people I know. None of faces we wear throughout our lives ever completely disappear. All the ages are there somewhere and sometimes if the light is right and I'm in the right frame of mind I can see them all.

How was I ever going to take all these photos down and who would I give them to? I could give some to Michael's mother and others to Fran's sister, Sandi. But what about my photos? I knew what Earl would say . . . do whatever you feel comfortable doing, although he might suggest I keep them in a folder in case I decide to write a magazine article to accompany the book.

I wasn't sure I could do that. I wasn't sure I could look at them without feeling heartbroken and kicking myself for being so obtuse and unaware. If I did keep them it would be in a new shoebox placed in the attic to be lost again and forgotten.

I sat there in a daze staring at all the walls, trying to imagine what Michael was thinking when he sat in this very spot, wondering how close to the surface the high school Michael would rise and whether he ever sat there wondering about his sanity . . . or at the very least his grasp on the present.

As I looked around for the second and third time, I noticed there were photos missing. I could tell because there were empty spaces on all the walls outlined in dust and less faded than the areas around them that had been exposed to years of light. There were blank spaces all around the room—missing photos of the young Michael, the high school Michael and me, Fran and Doug, even the matronly me.

There was one more room to explore and I dreaded what I might find. This Michael was so very different from my high school Michael. He'd become reclusive and odd, tormented by something, something from his past . . . similar in a way I suppose to Joseph Cornell. Whether it was a gene he received from his mother that snapped on at a certain age or was turned on by the psychedelic drugs, I would never know. He clearly had two faces, the one he showed at work and the one he kept in his apartment. Did he have the same two faces back in high school? The truth, unfortunately, had died with him.

I got up slowly and left the room. I stood in front of the third bedroom door and it took a while before I got up the nerve to reach out for the doorknob. It didn't turn like the other, it was locked. I searched everywhere for a key—through every kitchen and bedroom drawer—but I couldn't find one. I called Earl to ask what he would suggest. He said to call the doorman. He'd send up the super who might have a key and, if not, would be able to pick the lock.

I didn't want the super coming up. I didn't know what would be on the other side of the door and I didn't want some stranger gasping in surprise and then telling everyone in the building, especially Michael's neighbors who I would prefer remember him as a kindly but eccentric older man.

"What else can I do?" I asked Earl, after explaining why I

wasn't thrilled with his first suggestion.

"It's a typical bedroom door lock, isn't it? Not some sort of dead bolt."

"Yes, I mean no. It looks pretty standard bedroom issue to me."

Like the kind we'd installed on our own bedroom door when the kids were young and we wanted to make sure they didn't burst in unannounced.

"Then try picking it with a bobby pin."

I wondered whether any of the kids these days would know what a bobby pin was.

After hanging up on Earl, I went out to get something to eat and then to the drugstore to buy a package of bobby pins. I couldn't believe they still sold them and they hadn't changed in fifty years.

CHAPTER EIGHT – SHADOW BOXES

I spent almost an hour trying to pick the lock. I looked up ways to do it on the internet and while every video I watched made it look simple, it wasn't easy for me. I've never been mechanically inclined. I can string words together, break apart run-on sentences and sometimes when I'm lucky turn a nice phrase, but working with a screw driver or a hammer make me sweat.

I was about to give up and ask the doorman to send up the super when I heard a click and the door knob turned just like that, as if by magic. I don't know what I did that was different, but if I were a more religious person I might have imagined Michael watching from somewhere up in the ether and deciding I had been at it long enough.

The room was dark and I had to feel around for the light switch. I found one not far from the door, but nothing happened when I flipped it. The window was covered with a blackout curtain so there was no light coming in from outside. From the light behind me in the hall, I could see the shadow of a large table at the center of the room and a lamp standing next to it. I carefully walked over and turned it on. It was big and bright and for a moment . . . as I looked around . . . it felt as if I had entered into the workshop of some master toymaker.

The table was filled with hundreds of objects: small photos, post cards, pendants, colored paper, shiny paper, little trees, puzzle pieces, springs, stamps, medals, baseball cards, a little rolling pin, a tiny cake, small tins that looked as if they were a hundred years old, wheels from toy cars, pieces of cloth and jewelry, watch parts, doilies, lace, shells, buttons, spools of thread, tassels, doll clothing, doll pieces, heads, legs, arms, tiny cars, small balls, jacks, dried flowers, small baseballs, bats and gloves, tiny hats, little animals, small wooden clouds and planets, a couple of bright yellow suns and full moons, patches, magazine ads, golf tees, picture hangers, screws, a small green Gumby, tiny tools, little people, empty pill bottles, ribbons, toy soldiers, pocket watches, pocket knives, cracker jack prizes, pens and pencils, small letters made of wood and plastic, tiny stuffed animals, miniature mirrors, dice, small bugs and butterflies, keys, hearts of all sizes and colors, fishing lures, little models of the earth, tiny fish, small books, ceramic flowers, birds, miniature puppies, blocks, rocks, small wooden planes, halos, angels, starfish, old immigration documents that looked as if they'd been issued before World War II, small Christmas trees and ornaments, marbles, candies made out of glass and rubber, and lots of clock faces . . . miniature clock faces.

I could go on. Those were just some of the little things scattered around this large table in the middle of the room. The center of the table was clear except for Michaels tools—scissors, knives, different kinds of glue, tweezers, small hammers and nails, and a large magnifying glass with a light that hovered over the table which Michael could lower when he was working on something intricate.

All around the room, piled six feet high and two feet deep were shadow boxes, all of them completed and all of them—and I'm not an artist or an art critic—quite striking. There must have been three hundred of them, all different, and I didn't know where to begin. Earl suggested I inventory them, give each one a number and describe its contents.

"Don't you know a gallery owner from that article you did about retirees returning to art?" he asked.

I did and I called him. Gustave Alfimill Lucy, who everyone called GAL, had a small but well respected art gallery on the Bowery. When I called and described what I was looking at . . . and the circumstances that brought me here . . . GAL was excited at the prospect of a new shadow box artist.

"That's what happened with Joseph Cornell," he said, "and his work is in most every major museum. When they come up for auction, which isn't that often, they routinely go for six figures . . . sometimes higher. There hasn't been a shadow box artist at his level since he died in 1972."

He cautioned me about getting too excited because there had been a lot of Cornell imitators over the years and few of them got very far.

"If he has his own style and isn't simply another copycat that will help," GAL said. "I think the market is ripe for a major new shadow box artist . . . and his life story will count. It always does."

He couldn't get to the Upper East Side until the day after tomorrow and I planned to use that time to catalogue Michael's work. Like the photographs in the other room, there was a chronological order to Michael's boxes . . . the earlier ones, at least those pertaining to his earlier life, started in the corner to the right of the door.

The years moved clockwise around the room . . . chronicling Michael's life and times . . . until they ended at the wall behind me where the last one Michael made, representing the life of the Michael who had existed a few short months earlier sat alone on the floor.

There was room for more boxes and with all the supplies on the table, as well as the empty boxes in the corner waiting to be staged, it seemed as if Michael had a lot more art to create, suggesting to me that the descent into his eternal bath might have been more an accident than an intentional act.

I imagine no artist wants to take leave of life with his work incomplete, although I'm sure few artists ever feel as if they've completed their work. Perhaps there comes a point when they begin to feel too artistically exhausted to continue, when the inspiration becomes harder and harder to find, and they begin thinking it might be better to quit before their art suffers too much.

Could that have happened to Michael?

I started the inventory at the beginning. The first box, which had a date on the back below his signature—as they all did—was the made shortly after Doug had died, around the time he moved into his Park Avenue apartment.

The thing about shadow boxes, which I read about online—at least with respect to Joseph Cornell—is that the objects in each box are meant to present a thematic grouping with an artistic purpose or message which in most cases has some historic or personal significance . . . sometimes both. The grouping of the objects, the effect created by their relative heights and depth, as well as the background, are all intended to create a dramatic visual effect and tell a story.

It's not always obvious and like any work of art will lend itself to a myriad of different meanings and interpretations.

It seemed clear to me that Michael was trying to preserve and present objects that told the story of his life and times, a story with great nostalgic importance . . . certainly for him.

This first box had a large photo in the background, a black and white photo of American soldiers during World War II resting on a tank after what looks to have been an exhausting battle. In front of that was a Purple Heart. I assume it belonged to Michael's father who had served in North Africa during the war, although Michael said he didn't fight. He was responsible for bringing up supplies—ammunition and food—to the front lines. A soldier could certainly get injured doing a job like that during a battle.

Alongside the Purple Heart was an old ad for a hair dryer, one of those big contraptions that looked like a cross between a shower cap and a space helmet, the kind my mother used to sit under in the beauty parlor almost once a week back then. The woman in the ad looked as if she was having the time of her life as she sat there—her legs crossed—reading a magazine. I assumed she represented Michael's mother during better times. I didn't know for sure since I knew nothing about their early life when Michael was in elementary school. Perhaps she was more like the other mothers back then, regularly going to the beauty parlor to make sure her hair stayed puffed up high over her head.

Maybe her change was dramatic and sudden . . . like Michael.

The box contained a piece of old costume jewelry, a marcasite pendent. Michael's mother had a marcasite necklace she always wore. She held onto it sometimes like some kind of talisman. Next to that was a tiny abacus perhaps representing his father becoming an accountant after the war and beside that there were some small dinosaurs and a tiny Matchbox car. There was a little tricycle, an Alice in Wonderland watch, a tiny Pepsi Cola truck, a small Tweedie singing bird in a cage, a Howdy Doody head, the face parts from a Mr. Potato Head and a couple of toy soldiers . . . all popular toys in the early 1950s. The ones Michael must have played with as a young boy.

I wished I'd been more observant when I was in Michael's room since he had a bookcase filled with his old things. I vaguely remembered some model cars and a small metal cannon, but that was it. Mostly I remembered the baseballs, the trophies and the earthy and sweaty male smell.

I wrote a detailed description of the first box, more so than many of the others, simply because there was too many of them. I'd have to say that the first one was a relatively happy one, a box that looked back on the shadows of his early years and found very little out of the ordinary, nothing too disturbing, certainly not like some of the later boxes.

The next box had a photo of Albert Einstein on one wall. He was staring at two small framed photos of Elvis Presley and James Dean on the other. We both loved Elvis Presley and while Michael was a big fan of James Dean and any movie with war and violence, I was more in love with the Disney movies back then and their heroes like Fred McMurray in The Absent-Minded Professor and Tommy Kirk in The Shaggy Dog.

There was a small headline about Senator Joseph McCarthy on the floor partially covered by a model of an early satellite. In the foreground, up against one corner of the glass was a plastic McDonalds' restaurant advertising over 12 million sold. You had to go quite a way back to wind up with that number. They probably sell twice that much in a day now. There was two tiny baseball players with flexible joints, one crouching down as if to catch a pitch being thrown by the other. There was a small black and white photo of his parents on a tiny easel—their faces only—the kind you would take at the penny arcade. They were cheek to cheek and both smiling.

It was a work of art as far as I was concerned representing the world Michael was born into and spent his early years. It wasn't the kind of thing a student might do for a school project with some glue, scissors and a cardboard shoebox. This was a professional shadow box made of oak with the corners perfectly matched and a non-glare glass front fit into groves that Michael had cut into the ends of the frame. Some of the boxes were stained darker, but the majority of them were left in their natural state.

The next one I spent a lot of time looking at was the one where I first appeared. There was a photo of me dressed for the homecoming dance in 1965, the first dance Michael took me to. I remember how long it took for me to find that dress. Every one that I liked my mother didn't. Styles were changing in the mid-sixties and I was going for the sexy ingénue look. My mother was stuck in the late fifties and early sixties when dresses were still, as she put it, ladylike and proper. Those were her exact words. That meant no short skirts and nothing too tight. No scoop necks, nothing revealing, although dainty lace accents and softly shirred sleeves were acceptable.

It was a nice green dress with a pleated skirt and a belt that buckled behind me. Although you couldn't see it in the photo, it had a little scoop in the back that revealed very little, not even the hint of my bra. It wasn't my first choice, it wasn't even my tenth choice, but my mother turned out to be right. I liked the way I looked when I stood in front of the mirror waiting for Michael to pick me up. It made me look older and more mature.

I did look modest in the photo, which pleased my mother, and more importantly Michael loved it. If only my mother knew how immodest I would soon become. If she had any idea she would have kept me under lock and key.

I don't remember ever wearing that dress again, but I would in a minute if I still had it and it could fit me, which would be impossible.

I looked so happy in that photo. I don't remember who took it, but I'm guessing it was my mother who refused to let any special occasion go unrecorded. She must have shown me the photo and instead of letting her stick it into another one of her albums I gave it to Michael. I don't remember any of that for sure, it's just speculation, although I remember the dance very well. It was my first slow dance with a boy, my first make-out session in a car—driven by some upperclassman on the baseball team—and the night I really got to know some of the other guys on the baseball team and their girlfriends.

I felt like it was my initiation into the club.

I was expecting a photo of Michael from that night in the box as well, but there wasn't one. I remember how handsome I thought he looked in his blue suit and shiny black shoes. There was a little poster on the back wall for The Sound of Music which opened in March of that year. Michael knew it was one of my favorite movies. I wondered how Michael found a poster small enough for the box, although I assume anything is available on the internet for a price. He had the money and no one left to spend it on.

There were more toy soldiers and a jeep, no doubt representing the arrival of the first American combat troops in Vietnam. There was a helmeted police figure standing over a little black doll. The civil rights movement was at its height in 1965. There was a palm frond on top of a tombstone. I checked the internet and discovered that 1965 was the year of the Palm Sunday tornado outbreak in six Midwestern states that killed over 250 people.

There was a noose which I assume represented the hanging of the *In Cold Blood* killers in Kansas. A small electric guitar perhaps because that was the year Bob Dylan disappointed his folk purists by going electric. A miniature Yankee Stadium might have been intended to commemorate Pope Paul VI's visit to the Bronx since the Yankees lost their magic in 1965, beginning a long fall off their pedestal.

One wall was painted black and contained an outline of the New York City skyline. Obviously a reference to the Northeast blackout in November of that year. I remember being frightened like a lot of people, thinking it might be the beginning of a nuclear war, and Michael coming over to sit with my mother and me, my father being stuck somewhere in the city.

Curiously, there were a bunch of brightly colored balloons, plastic of course, rising above the dark city skyline. I wondered what they might represent. Perhaps the color and joy—balloons were always happy symbols in my mind—that would eventually return to the city after the long night of rioting and darkness. Or perhaps it represented our love which was just beginning, according to a note Michael wrote to me shortly after that first Homecoming Dance . . . destined, he said, to rise up to the heavens.

It was a box filled with history, events of great significance, except for me and the balloons . . . the only nostalgic representation I could see specifically from Michael's life. Was it his way of saying how important I was to him that year and how important the next three years would be? After all, I had the center stage in that box with history happening around me. My photo was what first drew the viewer's eye . . . along with the small bouquet of dried flowers at my feet and the balloons.

There were a lot of shadow boxes tracing our high school career. A number with baseball themes and objects I associated with young love like daisies and red hearts. There were balloons as well in almost every other box. There were more high school shadow boxes than our three years together warranted, possibly because time seemed to move so slowly back then. The four years of college flew by a lot faster than that.

If I were to describe all 323 of the boxes I'd need another 300 pages. Each one was different and each was more beautiful and interesting than the one before it. The most recurring object was the balloons. There were little plastic balloons, like the ones you might find on an ice cream cake. Small balloons that had never been inflated. Clay balloons and photos of balloons, some in color and some in black and white. Sometimes you could see them in the distance, at other times they were just outside a window, peeking in as if they themselves were curious to see what was in the box.

The last box was the saddest for me. It was dated four months earlier, shortly before Michael's death. Not surprisingly it was dark and devoid of color. It looked like he had aged the box with multiple layers of dark grey paint and varnish, perhaps leaving it for a while by a sunny window to cook it or putting it in the oven for a while so the paint cracked and appeared worn. There were balloons, as always, little plastic balloons he'd crushed and scattered around the ground. The strings that once gathered them together cut and strewn about. Lying alongside the balloons were a flock of fallen bluebirds . . . all on their side . . . and behind them a small cemetery with grey tombstones, some upended and others looking about ready to fall over.

There were other birds, parrots cut from books and perched in cages, arranged as if for a shooting gallery. Seagulls standing around looking lost and confused, crows eying them hungrily. None of the birds were flying. There was no sense of movement in the box unlike some of the others. Everything in it was so still and quiet it made me want to hold my breath for fear of disturbing anything.

It was night, but there were no stars and no moon. The ground was also strewn with rubbish and propped up in the corner was a very creepy little doll with a frightened porcelain face, her eyes opened wide as if she'd just seen eternity and had been terrified by its immensity. Besides her was a small fountain, cracked and dry. The sides of the box were covered with broken things, broken toys, a small cracked bat, a shattered mirror and a heart in pieces.

I was happy not to find a photo of me anywhere in the last

box, although some of the photographs Michael had surreptitiously taken of me over the years had appeared in other boxes. The only photo in this last box was of Michael playing baseball, the one he'd posted on Facebook. It was stuck on the wall at the back of the box and had been defaced by graffiti. He'd given himself a big black eye and a white beard. He was sort of dangling from a twisted and gnarled tree.

I needed a drink after writing the description for that box. Perhaps Michael did intend it to be his last. What a terrible black mood he must have been in.

I finished my list about an hour before GAL showed up for his appointment. We weren't friends or anything like that. I had written an article about his gallery when it was running a series of shows by seniors who had once been artists in college and were returning to it for the first time after decades away. He was grateful for the publicity and I suppose he agreed to come uptown to look at my late high school boyfriend's shadow boxes because he felt he owed me that much. I'm sure he'd been on a thousand wild goose chases over the years, humoring friends and acquaintances the same way.

However, as soon as he entered the room and looked around he covered his mouth and sat down on the chair.

"Who was this guy again?"

"Michael, my high school boyfriend."

"When did he die?"

"About four months ago, I'm acting as executrix of his estate."

He didn't ask me another question for a long time. He just stood up and walked slowly around the room, squatting down every few feet to get a better look into the boxes, which wasn't easy since he was older than me.

He went back to the chair and sat down, taking out a handkerchief to wipe his neck and a drink from a bottle of water he pulled from his bag.

"These are incredible . . . every bit as expressive and captivating as any shadow box I've seen by Cornell."

He sat there for another minute catching his breath and looking around.

"Azu," he said, startling me out of my own reverie, "this is like discovering gold. I wish he were around to talk to. I'm sure he had no idea how good he was."

GAF sighed loudly. "Why do they always die before they realize it?"

"I don't know," I said, handing him my list.

He took his time reading through it.

"Three hundred and twenty-three. That's impressive . . . in about twenty years . . . less. And you say he had a full time job?"

"Head of Compliance at Morgan Stanley."

"I don't know when he could have slept. He couldn't have had much of a personal life."

"I don't think he did."

I told GAL about Michael's wife and son.

He got up and took another tour of the room, stopping to examine some of the boxes that he'd missed before.

"Some of these photos are you, aren't they?"

"The high school ones."

"Some of the later ones as well."

I nodded and told him how they were taken without my knowledge.

"Joseph Cornell was also a little weird . . . more than a little. He was a recluse. He had a strange mother who believed that touching and sex were abominations. What was Michael's mother like?"

"A bit reclusive as well and depressed."

GAL nodded like he wasn't the least bit surprised. I told him about her now.

"What a shame. My mother had dementia before she died. It's like dying twice, first the mind then the body. Unfortunately, it runs in my family."

We remained silent for a while, both of us walking around the room looking into the boxes.

"I'd love to represent him . . . the estate. I'd make him my number one artist. It won't take long for him to be discovered. He'll take off with the first show."

"I'd like that . . . I don't think he should go unnoticed."

GAL spent the rest of the afternoon looking at each box to decide which ones should appear in the opening exhibit and talking with me about the prices. I couldn't help much there. He also had a hundred questions about Michael.

"The life of the artist is important," he said. "Buyers and

museums want to know about it. It's hard to separate Dali or Picasso's art from their lives."

Michael's life, unfortunately, was closer to Joseph Cornell than Dali and Picasso. Cornell was a recluse who lived his life through his art. Michael had his work life, his personal life for a while, but in the end—at least over the last twenty years or so—his life was his art.

"It's hard to believe you hadn't been in touch since high school," GAL said as he moved to the later boxes.

"It's true," I said. "Not a word."

"All those photos of you," GAL said, shaking his head from side to side. I'd already shown him the other bedroom with the wall of photographs.

GAL bit his lower lip while he thought it over.

"It's got to be upsetting to discover he was watching you for all those years."

I shrugged, shaking my head yes then no. "I was at first, but not anymore. I suppose because he took pains to make sure I didn't realize it . . . and none of the photos are very personal or revealing. They're just me in everyday life . . . walking down the street or standing somewhere . . . pictures anyone could have taken."

"And because he's dead," GAL added. "If you'd discovered it when he was still alive, I think you'd feel different."

"I suppose . . . I'd have asked him to stop."

GAL bent down to look at the box with a photo of me pregnant.

"Everyone thinks about their past and their past lovers," I said. "I've certainly had thoughts about him over the years."

"Normal thoughts like everyone else. This isn't normal."

"No, but the way I look at it, instead of just thinking about me from time to time he needed something a bit more tangible. He didn't need to contact me or to talk to me, he just wanted to see me from a distance . . . to remember me in more than his mind's eye."

"Spoken like a true writer," GAL said, moving behind me to the last wall of boxes. "It's very unusual, there's no denying that."

"People do the same thing all the time these days."

"What do you mean?"

"They look for people they once knew, they just do it

remotely through the internet. If he'd started now, Michael probably would have followed me on Facebook. And if I posted photos like everyone else he wouldn't need to find me with his camera. If you think about it, it's not much different from the voyeurism everyone practices now on their computers."

"It's very different," GAL said. "Traveling a thousand miles to spy on someone and take their picture is not nearly the same as searching for them on the internet."

GAL turned around from the box he was examining and looked at me.

"But it is the sort of eccentricity that helps make a great artist. My theory has always been that you can't become a really great artist without something being off . . . some quirk in your upbringing or personality. Dali and Picasso saw shapes and monsters when they were younger. Maybe for Michael it was his mother . . . or the way he saw the past in the present. He used shadow boxes . . . and your photographs . . . to travel back and forth between the two."

GAL sighed.

"Michael was truly a great artist. Normal people can't create things like this," he said, his arms outstretched as he panned around the room.

"He was perfectly normal in high school."

"Maybe or maybe it just seemed that way. I bet there were some things about him you didn't know . . . or overlooked."

"I'm sure there were things I don't know, but I'd have seen something if there was anything really wrong with Michael. We were very close. We spent a lot of time together, more than a lot. I couldn't have been that obtuse."

I suppose I sounded a bit defensive because GAL added, "I'm sure you're right, you were there, you would know better than me. But I've found over the years that some people are really good at hiding things . . . their fears . . . their perceived truths . . . particularly artists."

"I've thought about it nonstop over the last couple of months," I said. "I've interviewed Michael's old friends on the baseball team. No one noticed anything. Believe me, I've been racking my brain. I think I'd have seen something if Michael had a problem."

"The budding journalistic eye?" GAL asked.

"The loving girlfriend."

GAL nodded as he bent down to examine some of the later boxes again. The boxes Michael had made over the last five years had more depressing themes—some had universal themes involving climate change, war, refugees, disease and hunger. Some were more personal involving the effects of time on one's body and one's dreams. I did appear in some of those boxes.

There was one box that featured an old pocket watch with a shattered face and rotting food—wooden of course—and a photo of us at a high school dance. Scattered on the ground around us were wilted flowers, although in the midst of those were two colorful daisies.

Memories—for Michael—never wilted, not like the present. Apparently, shadow boxes did not require all that much subtly.

GAL didn't want to waste time. He wanted to mount a small exhibition in the next 30 days, bumping the one he had planned. He wanted to put Michael out into the world as quickly as possible. He felt, and it turned out he was right, that Michael would instantly become famous, favorably compared by all the critics to Joseph Cornell.

After GAL left I sat there with my eyes closed trying to peer into the past . . . to our high school years . . . to see what, if anything, I might have overlooked. Some small crack I had missed. Other than his mother and the early death of his father, I couldn't see anything out of the ordinary.

Certainly our breakup was odd . . . putting me on our swing like that, the one that held such fond memories . . . and doing it the day after my graduation at the start of the summer. Why not wait a week or two to see if his feelings really had really changed now that he was back home?

Yes, Michael's mother was different, he'd be the first to admit that . . . but it didn't seem to bother him all that much. He didn't talk much about it. He certainly didn't dwell on it. So she wasn't like the other mothers . . . always talking on the phone and planning for canasta games and dinners out. Sure she was quiet, and I suppose sad now that I look back on it, but I never thought of her as all that strange. Of course, I was sixteen and in love which seemed strange enough. I didn't really think much about her because it didn't matter, Michael wasn't his mother any more than I was mine.

I thought about what Sandi had told me about Michael having an aunt who was institutionalized as a young woman and confined there for the rest of her life. Fran told her that at some point they gave her a lobotomy and she turned into a vegetable. Michael must have known about her when we were going out—it's not something easily hidden within a family—but he kept quiet about it.

How is it Michael never weakened and told me about her? We swore we'd never keep secrets from each other. Maybe it's not the type of thing you tell your first love, not the one you imagine marrying and carrying your children. If the shoe were on the other foot I'd probably have stayed silent as well. We were terrible with secrets at that age and I'd have probably told my mother. Although she'd have promised to keep it secret, she might have "mentioned it in passing" to a couple of her good friends.

It's certainly not the kind of thing you want the community gossiping about.

Why would Mr. Perfect want to spoil his image? I didn't talk about the black sheep in my family. I had an uncle who never married and sometimes asked my mother for money. She never talked much about him and I rarely saw him. Michael knew my mother had a brother, but that was about it.

Could Michael have been afraid it might happen to him? That he might turn into his mother or his aunt?

If so, I never saw any sign of it. When we had serious conversations they were mostly about our love and our future which always looked rosy. Michael wasn't afraid of anything so why should I be? The world . . . our teenage world . . . was a safe and happy place. The outside world kept its distance. Time was endless. There were no conversations that touched upon our mortality or the possibility of a debilitating illness—physical or mental—nothing that could interfere with the long, rainbow arc of our imagined life together.

Michael never stood still in high school. He never stopped moving. He was always busy with something, whether it was with me, the team or the yearbook. He hardly had time to sit down, let alone think about things, and I always used to tease him about it. Perhaps there was a reason for that. Some people who carry around invisible fears are afraid of the quiet and the stillness . . . moments alone when disturbing thoughts can really make themselves heard.

Perhaps Michael heard those voices late at night when he was alone in his bed? If he did, he never said a word about it to me. How could I possibly know if there were? There was really nothing about our years together—nothing I could remember—that would have led me to doubt who he was or fear for the way his life might turn out.

While I waited for the show to open and helped GAL prepare the press releases and brochure, I bought a book written by Richard Yates, the writer Michael mentioned on his Facebook page, called *Eleven Kinds of Loneliness*. It was a collection of short stories that took place in New York City. They were about ordinary people who had to defend their dignity in the face of significant humiliations. After I finished it, I ran out and bought another collection of short stories entitled *Liars in Love*. I read it overnight. They were stories about troubled and fleeting love, as well as elusive truth and human frailty. They seemed fresh and timely despite their age and I found myself re-reading sentences that blew me away.

How is I had never read anything by Yates before?

I bought and read all his novels. His words were sparse yet filling, simple but poignant, and clearly autobiographical. There was something tragic in everything he wrote, his short stories as well as his novels, even if it wasn't always out front for everyone to see at first glance.

It's no wonder Michael was so attracted to him.

In a way he was like Michael. He never had much success while he was alive. Not one of his books sold over 12,000 copies and they all were out of print by the time of his death. He came close once to winning the National Book Award, but he didn't. In the end he died young, almost the exact same age as Michael.

It took an essay in the Boston Review, seven years after his death, to bring him the kind of acclaim and sales he deserved.

Michael's shadow boxes would do the same for him. He became famous within a week of the opening of the exhibit, within a month he was making the covers of newspapers and magazines around the country.

Irony, like history, is something life is condemned to repeat.

CHAPTER NINE – CAN YOU EVER REALLY KNOW SOMEONE

Can you ever really know someone? That was the big question for me. I think I know Earl. What he will say and how he's going to react in just about every situation. I'm sure he feels the same about me. But that kind of knowledge comes with maturity and forty years together. Is it any surprise that by our late sixties we have learned to see deeper and clearer into each other's heart and our own . . . other people's hearts as well.

I doubt the same can ever be said of us in our youth. I would confirm that soon enough when it came to Michael.

Meanwhile, I started reviewing my notes and outlining my story. For Michael, I was creating a character who found the present too painful, especially as he reached the autumn of his life when all kinds of aches and pains—not just physical ones—refused to let go, and the past moving further and further out of reach dragged him along with it.

The present is so uncertain at our age. You may not know when, but you certainly know the end is coming soon enough, and it could come as a surprise, without warning, and in an instant.

The past can sometimes seem like the best escape from that kind of uncertainty and pain, especially for someone like Michael, at least the character of Michael I had in mind, although the relief it offers can't last very long and works less and less the more you rely on it. The past is lost. It's not coming back, it's out of reach . . . gone by definition. Moments never return, neither do people, certainly not in the way most of us would wish for.

Trying to recapture the past only serves to screw up your present . . . and likely your future. You can wind up living . . . and dying . . . like Michael, out of step with the world around you, trying to keep up with the present while carrying a heavy piece of the past strapped to your back. That was the handle I was going for. Michael reaching for his past in the form of me and his shadow boxes. Michael trying to run from a present that was too painful to bear . . . largely because of the loss of Fran and Doug . . . towards a past of teenage bliss.

It's easy for most people to put the past in its place and not dwell on it—or in it—when the present offers companionship and a modicum of contentment with who you are, where you are and who you love.

Despite what Earl kept assuring me, I couldn't help feeling a bit guilty, as if an impulsive act on my part to call him in college or a simple turn of my head at the right moment might have changed the trajectory of Michael's life. It wasn't mine that would change in my imagination—or I wanted to change—just his.

I know it made no sense, but I imagined it a hundred times.

I imagined myself home for summer vacation after my sophomore year at college. I'd spot him this time coming out of the grocery store and walk up to him. We'd start talking. He'd confess to me he's gotten a bit too deep into drugs. He'd tell me how hard it's been with his mother now that his father is gone. You can tell things to a lover, even a former one, that you can't tell your baseball and college buddies.

I really had no one in my life at that time. I had good friends at school, I've always had friends . . . more male I'd say than female. I think that started with Michael. I'd been going out on a lot of dates, but there was no one special.

Michael and I would agree to meet later that night at a bar. We'd wind up back at the swing. We'd start seeing each other again, going slowly at first, as if it were all new and in a way it would be because we'd both be very different people now. The time and place would be different as well . . . at least our perspective of it. We are visitors now to this past, no longer residents.

The embers would still be there and while they might not ignite the way they once had, they would certainly be warm and glowing.

I didn't do drugs and I wouldn't continue seeing him, I'd tell him, if he does . . . at least not to the excess he has been. He would agree. The Michael I knew would have the strength of character to quit.

Perhaps he would have developed some quirks by now. He'd be quiet sometimes, quieter than he ever was in high school, and he'd stare out at times like he's looking at something only he can see. There would be moments when he'd seem full of self-doubt, which happens to all of us when we leave the nest, or maybe it's more anxiety and fear. But, hey, we are college students in an age filled with wars and riots. Anxiety is part of the times.

I'd try to understand the changes and accept them, at least that's how I see it in my imaginary alternate universe.

He might even have a panic attack or two, like Teal described, but we'd get through them. I wouldn't quit on him because he was no longer perfect. I'm too loyal a person for that. Over time, we'd become more friends than lovers because even in my imagination I'm destined to meet Earl. There can be no scenario, however far-fetched, that doesn't result in me marrying Earl and having our children and grandchildren.

The only thing that would change is Michael's life. He'd be more up about it, his decisions would be better so it's not surprising that his luck and life would turn out differently. He'd stay close to his old high school teammates, attend all the get-togethers, as well as the annual family barbeques which always culminated in a big softball game where everyone played . . . wives, kids, even the dogs ran the bases.

There would be no shadow boxes in this imaginary life, perhaps because he would never make it to the Joseph Cornell art exhibit or perhaps because he doesn't have the kind of pain—the loneliness and anxiety—required for the inspiration and perspiration an artist needs.

In my fantasy, Fran would be cured and Doug would go on to baseball stardom. Earl and I would bump into Michael and Fran somewhere—maybe in Florida with our grandchildren at Disneyworld—and they'd join our list of acquaintances who we would see once every two or three years for dinner, always laughing at the descriptions we had to offer of ourselves as teenagers.

I know I'm deluding myself in believing I could have made that much of a difference or any difference really. The arc of time and place pulls us relentlessly in the direction it wants to take us. I know that doesn't make sense for someone who believes in free will, but I believe a bit in fate as well . . . a fate that guides us based on where we are born, who we are born to and the DNA chance has provided to us. Believing in two opposite philosophies, seeing things in contradictory ways, is part of human nature I suppose . . . certainly when it comes to love and memory.

Perhaps his life would have turned out exactly the same no matter what moment I changed, although every detour, no matter how small, takes you in a slightly different direction and winds up in a very different place.

These were the kind of thoughts I was having as I sat there for hours and hours trying to turn my notes into a book.

In truth, I was getting nowhere. I couldn't find the right theme . . . drugs, bad luck, Facebook lies . . . nothing seemed to propel the story forward. I didn't want to write a soap opera story about the man who lost everyone and died alone . . . only to be resurrected as a great artist.

I was thinking about giving up and I might have if not for Earl.

"Do you have anything on the back burner waiting to turn to?" he asked when I told him what I was thinking.

I shook my head no. He knew I didn't.

"At least keep trying until the reunion. Who knows what ideas will come out of that?"

It was a couple of weeks before the reunion and I still hadn't made up my mind about going, notwithstanding that I'd sent in my acceptance and made our hotel reservations. I certainly wasn't going if I'd already given up on the story . . . whether it was a book or reduced again to a magazine article. I wasn't going to spend a purposeless evening talking about Michael's death and his new found fame as a shadow box artist.

He was already being heralded as the newest in the long line of great artists and writers not discovered until after their death. The art magazines were calling him the second coming of Joseph Cornell. They made it sound like a religious experience, like a reincarnation.

Indeed, Michael's photo, a more recent one obtained from human resources at Morgan Stanley, was put on the cover of New York Magazine. Nosy Nancy had called to tell me about it a few days before it hit the newsstands. The picture was backed up by a fluffy article about Michael's tough life, the dichotomy between his work and art, and his untimely death. It was the type of article researched quickly—while interest was hot—and which couldn't have taken more than a week or two to write.

It completely ignored the young Michael and made no effort to understand what happened..

"I wish he had made one of those shadow boxes for me," Nancy said over the telephone when I'd been silent for too long. "Then maybe I'd have enough to buy something in Florida."

It was a rainy Sunday, a week before the reunion, part of a week of rainy days. Unlike Florida where the rain always passes quickly, the dark clouds in New Jersey often seem painted up there, as if they will never leave. It didn't bother me all that much because nice weather tended to distract me from my writing and I was determined to stick with it a little longer.

However, it did keep Earl off the golf course and after three days he couldn't sit around any longer watching TV and doing crossword puzzles. He decided it was time to tackle the attic. We'd been talking about selling the house for about a year now because it was way too big for the two of us. Finding a small apartment in the city would mean being able to walk places instead of driving everywhere. It would also mean we'd save a ton of money not having to maintain a house that was growing old and in need of more and more help . . . like us.

Earl thought he start "lightening our load" in the event we did decide to downsize, starting with the attic.

He came across the shoe box at the bottom of a carton of old clothes my mother had packed up for me when she was selling her house. My mother told me she'd toss it if I didn't take it. I didn't need any more clothes and I was sure there was nothing in it I wanted. Still, I was too young to discard my past like that, at least not without going through it first so we brought it home. I never did go through the carton because we put it right up in the attic where it was ignored like everything else up there.

Earl brought the carton into my writing room. He pulled out a few items from the top, an old blouse, some worn t-shirts, a couple of sweatshirts and sweaters. You grow more sentimental in many ways as you get older, but not when it comes to things like that, not old clothes that will never fit again and are too worn to donate. I told Earl to toss the whole box.

He took it out to the garage and looked through it anyway just to make sure. That's when he spotted the shoe box at the bottom. He knew it was the one because it was covered with little hearts and flowers . . . daisies actually . . . drawn in the hand of a love struck teenager.

My mouth fell open when he brought it in.

"It was at the bottom of the box," he said.

"Where my mother placed it," I said, "no doubt hoping I would never find it."

She was very controlling in her own way. She tried to avoid being too outwardly judgmental, but she always found ways of getting her point across. She'd leave magazines open to articles she wanted me to read which supported whatever it was she was trying to get me to do or not do, or she'd talk loudly over the phone with a friend so I could overhear the conversation.

She couldn't bring herself to throw the shoe box away since it was my life and my memories. She wouldn't be comfortable with the guilt she'd feel if she did which is why she put it somewhere I wasn't likely to find it.

Earl didn't stick around to watch the opening of what he called my teen time capsule. Not that he wasn't interested, but he felt I would be more comfortable doing it alone in the first instance. I was too anxious to object.

The first thing I noticed was that the shoebox was almost empty. It was full the last time I remember putting something into it and sliding it back under my bed. Hardly any of the photos I'd put in it were still there. No homecoming dances, no baseball games, no beach photos and there had been quite a few of those. The only photos left were of the two of us taken at Michael's senior prom.

There were no love notes, none of the sweet little drawings of hearts and smiles Michael used to hand me in school sometimes when we passed in the hall. None of the little things he'd won for me at the annual fireman's carnival or the cheap rings and necklaces he brought me that I put into the shoebox after we broke up. Even Michael's varsity baseball pin was gone, the one I kept under my pillow that entire summer after he dumped me.

I didn't put it into the shoebox until I left for college.

The box was under my bed for the longest time. I used to look into every time I came home that first year on vacation, maybe once or twice the second year and once the third year.

Never after that, not that I can remember. I suppose that was when my mother decided it was time to "lighten up" my Michael memories by discarding what she determined to be unnecessary or inappropriate—which appeared to be most everything—and moving what was left up to the attic. She must have waited until my senior year in college or perhaps after I graduated and moved out. I can't be sure because I couldn't remember the last time I looked under the bed for it.

I have a vague recollection of asking her once where the shoebox was. It had to be one weekend after college when I'd come back for a visit. It was certainly before I met Earl. She must have told me she put it in the attic, I don't recall. I suppose it would have been a sign of weakness, immaturity really, if I'd gotten angry and climbed up the attic stairs to bring it back down.

I think that's a real memory, although I'm not sure.

I was surprised—the more I thought about it—that my mother didn't toss the whole box into the garbage, instead of hiding it at the bottom of a carton of old clothes. My mother always had a purpose for the things she did, at least when it came to me, and if she decided to keep it she must have had a reason . . . something she left in the box that might prove useful, something that might stop me from dwelling too much on the past or chasing after it again if my love life took a sudden turn for the worse.

She might have forgiven Michael for breaking up with me—that was a college rite of passage—but not for the way he did it. She considered those swings, as did I, to be hallowed ground.

There had to be a reason the shoebox escaped the trash heap and I started searching for it the moment I dumped its contents on my desk. I was looking for something I didn't put there, something my mother wanted me to see in the event I had any doubts.

There was one of the prom photos I had put in there after Michael had dumped me. Before that it was in a frame on my dresser. I was old enough by then to pick out my own dress. It was hard for my mother to stop me from wearing what I wanted. In fact, my father had given me his credit card and told me to buy whatever I liked. He knew I wouldn't go overboard.

She tried to influence my choice, but those days of obedience, at least when it came to my wardrobe—and what I did behind her back—had long since passed. The sixties had moved ahead and the styles were shorter, tighter and more revealing of a girl's figure, even if I didn't choose a dress with a plunging neckline, which I didn't. I was still her daughter and couldn't help absorbing some of her tastes. Later in life I was glad I did.

Michael and I were a good looking couple in the prom photo. Aside from being smartly dressed, more dressed up than either one of us had ever been before, we looked happy and very much in love.

To be young is bliss. To be young and in love is heaven. I read that somewhere in college. It's something you don't appreciate when you're that age, not as much as you should.

There were a few school mementos my mother had left in the shoebox that weren't tied to Michael. Some pins I'd gotten at the World's Fair in Queens I went to with my parents. There were tickets from my first Yankee game with my father and my old high school GO card. It cost fifty cents to join back then. There were a couple of yellowed copies of articles from the school newspaper carrying my byline, articles I couldn't remember writing. There were birthday cards from my parents and a couple of troll dolls. I used to love trolls.

There was the three foot long bubble gum wrapper I started making for Michael but never finished. I'm sure my mother had forgotten I was making it for Michael, not myself.

There was nothing out of the ordinary, not from the contents I had dumped on my desk, and I looked back into the box to see to see if I'd missed something. That's when I saw it . . . the letter stuck at the bottom. It was addressed to me with no return address, although I recognized Michael's handwriting right away even after all this time. I assumed it was one of the letters he wrote me during his first year in college, but when I looked at the postmark I saw it was much later . . . the start of his senior year, my junior year.

He never spoke to me after we broke up and he certainly never wrote to me. Although my memory is not what it used to be, it's still pretty good long term, certainly when it comes to something like that. I had no doubt I'd never seen this letter. It was addressed to me at home and postmarked a week before I would have normally left for college. However, I went up early that fall because I had volunteered to help with freshman orientation.

It must have arrived in the mail after I left.

There had to be a reason my mother didn't tell me about it, but couldn't bring herself to throw it away. Did she keep it hidden for a year or two—until the coast was clear—before putting it at the bottom of the shoebox? Did she wait until she was sure I had stopped looking into it and wouldn't be too upset if I found out she'd moved it up to the attic?

I could hear my heart beating in my ear. What was in it she didn't want me to see? I had to assume Michael was reaching out for another chance—one I'd gladly have given him back then. I wasn't serious with anyone at the beginning of my junior year. It might not have changed anything in terms of the arc of my life— and Earl's—but it might have made it easier for Michael to let go.

I was a basket case the summer we broke up and it certainly affected my first term at school. I assume my mother wanted to make sure I didn't slide back and let it happen again. Or maybe she'd heard things about Michael . . . and his mother . . . and thought it was still her job to protect me.

Whatever her reasoning, it wasn't her decision to make. She couldn't protect me from the pain of love, no mother can do that, certainly not anymore, not with all the different boys waiting for me in college. I know I'm old and mature now . . . a mother and a grandmother . . . so I should be able to understand it . . . the desire to shield those you love from pain, but all I could feel was the anger of a young twenty-year old girl rising in my throat like bile.

The letter was open, which was no surprise. I wondered what she was hoping when she put it in the shoebox and put the shoebox in the attic. Was she hoping I'd never find it . . . that it would find its way to the dump before I ever saw it . . . or was she hoping when I finally did read it I'd be old enough to understand and appreciate her motive?

My hands were shaking as I unfolded it.

It was dated September 1, 1971. Michael's handwriting was unmistakable—small, script letters slanting hard to the right. I never had trouble reading it, I suppose because I had gotten used to it over the years. I'm surprised my mother could. I wondered how long it took her to decipher it.

I still had no trouble reading his handwriting. For a moment I felt as if I were back in 1971, my hands trembling with anticipation.

Dear Azu,

I hope this letter finds you well. I saw you over the summer walking into the A&P. I was going there to buy some food for my mother. She never leaves the house these days. I have to arrange for people to shop for her when I'm at school. There are people you can pay to do that and all kinds of other things, believe or not, but I still have to come down some weekends to help her and keep her calm. She likes it when I'm around. I decided to wait until you left before going in. I don't know why exactly. I still feel badly about how it ended . . . how I ended it . . . and I suppose I didn't want to bring those bad feelings back to you. Sort of like pulling the scab off a wound that's finally healing.

That was one of the ways I imagined it would happen back then, but Michael wouldn't let it. I didn't buy his reason. Did he really think I was still nursing my wound two years later?

There had to be more to it.

Besides, I didn't trust myself. Falling back into your arms, which I would have surely done the instant you smiled, and you always had the best smile, would have been bad for both of us. My life is too crazy now. I barely have enough time for my coursework. You are much better off without me.

I don't know if you've heard, but my mother has had some problems, emotional problems more than physical ones. She's always had some problems when I was growing up, but we never talked about them. She tried to hide them from the neighbors and keep to herself. It was a real effort for her sometimes when you came by and if she couldn't keep it together she'd stay in her room. Do you remember that? I'm sure you do.

There were days she wouldn't get dressed or leave the bedroom. Days she wouldn't eat. Days she looked so sad I didn't want to go to school. My father always made me go. He knew how to take care of her. He knew all of her issues. Fortunately, the really bad moments always passed and things got better, never good, but better.

I bet you're surprised to hear that Michael's perfect world wasn't so perfect.

No Michael, I'm not, I answered silently to myself some fifty years later. I wasn't that naïve even at sixteen. I knew his mother had problems, although not the full extent of them. I knew his father was challenged . . . and that life wasn't perfect at home. I just thought it was perfect for Michael and me.

Nothing else mattered.

Although I certainly realize just how bad it really was. Reality is not always easy to see when you're a teenager in love.

She got worse after my father died and worse still after I left for college. She called me most nights and I did come home a couple of weekends without letting you know. I never told you about it because she really needed me, my whole attention, and I didn't want to spoil us, our happiness, and make you or anyone else feel sorry for me. The bad moments always passed, although they became more frequent and lasted longer without my father around.

The scariest part for me . . . the scariest part that I've never told anyone, not you, not even my parents . . . was that I knew exactly how she felt.

What does that mean? I wondered. The college junior inside me wondered because she was reading the letter as well, although the Medicare me knew what had to be coming.

Last summer she tried swallowing some pills and drank too much of my father's old whiskey, but all she did was get herself sick. Unfortunately, that kind of thing . . . suicide and depression . . . fear of things that may or may not be there . . . runs in my family.

I never told you this either, but my mother had an older sister. I didn't learn about her until I was 14. Can you imagine not knowing you have an aunt . . . who was alive . . . at least for a time while I was alive? Up until that moment I thought my mother was an only child. I only discovered it when I overheard her talking to my father. It seems her sister had some problems and they committed her to a public mental institution. She spent most of her life at Pilgrim State Hospital, had a lobotomy, and died a couple of years after that. My mother eventually told me the truth . . . she killed herself.

I did some research the other day and found out she was institutionalized at the age of 21. The same age I am now.

This was the real reason he didn't come up to me at the A&P. He was trying to protect me. I had a hundred notes from Michael during high school and lots of letters during his first year in college, but in none of them did he ever sound this worried, not even close. Perhaps smoking all that pot was making him paranoid, making him feel as if he was about to turn into his mother . . . or even worse, his aunt.

Michal was nothing like his mother, I would have told him while holding tightly to his hand if he told me his secret that day in front of the A&P. I'd have reminded him how much he took after his father . . . not only in his looks, but in his athleticism and academic accomplishments. Sure his father was irritable and unhappy, but that was because of the burden he had to bear with his mother. I would never be that kind of burden to him . . . nor would he to me.

My mother knew what would have happened if I'd read this letter, I'd have called Michael and taken a road trip to Cornell to see him. It wouldn't have scared me away. It might not have changed my destiny, but it wouldn't have scared me away.

I suppose it could have changed things.
She had to know that.
Unfortunately, there was more to come.

It's been a depressing time, as you might imagine, and I went to the college mental health center to talk to someone. So much has happened since my father died and you left my life . . . I know I pushed you away . . . none of it very good. I suppose that's why I started smoking so much grass and experimenting with some stronger stuff. The drugs do make me feel better. For a little while they take me out of myself. Does that make sense? Sometimes you need to get away from your own thoughts and visions, particularly if they start following you from your dreams to your window.

Visions? Window? I didn't like the sound of any of that.

People like me, people with my family background, have to be more careful. That's what the counselor told me. Stay away from the hard drugs he said. Even too much pot could aggravate the feelings I've been getting. Sure, he said, they may make things seem better in the moment, but you can wind up feeling a lot worse when you come back down. I listened to what he said, but I didn't really listen. It's not so easy when you're on the inside looking out.
Sometimes I wonder if it isn't already too late.
Of course, I didn't tell him everything.

I heard Michael's voice in my head as surely as if I was back in high school, although I had a terrible sense of foreboding. I suppose I knew there was something much worse coming—the "everything" he hadn't told the counselor—and unfortunately I already knew how it would turn out. I wished I could reach back there to warn Michael to stay away from the hallucinogenic drugs and to wait for the more helpful ones that would be coming soon like Prozac. I'd have reassured him that everything would all be alright. I'd have lied even if I were reaching out from the future and knew exactly how it would turn out.

I have a secret to tell you. Something I should have told you that day in 10th grade when I saw you sitting there in study hall and tugged on your ponytail, not knowing how much that moment would change my life. Being great in baseball, and I always was since I was little, is all about your eyes, seeing the ball clearly, seeing the stitches if you're lucky, and having quick reflexes. It's almost as if I could see the ball coming at me in slow motion. Hitting and fielding was always easy. I never had to think about it.

It makes everything easier when you're good at sports. That's what people see, that's what they talk about. It's all they notice and remember. Wear a smile, practice it in the mirror so it looks natural, and it all becomes true. Sports were a gift, not something I earned. My looks were also a gift. The grades were easy as well. There are different kinds of intelligence and emotions, I took a Psych course about that, and one doesn't necessarily correlate with the other.

Why I got those gifts I don't know, but there were other "things" that came along with them. Eyes that could see the seams of a baseball coming at you at 70 miles an hour could also see things that others couldn't . . . or didn't.

Every silver lining has a dark cloud. I know that now.

My secret, the one I never told you or anyone else, started my freshman year when you were still in junior high and I was looking and hoping to find someone exactly like you. I remember it like it was yesterday and I suppose considering the expanse of time it was yesterday. I was about to leave the house to play baseball. It was just a pickup game. My father was at work and my mother was in the bedroom having another one of her "headaches," which is what she used to call them. She needed absolute silence and darkness, not always easy to find during the day, particularly when there's a teenager running around the house.

I was in the kitchen getting some water for the game . . . a game I never made . . . because I noticed something out the window. It caught my eye and it felt as if it were pulling me toward it. I know this is going to sound strange, but I saw a string of balloons, six of them, right outside the window. They were all different colors. I wondered for a moment if someone was having a birthday party and they'd gotten loose. Then I realized they weren't just hovering outside, not drifting with the breeze, but pressing against the window, blinking and pulsating as if they were alive, as if they were watching me while I was watching them.

It suddenly dawned on me that they were filled with poison gas—I don't know how I knew it or why, but I did—and the only way I could stop them from coming in, bursting in through the screen, was to keep my eyes focused on them, staring them down until they felt my resolve and decided to move on to someone else. Eventually, after what seemed like an hour, but was probably no more than five or ten minutes, they backed off, rose above the window and drifted away. I followed them for a long time as they faded in the distance. I refused to move until they were completely out of sight and I wouldn't leave the house for the rest of the day.

I never told anyone. Not my father, certainly not my mother, not any of the guys, not you, not the counselors, not anyone. Partly because I wasn't sure whether they were real or imaginary. They seemed real, but I couldn't imagine how they could be. Either way I knew there was a big risk in telling, an enormous risk . . . and I was determined to keep it secret forever.

I put the letter down and looked out the window. It was almost as if I expected to see those same balloons staring back at me. What a terrible thing for Michael—a boy at the time— to have experienced and kept to himself. Back then there wasn't this big push for kids . . . for anyone really . . . to be open about their private thoughts and feelings, their fears and anxieties. If it wasn't a cut or some visible bruise the school—no one really—was very interested.

Families didn't talk about mental problems. I suppose Michael's family is a prime example of that. Families hid their problems behind closed doors . . . sisters who talked to themselves and wound up institutionalized, uncles who committed crimes and went to jail, children who stayed at home because they couldn't stop banging their heads against the wall and mothers afraid to leave the house. People kept illnesses—especially the ones you couldn't see or explain—secret. They considered them an embarrassment, a punishment from God, a failure of some sort on their part . . . whether it was a failure of love, character or upbringing.

In any event, it was a secret to be kept at all costs.

It didn't happen again for the longest time. But it did the Thanksgiving after we met, despite the boundless happiness you brought to my life. Or maybe because of it. Maybe I didn't deserve to be so happy, not without the "vision" to remind me of the danger. I often wonder if it's similar for my mother and what tormented her as she got older. I can't ask, not the way she is now. I suppose it doesn't really matter anyway. They were the same balloons this time as well with the same poison and I had to watch them longer before they finally gave up and rose slowly to the heavens.

After that they weren't always balloons, sometimes they were birds outside the window, hovering place, waiting for me to leave the house. Once they were butterflies, another time they were soap bubbles . . . soap bubbles with eyes.

Fortunately, when they were gone, they were gone so they were easy to hide, relatively speaking, at least back then when the world was filled with baseball, high school . . . and you. People would be surprised at how easy it is to look and act normal, particularly when you are most of the time, particularly when you have an easy swing that sends balls flying over the fences and a smile that's always easy to return, particularly when you always do well in class and know that whatever it is following you around, that's always there even when you can't see it, doesn't leave a clue or a mark.. There's no bruise, no burn, no sound, nothing to indicate you're being watched. All you have to do is be quiet about it and listen to everyone else's problems.

People like to talk about themselves and be seen much more than they like to listen and look. They never look close enough to notice what's not being said or to ask the right kind of questions. No one did in high school, not once.

There were times I was hoping you'd notice something and ask me about it. I'd vowed never to lie to you if you did.

I suppose what I saw, the visions as I think of them these days . . . they almost sound like a gift from God that way and perhaps they are a tradeoff for the other gifts . . . might have a simple explanation. I've been thinking a lot about it lately. What if it was a young boy's way of trying to get more attention in a house filed with secrets and silence, a house where his father was focused on his mother and his mother was focused on some other darkness? What if I brought it on myself because I added to that silence, sensing my mother's unhappiness as I grew older, but never once asking about it or saying a word? Maybe this is what happens when you internalize that kind of thing? What if the same thing happened to my mother for staying silent about what was happening to her older sister?

These kind of crazy theories, and I know they're crazy, I keep to myself.

Anyway, it got worse freshman year at college. I suppose all that pot didn't help. Nor did the acid I dropped on two occasions. I never told you that either. I wrote some of it down in a letter once, but crumpled it up instead of sending it to you. I still keep it to myself. I won't tell the truth to the counselors at school. Telling them I'm feeling tired and sad is all they need to hear. They aren't interested in much else. I suppose they don't have the time.

If the counselors think you're a little depressed and smoking too much dope, it doesn't really concern them because they think all of us are a little depressed—depression being as common as a cold in school—and most of them have their own pot issues.

Our breakup, my breakup with you, was never about someone else, not really. It was an impulse, a certain comfort in proximity . . . having someone like Georgina nearby when I needed someone . . . almost like the pot. There has never been anyone else who made it as easy as you did to keep it at bay. The guys on the baseball team, my drug buddies in college could sometimes, but it wasn't them I focused on during the nights I lay there trying to block it out. The coeds in school see their own visions when they get high and in the end they are interested in little more than a good time.

The highs never last that long, certainly not long enough.

I don't want to turn into my mother and force you to play the role my father did for all those years. How could he be happy as my mother grew more reclusive and distant? You didn't know what she was like when I was younger and could still find her energy and smile . . . at least that's the way it seemed when I was little. There were many years like that, years I suppose where she was better able to hide it. The smiles disappeared by the time I turned 13. I'm sure that's why he drank so much and you found him so irritable. I'm sure that's a big reason he died so young. I almost think he wanted to die. He'd had enough, more than enough. He was too loyal to leave any other way.

I don't want that for you, not even the chance of it.

So here I am entering my senior year, still thinking about you . . . as I so often do . . . wondering if I am my mother and whether there is a way out. Some things are so deep down inside you, they're beyond anyone's reach, even your own.

If I knew it wasn't true . . . if I knew they'd leave me along soon and go away . . . you'd be the first person I'd call to beg you to take me back. But some things are not meant to be . . . not every live is about love and happiness . . . that much I've learned in college.

With All My Love Forever,
Michael

My hands were trembling when I finished and my cheeks were soaked. "With All My Love Forever" was how he used to sign all his letters that first year he was in college. It felt as if only a moment had passed since he sat down to write me this letter, not fifty years. It was as if he were talking to me across a bridge of time . . . that moment alongside this one.

How is it possible I didn't see any of this? I thought I knew him so well. I watched him play ball and walk down the hall. Almost every day for three years. I stared at him lying in bed after we'd finished fooling around, his back smooth and unblemished, except for that little half-moon beauty mark on his left shoulder blade. Running my finger along the tan line left by his uniform. We sat there for hours on the swing talking about us and our future, our words punctuated with kisses and laughter.

If there was any doubt in his eyes, I never saw it. I suppose because I was only looking for any doubt about me—my reflection in his eyes—not anything else.

Clearly, I didn't look close enough at Michael or listen carefully enough, not with the kind of eyes and ears I would have one day as I grew older. Unfortunately, I only had the 16 and 17-year old versions and they were still unpracticed in recognizing the darker aspects of life.

I couldn't blame myself, Earl said, because I had no experience with mental problems at the time. If there was issues like that among any of my relatives they'd been hidden from me as well. I had no idea, he reminded me, what to look for or whether there was any reason for me to look at all.

Young children and old people, he reminded me, didn't receive the kind of attention they need when it came to diagnosing mental illness.

"Not then," he said, "and it's not much better now."

I'd read the same articles he had confirming that. Even parents can be too close sometimes and too tired to notice.

I never really questioned Michael about those days, and there were a few of them, when he didn't come to school, cancelled a date because he wasn't feeling well or had to help his mother with something. Were those signs? Should I have pressed him for more information? Of course, it never dawned on me that there could be another reason for any of it or that Michael would be anything but a hundred percent truthful to me.

"Easy for a high school sweetheart to overlook," Earl kept repeating, but I still couldn't understand—or accept—how the 17-year old me could be so obtuse.

"What about all his friends on the baseball team," Earl said, "as well as his coaches and teachers. There's a whole village that missed it . . . and they missed those kinds of things all the time back then."

He was right, it was true. There was a real stigma to mental illness. People didn't want to hear about it. They didn't make much of an effort to understand. Mostly they gossiped about it like the bad fortune had to be well-deserved.

I ached for Michael . . . and I ached for myself as well . . . for my failings as a first-lover and the bright, intuitive, understanding girl I thought I once was.

Earl nodded when I told him that, poured me another drink, and left the room to give me some more space.

"I'll be on the patio," he said, picking up his Golf Magazine, "when you're ready to talk more about it. But I'll tell you one more thing I'm thinking before I leave."

I looked up from the chair hoping he'd have the right words, as he so often did, although I know there were no right words this time that would make me instantly feel better, as did Earl because he didn't even try.

"This is all the more reason you need to go to the fiftieth reunion. You need to write this book and put the truth out there. If you don't, he'll just be the great high school baseball player who became a great artist . . . with a little bad luck in between. It's an important story that's not limited to Michael."

I nodded because Earl was right. I knew he was right before he even said it. Whether I did it at the fiftieth reunion or later in a book, the truth needed to be out there.

I sat there thinking of this refrain one of my friends down in Florida liked to repeat every morning after we did our laps in the pool. Every morning is bliss, she'd say, even if the night is filled with pain. I agreed with the sentiment . . . the importance of living in the moment, the good moments, but it didn't do much good. It wasn't the present I was feeling badly about or the future, it was the past.

I'd always thought of the past—history really—as something fixed and inert . . . unchanging . . . far from that uncertain edge inhabited by the present and the future. How could I have been so wrong? It turns out the past, just like the present, is not always what it seems. It's just as fluid, changing from moment to moment with the turn of a shovel, a new scholarly treatise . . . or the discovery of an old letter.

CHAPTER TEN – RECOGNITION AND REMEMBRANCE

Michael's shadow box exhibit sold out within ten days, most going for the high five figures and two for the low six figures. There were almost 300 boxes left and GAL had no doubt—since no new ones were ever going to be made—that the prices would climb significantly.

Representatives from the Museum of Modern Art and the Met came to the apartment to view the boxes. They each purchased two, two from the sixties and two more recent ones. Michael was the talk of the art world. There's always something special about an unknown artist being discovered after his or her death. ARTNews did a front page story about Michael's shadow boxes and the many parallels between his life and Joseph Cornell's.

Even the Bethel Woods Museum, built to commemorate the Woodstock concert, purchased a box representing the late sixties . . . as Michael saw it and his life in it. The one they purchased had an original Woodstock ticket inside, along with a model of the Apollo moon lander. There was a toy 747 jumbo jet, a car falling off a bridge representing Chappaquiddick and a little replica of the Stonewall Inn. The more personal items in the box included a stone pipe for smoking grass, a photo of me in a bikini, and a photo of him in his old high school baseball jersey smoking a fat one.

There was also a small doll wearing glasses with a hole in her head.

I had no idea what that might represent unless it was Michael's aunt. A little research confirmed that she had died in 1969. Whether she had a lobotomy or not, and how she died, was information they would only reveal pursuant to a court order.

Not surprisingly, there was a small red balloon hovering in front of the full moon, a moon with the first man standing on it.

The interest in Michael extended beyond the art world and a week before the 50th reunion his photo was on the cover of Time Magazine. It was a photo lifted from his bio at Morgan Stanley. He was wearing a blue suit with a dark red tie and looked every part the senior vice president in charge of compliance. He looked nothing like a recluse or an artist, but that was the point of the story.

In today's urban society, the author wrote, reclusive people are not easy to spot, not like the agrarian hermit a few hundred years earlier who lived in the woods, his hair wild and matted, his clothes in tatters. Today's recluse could have a job and appear almost normal during the work day. It was their seclusion outside of work, what they did or didn't do in their private lives that marked them as reclusive.

It could be the result of having experienced something frightening or having watched something horrible happen to someone they loved. Becoming a recluse in that case, she wrote, was a form of Post-Traumatic Stress Disorder. It could be something less dramatic like growing up feeling much more comfortable alone with your own thoughts and playing your own games. It could start with an unease making small talk or a concern that your eyes gave too much away.

Perhaps growing up in a big family might give someone an obsession with privacy. Or it could be the result of excessive feelings of inadequacy or a concern that there's something wrong with you or at least very odd that no one else can see because it isn't obvious or that will become obvious if you stand too long in the light. The best way to keep a secret like that is not to spend much time with anyone else.

The author concluded that more and more people these days live lives with various degrees of "reclusive-ness"—lives of quiet reclusivity is how she put it, torturing a famous line by Thoreau. She warned her readers it would become more common as it became easier to access the world, the entire world . . . from working to ordering food . . . without ever having to leave your room.

You could live your entire life that way these days if you

wanted.

Michael was a successful athlete and student who lost his father at a young age, she wrote, who was forced to help care for his troubled mother, and helplessly watched as his wife and son died way too young. He kept up his work, his external life, because he needed to earn a living—and he could, not everyone can—but he secluded himself when it came to everything else because he'd had enough of modern life.

The author didn't find it surprising he kept to himself after a personal tragedy like that. What she did find surprising was that instead of sitting around watching television, roaming the internet, doing crossword puzzles and feeling sorry for himself, he channeled his energy into shadow boxes . . . displaying his life and history through his own reclusive eyes.

I thought it was a terrible article, although it did contain some basic truths. Most of them didn't apply to Michael, at least to my thinking. What did she really know about him? Little more than she could have found out by talking to a few of his co-workers, the doormen at his building, and perhaps an old classmate or two? She didn't know the truth because I wouldn't tell it to her when she called to interview me. I declined, explaining that I was working on my own book and my agent did not want me talking to the press, not yet anyway.

"So much for her investigative psychology," I said to Earl, tossing him the magazine.

"She's speculating based on what she does know," Earl said.

"She reading tea leaves."

"She's working with what's out there."

"She has a few pieces of a much larger puzzle and pretends she can see it all. That's arrogance, not insight."

Earl nodded this time. He wasn't going to argue with me. He'd been patiently listening for days now as I complained about everything being written about Michael. He and I were the only two people in the world at the moment who knew the truth.

"Her last line is alright," I said, trying to sound a little less frustrated, as I reached out and took the magazine back from Earl.

"What does she say?"

I read it out loud. "One of the most important lessons to be learned from Michael, perhaps the most important lesson of all, is that art is everywhere, it's in each and every one of us, no matter how disappointing or troubled the other parts of our lives might seem, if only we can find the strength and a way to express it."

"That's very true," Earl said.

The article mentioned me and my role in the discovery of the shadow boxes which was an example, she pointed out, of the serendipity of life, particularly Michael's life. If I hadn't joined Facebook, become curious and investigated Michael's death, who knows what would have happened to the shadow boxes. Most likely some moving service would have been retained to clean out the apartment and the boxes would have been tossed into the trash.

I handed Earl back the magazine so he could read the full article.

"She mentions I'm writing a book," I said. "I'm sure my agent is happy about that."

Earl thought it was ironic that I was finally getting to fulfill my dream of writing a book and it would be about a high school boyfriend who had been out of my life for fifty years and who was guaranteed to get mentioned in my obituary long before Earl was.

Earl laughed about it. He didn't mind, he said, as long as he got mentioned somewhere.

I gave him the fish eye in response and he apologized.

"Sorry, bad joke."

Earl came with me to the 50th reunion, as he promised, which was the third Saturday in June, a glorious early summer evening under a canopy of stars, a tent set up just in case at the back of the Hilton Hotel. The Hilton hadn't existed when we were students, the county was still relatively undeveloped. There were no big hotels, no large apartment or office buildings and no shopping centers. E.J. Korvettes and Grants were the only two big stores in the county. Now there were large chain hotels, big office buildings you could see for miles, and two enormous malls, one being second in size to the Mall of America, the largest in the country.

We drove up early and while Earl checked into the hotel I went to visit Michael's mother. I brought her one of his first shadow boxes, one with a photo of his parents in younger and happier times standing beside Michael in his t-ball uniform. There was also a small doll—Michael the artist liked small dolls—peeking out from behind a bush. A round window looked out on the ocean, as if it were a porthole. There was a battleship in the distance. Michael had also added a little green parakeet, a replica of Aladdin's lamp and a small table with a tiny box of corn flakes, a small milk of carton and three bowls.

The TV was old-fashion with rabbit ears on top.

There were no balloons. They weren't in Michael's life yet.

I tried to imagine what the small doll might signify. Perhaps Michael almost had a sister. What if his mother had lost a baby at birth when Michael was four or five? Perhaps she changed after that. Wouldn't his mother and father have discussed it with young Michael . . . you know, the angel taken by God to heaven? Perhaps not. What if it became just another family secret, something else for Michael to wonder whether it was real or imagined?

It was all speculation, I know, but that's the nature of art and shadow boxes in particular. I certainly wasn't going to ask his mother, assuming she was in the moment when I got there.

I also brought her four magazines with stories about Michael, two of them with him on the cover, and two with pictures of his shadow boxes. I told her how famous he'd become and how rich. I asked her what she wanted to do with all the money, but she didn't respond. She hardly looked at the box or the magazines. When she wasn't looking at me—passed me really— she was looking up at the sunlight.

As her newly appointed guardian, I learned Michael had set up a trust fund for his mother many years earlier which contained more money than she would ever need. The first thing the attorney wanted me to do was make a will for her, as the trust provided for the remainder to go back to Michael upon her death, and with Michael already dead everything of Michael's belonged to her, his nearest—and as far as we could tell—only relative. With all the new money coming in from the sale of his shadow boxes there would be a big pot to distribute after she was gone.

"If she doesn't bequeath it somewhere in her will," the attorney told me "it will wind up going to the state."

We talked about a charity, something that might appeal to Michael and his mother. The attorney had suggested an art foundation or a museum. I said I would talk it over with Helen, although we both knew that would be pointless.

I read to Helen from the article about Michael in ArtNews which spoke glowingly of his artistic work and sensibilities. It called him one of the major new artists of the twenty-first century.

I looked for any light in her eyes to indicate some of it was getting through, but I didn't see anything. I handed the magazines to the aide and asked her to show them to Helen if she returned again to the moment.

"She hasn't," the aide said, "not since the last time you were here. She's hasn't said a word in a month."

The aide bent down to study the shadow box.

"People pay money for this kind of thing?"

"A lot of money."

"How much is a lot?"

When I told her she stood up and fell back against the wall, as if she'd lost her balance.

Helen looked frailer than she did the last time I was here. I couldn't wait too long to do her will and wrote myself a note to do it right after the reunion. When I told Helen I had to leave it looked for a moment as if she was reaching out to stroke my cheek, but all she did was grab at something imaginary in the space between us and squeeze it tight. Then she opened her hand and watched it fall to the floor, nodding and sighing at the same time.

Perhaps it was an imaginary bird or a butterfly.

Earl and I had taken a room at the Hilton, along with a lot of Michael's former classmates, many of whom had scattered around the country over the years. Sixty percent had moved away according to the reunion booklet we were sent in advance listing the attendees and their addresses. The fact that forty percent stuck around the same area code was what really surprised me.

When it came time to get dressed and go downstairs for the cocktail hour, Earl didn't move. He just sat there in the bed watching a golf tournament.

"You'd better get a move on it," I said.

He turned off the television and smiled up at me.

"Here's what I propose. You go to the cocktail hour alone. It'll give you time to talk to people . . . use your writer's eye to gather some ideas. Decide what you want to say or not say. I'll come down for the dinner part, but only if you call me. Otherwise, I'll just order up some room service and hear all about it when you get back."

"You don't want to go?" I asked, trying to sound more disappointed than I felt.

"I want to do whatever works best for you. Whatever you

really want?"

"OK," I said.

"OK what?"

"Ok, I agree, I'll give it a try. But you'd better be dressed and ready when I call because I'm going to be calling you the moment they finish passing around the hors d'oeuvres."

"I will be ready," Earl said with his Cheshire grin, which I found a bit eerie because he always seemed to use it when he could see something I couldn't.

I went into the bathroom to finish putting on my makeup. I knew Earl was right and I was better off alone. I was happy to have him here with me in the hotel, on the other side of the bed where I could talk things out with him, but it would be a lot easier for me if I didn't have to introduce him every time I met one of Michael's former classmates—and mine—and it would certainly shorten the obligatory background question and answer session intended to bridge a 50-year gap in five minutes.

Earl and I had spent the week discussing what I would say . . . or not say. My original idea was to tell everyone the complete truth about Michael right off the bat to use a baseball analogy. Tell them about the letter and the illness he suffered in silence. Probe their memories to find if anyone had an inkling. I thought it was important for the class to find out—on this 50th reunion of the high point of Michael's life—what I'd missed . . . what we'd all missed.

Why should I be the only one feeling complicit?

I thought the truth would better serve Michael's memory, whatever the moment and whatever the circumstance, and remind us of the importance of being ever vigilant about these kinds of things when it came to our grandchildren and friends.

Earl wasn't so sure. He didn't argue against it, but he did encourage me to think it over, not just from my perspective, but from theirs . . . and from Michael's.

"You're going to be surrounded by all his classmates and their memories . . . so rosy that far in the distance. They're going to be holding tight to the past, looking for an old friend's face and voice behind the wrinkles and age spots, someone to share a good memory at a time when there are not a lot of new ones being made. Is it the right time to confront them with a whole different truth . . . to point out what they missed and misunderstood? To shatter a moment they've come to honor and celebrate?"

I shrugged every time he'd talked like that over the past week. I didn't know the answer. It was certainly too late for me to hold onto any delusions. What did I owe to Michael . . . and to his class?

"Make it a game-time decision," he suggested. "Wait until you're there. See how it goes. Don't go with your mind made up . . . that's all I'm saying."

He compared it to a golf game where you have to take into account the weather, the condition of the fairways and the greens, as well as how you've been hitting the ball before you decide on the club and the shot.

The truth should be told, Earl had no doubt about that, he just wasn't sure the fiftieth reunion was the right place and time. He thought the book—generic, fictional, naming names or using pseudonyms, however I wanted to do it—offered a much better and kinder opportunity.

I told him I would keep an open mind, although I carried a copy of Michael's letter down with me in case I decided to say something. I wanted to be ready to show it to the disbelievers because I knew there would be many.

I didn't dress the way I normally do these days, which is a lot like my mother. When I was younger I would have called it dowdy and frumpy . . . not anymore. Now it feels more appropriate to my age and body. However, for tonight I had bought all new clothes, clothes I might have worn back in college—a few sizes larger, of course—including bell bottom jeans, a designer version anyway, a purple camisole, a white linen shirt and a head band, not the beaded kind I used to wear senior year in college, which I'd have paid any price for if I could find one like it. This was a simple red ribbon headband.

I used to wear tie backs with ribbons all the time in high school. It kept my hair out of my face. Michael thought I looked cute that way, as did my mother, and it gave Michael the opportunity to give it a little tug whenever we passed in the hall. I still liked the way it looked fifty years later, even with my hair shorter and grey.

Cute is not confined to the young . . . just naiveté and unreasonable expectations.

I like to say that my expectations are lower now than they ever were before . . . and getting lower every year. I'm satisfied these days with the flimsiest of promises . . . an ordinary night out with Earl, a quiet walk around the lake or a call from one of the grandchildren.

Still, as I rode the elevator down to the cocktail hour I had visions of something more than the typical reunion I'd seen over the years in the movies and on TV. I was hoping for something more intimate with deeper more stimulating conversations, conversations that weren't all about nostalgia . . . that didn't make me feel as if I had stepped into an old black and white photograph.

Don't get me wrong, I fully expected to talk some about the past, but I wanted to talk about other things as well, like how the past can change when we look at it from a distance and with older eyes. I wanted to talk with people from my own generation—who I knew back then and who knew me—about how far we'd come, what we'd seen and learned, and where we went from here.

I didn't want to talk a lot about material things. I didn't want to compare beach houses or travels abroad. I didn't want to talk, at least not too much, about children and grandchildren. I didn't want to hear about doctor's visits and assorted aches and pains. Or complaints about what the world has come to with computers and smartphones that don't require the kind of literacy and speaking skills we worked so hard to master.

Sure, I wanted to talk about us and our stories of progress—much more than I wanted to talk about our decline—but I also wanted to get philosophical and explore what it all meant. Sort of like sitting down with a really good book, except being inside it, a part of the narration and dialogue . . . in the middle of all the action.

I'd been reading up on us the last week . . . us being the elderly, although a lot of commentators suggested that reaching your late sixties was really the beginning and that we were closer to middle age than old age. While we might share our accumulating years and historical context—perhaps a host of opportunistic aches and pains as well—we were still young enough to have different dreams, different capabilities and our own paths.

We were still learning, one author wrote, and our lives—even at our age—remain interesting and complicated. The difference at our age is that the parts—the issues— seem simpler and more manageable because of the literacy we older folk bring to this stage of our lives.

I was curious to see who I'd recognize and how I'd feel. Who I would like and dislike? Would I still feel the same way about people as I did in high school? Everything I'd read suggests who we are when we reach old age is pretty close to who we were when we were young . . . that there is a consistency of self that travels across time.

Perhaps our collective wisdom—108 of us having survived a 50-year journey with 5,000 total years of experience—could help me . . . us . . . understand how we got here from there, why our lives turned out the way they did and why someone like Michael didn't make it.

I had my little notebook with me and I intended to write things down so I could include a reunion scene in the book. Perhaps at the end, particularly if I were to conclude that we as a class and as a society bore some responsibility for failing to encourage Michael to come forward as a child and for failing to see what we should have if we'd made an effort to look more closely.

Stepping into the room was like stepping into one of Michael's shadow boxes.

As I first looked look around, all I noticed were the objects.

There was a wall of posters from 1968 movies including 2001: A Space Odyssey, Rosemary's Baby, Planet of the Apes, Barbarella, Chitty Chitty Bang Bang, Oliver, Funny Girl, Yellow Submarine and the Night of the Living Dead. Apparently, the reunion committee had very diverse tastes.

There were album covers scattered everywhere, real album covers that classmates must have taken from their collections or the reunion committee found online. Just looking at the tables near me I saw The Beatles White Album, Astral Weeks by Van Morrison, Electric Ladyland by Jimi Hendrix, Beggars Banquet by The Rolling Stones and Bookends by Simon and Garfunkel. There were dozens of others on every table by all the groups we grew up with like The Band, Johnny Cash, The Kinks, The Beatles, The Velvet Underground and The Zombies.

There were lists everywhere neatly printed on large pieces of poster board and set up on easels. There was a list of television shows . . . American Bandstand, Bewitched, Candid Camera, Family Affair, Get Smart, Green Acres, Gunsmoke, Hogan's Heroes, I Dream of Jeannie, I Spy and Mission Impossible, among others. I was addicted to That Girl back in high school. Michael was a big fan of Mannix.

There was a list of top songs . . . Born to Be Wild by Steppenwolf, Piece of My Heart by Big Brother & The Holding Company, White Room by Cream, Sympathy for the Devil by The Rolling Stones, Hey Jude by The Beatles, All Along the Watchtower by Jimi Hendrix and Sittin on the Dock of the Bay by Otis Redding. Louie Armstrong had a hit that year with What a Wonderful World, as did the 1910 Fruitgum Company with Simon Says.

I liked all kinds of music back then, even bubble gum pop, although Michael preferred the heavier psychedelic stuff from groups like the Stones and the Doors. I realize now that many of their songs were about drugs which I don't think I realized back then. I wondered if Michael did.

There were book lists and sports lists that included all the top teams and players in baseball, football and basketball. If Michael were here now I could see him and his baseball buddies arguing who was better back then than and how they compared to today's players. Michael may have been a baseball god, but he also enjoyed football and basketball, playing as well as watching.

Of course, 1968 was a big year in the news and there were headlines cut out from newspapers and magazines taped to the walls. They dealt with Martin Luther King Jr.'s assassination in Memphis, Robert Kennedy's assassination in Los Angeles, North Vietnam's Tet offensive, North Korea's capture of the USS Pueblo, the three US medal winners who stood on the podium at the Olympics with their fists held high, and Apollo 8 orbiting the moon with Lovell, Anders and Borman becoming the first humans to leave the earth's orbit.

There were photos from our high school football games and The Fantastiks, the school musical in 1968. There was a wall of photos devoted to our teachers. I wondered how many of them were still alive. None of them were going to be in attendance, the reunion committee let everyone know that. My favorite English teacher, Mr. Pollard, who had to be in his early thirties when I had him in 10th grade, would be in her mid-eighties by now. I wondered if he was enjoying retirement in his own Florida community without any thoughts about the effect he might have had on me or anyone else in the class. He was the teacher most responsible for my interest in writing.

There were balloons everywhere, which I thought a bit ironic considering Michael's letter, and a large banner welcoming the Class of '68. It could have been a graduation party or an end of the year school dance, all I had to do was close my eyes and ignore the throbbing in my right knee.

At least I could have pretended it was just another graduation party until I looked under the banner and saw the Wall of Remembrance honoring the class of '68 members who had passed away. It wasn't necessarily complete since a lot of people hadn't responded and others couldn't be found. There was no way of knowing if they were dead or alive. The reunion committee's newsletter made that clear.

The photos of the dead had been cut out of someone's yearbook with their names printed below. No date of death, no cause of death, and no short bio to tell us what they were doing before they met their maker, although I knew that Rich Fenton, a running back on the football team and a back-up catcher on the baseball team, had died looking the same as he did in the photo in Vietnam. It was two years after he graduated, when our ties were still intact enough for the news to spread quickly.

At the center of the Wall of Remembrance was a large poster-size photo of Michael, not his baseball photo from Facebook, but a similar one of him fielding a hot line drive . . . a smile on his face as he snatched it out of the air. It must have come from one his teammates. On either sides was a framed cover from a magazine, Time to the left and Art World to the right, both with his Morgan Stanley photo. He didn't look much like himself because he wasn't smiling and he was wearing a suit, although he wasn't hard to recognize having retained his good looks right up until the end.

"I'm sure they're right," a voice said over my shoulder, "there are probably a lot more."

I turned around and a woman who looked ten years older than me extended her hand. She was dark and leathery, like she'd spent far too much of her youth lying in the sun under one of those silver reflectors that were popular when we young. We were all given nametags with our yearbook photos on them, but I hadn't put mine on. Neither had she. I couldn't bear the thought of walking around with my past pinned to my chest like that.

"I'm Peggy Noonan," she said. "Couldn't wear my nametag

either, afraid of ruining the dress. It was quite expensive." She stepped back to give me a better look and I smiled.

"It's lovely."

It looked as if it were a size too small. Every bulge the years had added was visible, as if time had turned her into a topographical map.

"Thanks. Got it wholesale. My husband, God rest his soul, was in the garment business and I still have some contacts."

I looked Peggy up and down but I didn't remember her, not even the name.

"Azu," I said.

"I remember you. You're still wearing a red ribbon in your hair."

"Not any more, just for tonight."

"Still looks cute. You used to have long hair . . . almost down to your waist, right?"

I nodded.

"You weren't in our class, were you?"

"No, I'm a sixty-nine."

"Right, you went steady with Michael," she said. It wasn't a question, it was an answer. She stepped up beside me so we could both stare up at his photo.

"He was a sophomore when we met. I was a freshman."

She nodded like it was something else she already knew.

"Every year it was the same thing," she said, "the upper class boys chasing the freshman girls. I don't know why . . . I suppose because they were like shiny new cars . . . and easy."

I didn't know how to respond to that. It never dawned on me that the upper class girls might resent me. Maybe Peggy had a crush on Michael. Maybe she even went out to a movie with him freshman year and he never asked her out again. I really didn't know what Michael did in ninth grade. I don't remember asking or if I did I don't remember his answer.

I never had that kind of problem with Michael when I became a sophomore because we were exclusive from our first date until my graduation.

"We were all jealous," Peggy said, "pretty much every girl in our class. We all had a crush on him."

"Me too," I said.

"Too bad he's dead. He's one guy I'd have liked to see."

Needing to move away or change the subject, I decided to try changing the subject first. At my age being rude is not an option. It's no longer in my DNA.

"What about your high school boyfriend?" I asked. "Who was he?"

"Cliff . . . ran track. Wasn't very good."

"Is he here?"

"No."

I nodded as we remained standing side by side looking up at Michael. I wondered how much she knew about his life.

"Did you marry him?" Peggy asked, giving me the answer.

"No, we broke up after his first year of college."

"Did quite well for himself," she said, pointing at the two magazine covers.

I nodded.

"Most famous person in our class . . . only one really who's amounted to anything. I googled almost everyone's name and he was the only one who came up on top."

I nodded again.

"How did he die?" she asked.

"Drowned."

"A shame . . . he was a pretty good swimmer if I remember."

"Passed out I think."

"Aging sucks."

"Did you read either of those magazine articles?" I asked.

That was another thing I was curious about. How many people here, other than Michael's friends on the baseball team, knew his story?

"No." She cleared her throat and pointed to another one of the photos on the wall. "That's my old high school boyfriend . . . Cliff Dobbins . . . his parents used to own the stationery store next to Volante's Pizza."

"I used to go there all the time."

"Who didn't? It was the only local place around to buy school supplies."

I didn't recognize the name at first, but I remembered Cliff from his photo. He was always working at the store when I came in to buy something and we always talked, never about school, about other things, although I couldn't remember a single subject at the moment. I think he had a crush on me, but he wasn't going to go up against Michael so he didn't try. No one ever tried.

"We split the summer after graduation. He went to college. I had to work, we had no money. Got a job as a receptionist."

"How did Cliff die?"

"Drowned scuba diving," she said. "I guess we have that in common . . . drowned first loves."

"That's unfortunate," I said, not feeling as if we had anything in common.

We moved along the wall in tandem as we examined the photos of the other dead. They all looked familiar, but they also looked unfamiliar, like they belonged to another time . . . another century . . . which I suppose they did.

There was only one woman on the wall. Carolyn Kent. I didn't know her well, although I'd heard she died in a car accident returning from college after graduation.

"Funny," Peggy said. "I don't remember anyone else on the wall."

"It was a big class."

"Not by today's standards. We had two-hundred and sixty-seven students in our graduating class. My kids' school had over seven hundred. Of course, that was a while ago as well. They're both married now. I have four grandchildren. You?"

"Three."

"So much easier than real children. You get to give them back when you're tired . . . which doesn't take much these days."

I nodded and smiled. I intended to write that line down as soon as I had a moment.

"I was on the reunion committee," Peggy said.

"Well, you guys did a great job."

"We couldn't find eighty-eight classmates. They say that's pretty normal for this kind of thing. They told us to figure about fifteen percent of the class should be dead by now."

"Who's they?"

"Classmates dot com. There are all kinds of sites out there that help with this," she said, walking us slowly back to Cliff's photo. "That means at least forty. The ones on the wall are just the tip of the iceberg."

"I'm sure they're right," I said, deciding I could leave now without appearing rude. I looked around for someone . . . anyone . . . and spotted Max at the bar.

"Cliff was misunderstood," she said.

"How so?"

"He was the stationery store kid to everyone, but he was much more than that. Do you know he liked to run all the time . . . before that kind of thing became popular?"

"I didn't."

"And he wrote me poems . . . love poems."

"Very nice. Did you keep any of them?"

"No, they got tossed years ago. My husband was the jealous type."

I looked around again to make sure Max was still there.

"Excuse me," I said, "I arranged to meet an old friend at the bar and I see him there now. You remember Max, he played on the baseball team."

Peggy shook her head no without taking her eyes off Cliff.

"It was nice seeing you again," I said.

"You too," Peggy said without turning her head. She just stood there in front of Cliff's photo, her lips snapped shut, as if she were angry at him for not living long enough to see if he could bring out that young girl in her one more time.

"Alone?" I said, coming up beside him at the bar.

"Yep. I'm glad you came."

"I was hoping to meet your wife," I said.

"She's not a big fan of this kind of thing."

"Reunions?"

"Nostalgia. She not the sentimental kind . . . not when it comes to the distant past. Had some tough times growing up, refused to go to any of her reunions. Says she keeps in touch with the people she wants to and that's enough, although she did want to meet you . . . maybe another time."

"So who are you here to see?" I asked Max.

"No one in particular. The guys from the team for sure, but we keep in touch so it's no big deal."

"You went out with a lot of different girls if I remember correctly."

Max nodded.

"There must have been a special one?"

I felt bad that I didn't remember.

"Was it that cute cheerleader, the petite one . . . the captain . . . what was her name, Linda . . . Linda Hunt?"

"Hutton . . . Linda Hutton. She my first and I was hers. It was eleventh grade. It's funny how you never forget that moment. I can remember everything about it. From the way she smelled when I started kissing her neck to the look on her face when she realized I was completely undressed."

"No you can't," I said, thinking how nervous Michael and I were and how much trouble he had unhooking my bra, "especially when you're in ninth grade."

"Really?" Max said. "Wow. We all wondered about that. We asked Mike all the time, but he wouldn't saw a word. All the other guys talked about every kiss and every time they felt anyone up . . . like it was a sporting event, but not Mike. He didn't brag about that sort of thing. I suppose he didn't have to."

The bartender brought us our drinks. Two scotches . . . his neat, mine on the rocks.

"He didn't like to brag," I said.

"Or talk about himself," Max said. "He'd talk plenty when it came to baseball, but never about personal things. He kept his own counsel when it came to that."

I nodded into my drink.

"He never talked about his mother and I called for him often enough to know she was a bit . . . ."

"Different," I volunteered.

"Strange. All the other mothers made you sit down and eat something so they could ask you a million questions . . . like you'd give up the truth about their son for a couple of Rice Krispie treats."

"And Michael's mother?"

"She'd nod, smile sometimes, but she didn't talk much. All the other mothers were always in the kitchen. Most of the time I came over she was in her room. How was she with you?"

"Pretty much the same. I thought she was shy back then," I said, "and unhappy."

It sounded like the perfect moment to tell Max about Michael's letter, about the secret he kept from all of us, his mother's secret as well, but I couldn't bring myself to do it. It just didn't feel right.

"I always admired that about Mike," Max said. "I suppose he was like his mother that way. Silence didn't bother him. He didn't have to say every single thought that entered his head, not like the rest of us."

Max took a sip of scotch.

"The more I think about it, the more I realize I didn't know a lot about him . . . what was going on in his head. That interior monologue stuff they talk about now. I suppose it's that old saying . . . still waters run deep. Why else would a guy like that kill himself?"

Max looked over at me waiting for my reaction. I nodded. I couldn't bring myself to pull out Michael's letter or to tell him I had a theory. Maybe it was too early in the evening. Maybe I hadn't had enough to drink. If I told him, the baseball team would have to know. Soon everyone would.

Would that be all that everyone would talk about? Or would it get five minutes of conversation before everyone moved onto their own lives and memories. How would I handle that? Earl was right, I hadn't really thought it through. I wasn't ready to let it out, not now, not like this.

I'd be more motivated to write the book if I kept it inside for now, let it build up steam . . . like I was some kind of pressure cooker.

"Azu, where did you go?" Max asked after what must have seemed like a long silence to him, although it was hardly a moment to me.

"Just thinking about your question," I said. "Did you ever notice anything odd about Michael back then? Anything unusual?"

He shook his head slowly from side to side.

"You knew him as well as I did," Max said, "even better."

"Other than Helen."

"Helen?"

"Michael's mother."

"I don't think I ever knew her name."

Max looked down into his nearly empty glass.

"He was the only one of us without a brother or sister," he said. "I'm sure he felt bad about that."

"Did he ever say anything about it to you?"

"No, just thinking out loud. Max looked sad. He'd lost Michael a long time ago. Why should I take him away again, especially during a party celebrating a milestone like this?

"Is Linda Hutton coming?" I asked instead.

Max nodded. "She's on the list of attendees." He looked

around. "I haven't seen her yet."

"Coming with her husband?"

"No."

"I'm surprised your wife let you out alone."

"She doesn't worry about me, I'm as faithful as a lap dog"

"That wasn't your reputation back in school," I said and we both laughed.

"Scouting out old boyfriends and girlfriends is the number one activity at these reunions," Max said.

"How would you know?" I asked. "How many of these have you attended?"

"This isn't my first fiftieth reunion, it's my fifth."

"How's that?"

"I've gone to the last five class reunions. The administration likes to have a current teacher attend. Since I'm also a former student, I seem to be their first choice. I don't mind. It's been interesting seeing what happened to some of the upperclassmen, particularly the ones who used to pick on me."

"What happened to them?"

"They got old . . . lost their steam, turned into blowhards who spent the evening colorizing their past. Half of them thought they were nice guys in high school, the other half thought we were my best friends."

"So you're like Mr. Nostalgia," I said.

"Tell me about it . . . except this one's different . . . this one's mine. Being an observer is a lot easier than being a participant."

"You mean like me?"

"You're not an observer."

I nodded. I wished I was just a journalist working a story.

Max turned around with his drink in hand and leaned back against the bar. I picked up my scotch and did the same. This way we could study the room.

"Do you recognize everyone?" I asked.

"Hardly anyone."

"You recognized me."

"I saw you a couple of months ago . . . although I'd have recognized you anyway. I spent as much time with you as I did with any of my girlfriends."

Everyone was talking in small groups. No one was standing alone, not like the school dances. The basketball players were in their old social circle. Their wives standing behind them looking less bored than I would have imagined if I were writing this scene. The band students were congregating together as well. I didn't see any of the guys from the baseball team yet.

I could see Max out of the corner of my eye scanning the room for Linda.

"How come Michael got the only big picture on the wall?" I asked.

"Because the guys from the team did it. We found the picture and blew it up. The committee didn't object . . . after all, he was the Prom King, the one person most everyone knew and were sure to remember. I bet most people remember you almost as well. You guys went together . . . sort of like bacon and eggs."

"Who was I, the bacon or the egg?"

Max laughed. "I'm sure most figure you guys got married, had a slew of kids and Michael was tearing up the senior league in Florida, at least until he started appearing in all the magazines . . . and they got the reunion list."

Max ordered another scotch and I switched to chardonnay. I had a tendency to talk too much if I have too much to drink. I can become the queen of sentimental dribble, at least that's the way I usually felt the morning after.

"There's Linda," he said, gesturing over to the sign-in table.

"How can that be her? She was such a petite thing in high school. It looks like she's put on a hundred pounds."

"She's still short."

We both stared at her. The weight looked unnatural, as if she were wearing some kind of theatrical padding. Perhaps because the last time I remember seeing her she was wearing a short skirt and tight sweater doing cartwheels and waving pompoms. Her posture had suffered as well, her shoulders hunched forward as if they were straining to stay upright, when it was always striking to me how straight she used to stand on the gym floor. It looked as if she'd had a hard life, but that was probably my writer's imagination.

We all age differently. How we do doesn't necessarily reflect how we lived . . . although I suppose there often is some correlation.

"I suppose I should go over and say hello," Max said. He leaned closer to me as if he were about to confess something. Perhaps Linda and he had been talking a lot over the past year.

Perhaps his marriage wasn't as happy as he let on.

"No one comes to these things for intimate conversation and commentary. They'll talk a minute or two about love and work, Freud's favorite subjects, but if you're not ready to relive every moment of their past, at least the one they imagine, they'll just move on to the next person. Everyone saves the analysis and comments, if any, for later when they're in bed or a few days after when they get back home."

"Aren't you the fiftieth guru," I said, smiling and reaching out to touch his arm.

"It would be a lot easier if Mike was here . . . for me anyway."

"Me too," I said.

I always liked Max, he always treated me with respect. I never felt his eyes scrutinizing my body parts all the time like I did with some of the other guys on the team. He loved Michael almost as much as I did and now we shared that lost love in a way no other two people could understand. Those kind of connections mean something.

"These things are harder than you think," Max said. "They tend to be a big letdown."

I know I was already feeling a bit let down, mostly because Michael's letter was still sitting there in my back pocket and was likely to for the rest of the evening.

"I can guarantee you one thing," Max added, lowering his voice even more, "you won't find any of the answers you're looking for . . . not here, not tonight."

"What answers?"

"About Michael . . . and you . . . about that time in our life," Max said. "The things that we missed . . . and miss. This isn't the right place or the right time."

I studied Max's eyes to see if he was hiding anything, if he knew more than I did back then but had been sworn to secrecy. It didn't appear that way. It just looked as if he'd had enough of 50th reunions . . . as if after having attended five he couldn't bear it anymore.

"The best thing you can do tonight," Max whispered, "is to keep moving. I call it riding the mingle merry-go-round."

"Very alliterate."

"As emotional and delightful as those days in high school may have seemed," he said, "they have little relevance to our lives now."

"Isn't this one of those intimate conversations and commentaries you said I wouldn't be having?"

"Maybe," Max said, "but that only applies to classmates, not underclassman like you."

"You're funny Max," I said. "How come you weren't this funny in high school?"

"Maybe I was and you didn't notice."

"Quite possible," I said since I rarely stepped far from Michael's glow.

Maybe pledging myself to one boy for all my high school years was a mistake. Perhaps that's why my college years were such a bust . . . romantically speaking. I had learned Michael and no one else and, as it turns out, I didn't know him all that well. Perhaps I was always standing too close . . . holding on too tight to notice anything out of the ordinary . . . too demanding of his strength and success to allow him to show any weakness or to reach out for the kind of help he needed.

Perhaps my expectations and the pedestal I put him on gave him no choice but to hide his defects.

Young love can be like that.

Although no one on the team appears to have seen anything either, nor did the teachers or his coaches. You'd think friendships and student-teacher relationships would be a lot less confining and a lot more observant.

"It's time for me to mingle," Max said, "starting with Linda." We both looked at her struggling to pin on her nametag. "But I'll leave you with two final thoughts, two things I've learned from my vast experience with fiftieth reunions."

"Another commentary?"

"Precisely. First, every paradises is lost . . . starting with youth. In the end, it's almost as if it never existed."

"Depressing, although I'm not sure I totally agree. It may no longer exist, but the memories do and that can feel real sometimes, as do the effects. They leave a mark."

'That's very different. How it affected you and what you remember is not the same as trying to revisit it. It's gone . . . gone forever . . . you have to acknowledge that."

"OK, point taken. I hope Max's second rule of reunions is a bit more uplifting."

"I don't know, depends on how many drinks you've had. It's

also a bit contradictory of the first rule."

"Inconsistency, I love it," I said.

"The second is this . . . time is sometimes a place . . . certainly it becomes one at a reunion. You can stand in this room . . . inside this moment . . . and reach out to touch your past, your present and your future all at once. It's one of those rare places in time where every moment is within reach."

"Wow, that's good," I said.

"It's not mine, I stole it from Proust."

Linda finished adjusting her pin and looked around. She spotted Max right away.

"This school and this town," I said, "really nurtured me as a young girl. I missed a lot of things I shouldn't have, I know that better now than I did before, but it's still a place and a moment I can never escape."

"You did a long time ago," Max said. "Coming back here to see it again . . . and some of the people who were in it with you . . . doesn't bring it back. It's just a twinge of nostalgia. You get them more often as you get older and more of your life is behind you. But it can't hold you for long. Nostalgia is like a shooting star . . . to mix my metaphors. It burns bright for an instant and then it's gone."

I nodded, although I knew that wasn't true for everyone. Maybe for most normal people. It certainly didn't seem like that way for Michael.

My mind was made up, I wasn't going to tell anyone the truth about Michael, not tonight. It would be a lot easier for Max—and me—if he read it in my book.

Max gave me a kiss on the cheek and whispered in my ear, "Remember circulation is the key to avoiding disaster." Then he walked off with an imaginary tug on my pony tail. I turned around to face the bar and ordered another glass of wine, determined to sip this one much slower.

I opened my little notebook and wrote down some ideas I'd gotten from Peggy and Max, as well as some lines from our conversation. I thought about calling Earl and inviting him downstairs in light of my decision, but I figured he'd be happier up in the hotel room not having to listen to the same conversation over and over again about work and family. Besides, I'd have a better opportunity to add to my notebook if I was on my own.

I wasn't sure how much longer I would stay anyway. I didn't see the point in it. There was no one I really wanted to see and I didn't relish the thought of everyone coming up to me to tell me how lucky I was to have landed Michael in high school.

I stood there at the bar looking around the room. I still recognized almost no one, even when I tried squinting and looking through the layers of time to find their younger expressions. Even when I managed to find it and they became familiar again, I couldn't come up a name or very much about them.

My world in high school was a lot smaller than I thought.

Two-hundred and sixty-seven might be a small class in comparison to most schools these days, but it's still a lot of people to know and remember. I'm sure I knew Peggy back in high school, but I couldn't remember the context where our paths had crossed. Was it in class or somewhere else? A job perhaps or a dance? Maybe she dated one of the other baseball players for a while or was in the stationery store hanging out with Cliff when I came in?

Without context these days I'm lost.

"I had a big crush on you in high school," a deep voice said.

I felt someone slide up next to me at the bar.

When I looked over, a very well preserved man was standing there. He was wearing his name tag with his high school yearbook photo—William Campbell. I remembered the name right away because he was in all of my classes. Some of the kids called him the brain, as if that was all there was to him. I didn't need to look at the old yearbook photo pinned to his chest because he had changed less than any person in the room . . . at least physically.

Yes, he was older, much older, but his face wasn't lined, at least not like everyone else. His skin was relatively smooth and unblemished. There were some age spots on his hands—mine were covered with them—but there were none on his face. His nose hadn't expanded over time, there were no bags under his eyes, and his chin wasn't sagging low enough to obscure his neck.

He had put on some weight, he was awfully skinny in high school, but not enough to bulge in places where they always seemed to bulge these days . . . around the hips, the stomach and in the rear. He looked fit, not the least bit tired or achy. Slightly greying hair and a slight stoop were the only concessions he'd made so far to his autumn.

"Billy, you look great."

"I won't lie to you," he said, "you've changed in fifty years. If I hadn't seen you talking with Max, and that red ribbon in your hair, I'm not sure I'd have recognized you."

"You mean I don't look eighteen anymore?"

"Not without the pony tail."

He stared at my face, moving closer than the two feet of social space deemed acceptable in most social situations. I'd written an article about that once.

"But I still see the girl in there."

He used his pointer finger to trace my eyes and mouth in the air between us before backing away and leaning against the bar.

"I had a crush on you for three years."

"Three years?"

"A moment in time looking back at it."

"True."

"You were always nice to me . . . not everyone was."

"You led that review class for the geometry regents. When was that, ninth grade?"

Billy nodded.

"It made a big difference. You helped me get it. You were a wiz at math."

Billy nodded again.

"What ever happened to that baseball star you dated?"

"Michael."

"You two were inseparable. Did you get married?"

"No, we broke up after high school. He's dead," I said, pointing to his photograph on the Wall of Remembrance.

"I didn't get over there yet. Sorry to hear it. He was a nice enough guy back in high school . . . despite how easy everything was for him. He really hit the gene lottery."

"Looks can be deceiving," I said.

"Don't I know it, no one paid much attention to me back then. I was the skinny kid always carrying a ton of books."

"I remember."

"I didn't have my first kiss until college . . . things were much better there . . . at MIT."

"I'm glad to hear it."

"What happened to him?

I told him about Michael's death, the shadow boxes and his

new found fame.

"Wow," was his response before calling over to the bartender to order a bourbon straight up.

I should tell the truth to one person, I thought, just to see their reaction. Someone like Billy who wasn't on any of the teams, wasn't a friend of Michael's and was more or less a loner. It wasn't hard to intuit that any conversations he had tonight would be about how much he'd been ignored in high school and how great his life had turned out.

"You know," I said, "everything wasn't always easy for Michael."

"How's that?"

I told him about his mother and the visions he had as a child.

He raised his hand to his chin, nodding while he thought it over. Then he took a sip of his drink.

"That's too bad," he said, looking down for a moment as he swirled the bourbon around in his glass.

"So tell me about yourself," he said "what have you been up to?"

I suppose I shouldn't have been surprised that Billy wasn't curious or interested. Michael wasn't a part of his high school experience. I was surprised he considered me to be. I'm sure he hadn't thought one second about Michael in the last fifty years.

I answered his question. I told him what I'd been doing the past fifty years. I told him about Earl and my family.

"Funny, I never saw a byline by you, but I don't have time to read those kind of magazines. I got involved in missile guidance systems after college. Top secret stuff but for private companies so I got paid well . . . a fortune really."

"That's great."

"Never found the time to marry. I've been living with this woman for the past twenty years. She had a doctorate in mathematics."

"How nice."

"I retired about two years ago. I'm working on a book about missile guidance . . . command to line of sight. We call it CLOS. It's a system that uses angular coordinates between the missile and target to insure accuracy."

"Sounds complicated."

"It's really not, not for me."

"I'm not surprised," I said, excusing myself to say hello to Griff who I spotted across the room.

Billy lifted his drink as if he were making a silent toast to something. I smiled and lifted mine back. It felt like a salute.

I didn't know Billy well enough back in high school to know if he was like this back then, but I suspect not. He'd come back to prove something.

I didn't know how many conversation like that I could stand to go through. I know I couldn't expect every conversation to be like the one I had with Max, but I didn't want to hang out at the bar any longer and be a stationary target. I'd rather be on the mingle marry-go-round for a while where conversations were all about family and work and lasted no longer than it took to cook a soft boiled egg.

I was stopped five times on my way across the room to Griff by classmates I should have recognized, but didn't. They all expressed their condolences about Michael, as if I were his widow, and I accepted them as if I were. I suppose as the executrix of his estate and the guardian of his mother I was the only one around to receive any of their expressions of sympathy.

They expressed their admiration for his shadow boxes as well and his "well-deserved" and new found fame. I accepted those compliments as well.

By the time I got to Griff, he had collapsed into a chair.

"You look awful," I said.

"Thanks, that's the tenth time I've heard it since I walked in."

"How did the surgery go?"

"Fine, they said they got it all, but the chemo's a bitch." He cleared his throat and took a drink of water. "I'm not allowed alcohol at the moment . . . another bitch."

"I can't imagine being at a fiftieth reunion without it," I said, raising my wine glass to his health.

"Tell me about it. Look me up in about six months and I'll be back to being a bull in a china shop again."

"Good, I look forward to it."

We talked about Michael's sudden fame which happened after our interview.

"I went to the gallery to look at some of those boxes," he said. "A lot of baseball . . . and you."

"There are a lot of others with his wife and son . . . and no baseball."

"Where's your husband?"

"Upstairs . . . which is where I'm headed."

"Don't go just yet," Griff said. "They boys are meeting under the tent for a baseball team photo . . . fifty years later, isn't that the biggest bitch of all."

Griff stood up with some effort and accepted my arm as we headed slowly out there.

"How did it happen?" he said. "How did we get so old this fast?"

"I've been wondering the same thing."

"And what's the noted journalist come up with?"

"I read somewhere that time seems to speed up as we age because every year becomes a smaller and smaller fraction of the best measuring stick we have . . . the length of our lives."

"In English please."

"Age five took so long because it was twenty percent of our life. Fifty to fifty-one flew by because it was two percent."

"You don't have to be a philosopher to figure that out," Griff said. "What else have you got?"

"When we were young everything was new and the memories got stored individually and with more detail. They get to take up a lot of space and are more emotionally charged. When we get older there's less room up there," I said, tapping my forehead, "and we have to store the memories in larger groups and with less detail."

"So looking back on our lives," Griff said, "the later years seem to have fewer memories with fewer details and seem to have passed faster?"

"Precisely."

"I don't buy that either."

"There was another theory I read about recently that I liked. It's called Losing Time. Want to hear it?"

"Do I have choice?"

"No. When we were children and wanted to draw a picture or build a toy fort we did it and it didn't take long. But when we become adults all our projects take a lot more time and thought, whether it's building one of your skyscrapers or balancing the checkbook . . . which makes us feel as if we've lost a lot more time getting things done . . . giving us less time and making it feel as if it's moving faster."

Griff laughed at that one.

"There wasn't a building I worked on that didn't lose time. I should be a hundred and fifty years old by now."

"I've got one more," I said.

"Boy, you've really made a study of this."

"I'm writing for the senior set these days."

"Go ahead," Griff said, waving at the seniors on the baseball team who were assembling at the entrance to the tent.

"Time seems to pass the fastest between thirty and sixty."

"Ok, I'll bite, why is that?"

"Because our lives our crazier during those years . . . personally and at work. We're under pressure . . . particularly time pressure . . . which causes subjective time to accelerate. When we're young or old and not working as hard the time pressures are less and time seems to slow down."

"Well, I'm officially old so I can't wait for that to happen."

"I suppose that's why many older people say they find this stage of life so happy."

"I can't wait for that either."

With that the team gave a cheer when Griff and I finally arrived and they assembled for a team photo. They tried to recreate the last one they took after winning the championship, but there were a number of teammates missing, including Michael, who had stood front and center for that one.

I got hugs from everyone on the team and for some reason none of them had aged very well. Perhaps that was one of the side effects of playing so many sports when you're young. Too much sun and too much pressure to perform at too young an age. Max looked the best which was a good advertisement for the health benefits of a career in teaching.

The stories about the practices and the games brought smiles and laughter, as did the mention of Michael's name. I didn't have the heart to say anything to burst that bubble.

They insisted I be in one of the team photos before they went back to the party.

"After all," someone said, "you and Mike were attached at the hip back then."

"Yes, we were," I responded.

In a very different way, now we are attached again.

They made me stand at the center, in Michael's spot, and both

Max and Griff promised to send me a copy.

Before we split up, one of the guys went around soliciting donations for a scholarship in Michael's honor. I told him that the estate would be happy to make a contribution, as would I. After that, I escaped the tent and found a way back into the hotel without having to pass through the reunion.

One thing is clear, I told Earl later that night as I lay there unable to sleep, intent on stopping him from drifting off until I was ready.

"That you are glad you came," he said, "and went without me."

"No . . . well, yes to the first part."

"That you feel badly having told only one person the truth about Michael and he didn't seem to care?"

"Yes, but he didn't really know Michael. Knowing about someone is not the same thing as knowing him."

Earl rolled over onto his side and looked up at me with those sleepy welcoming eyes of his . . . the ones that always drew me in at night when we were younger.

"OK, I give up," he said, "what's clear?"

"Except for the baseball team, no one seemed particularly upset about Michael's passing . . . or his life. Even the people who said they'd read the magazine articles and knew how hard his life had been."

"Your experiences back then," Earl said, propping himself up on his elbow, "as emotional as they were to you . . . are not all that relevant to their lives . . . back then or now. They had their own emotional experiences to carry forward and look back on."

"All they wanted to do was talk about themselves."

"Point proven."

I had expected an outpouring of grief for Michael and our past—my past—setting myself up, of course, to be disappointed.

"And I've been thinking about how old everyone looked, really old, except for Billy. He's the missile man I told you about."

"It's hard to hide the outside part," Earl said, "not like everything else that makes us who we are. I once read that we all think of ourselves as half our chronological age."

"I like it when you talk literary to me," I said, snuggling up against Earl.

"I guess the older we get, the larger the disparity."

"So I'll think I'm fifty years old when I turn a hundred."

"Mentally," Earl said.

I sighed and rolled onto my back.

"Someone once wrote," I said, "I think it was Updike . . . that we are closer to heaven at the start of our lives than at the end."

"I guess this is going to be a long night," Earl said, getting up, opening the tiny refrigerator and taking out two little bottles of scotch. "I guess we'll splurge." He poured them into two plastic glasses he got from the bathroom.

"What else did you discover," he asked, handing me one.

"That nostalgia is a wasted emotion. It has a lot of promise, but in the end it leaves you unsatisfied."

"You can't avoid it. It's part of the human condition."

"It never seems to bother you."

"My life was nothing special until I met you."

"That's not true."

We both knew it wasn't true. Earl was a happy kid, a good student, a letterman in high school and had a lot of good memories of his summers at camp. He had a high school sweetheart as well.

"Some people are immune to it," he said, "like poison ivy."

"It's not quite the same thing."

"You think about it too much," he said. "You think about everything too much."

I couldn't argue with that.

"When you are in the throes of it," he said.

"Of what?"

"Nostalgia . . . when you're in the throes of it, it's hard to let go. Michael wasn't unique in that regard. There's a guy I play with sometimes who spends all eighteen holes talking about his college days."

"As if his past is present."

"Exactly."

"I looked it up the other day," I said. Nostalgia is a Greek word, nostos means homecoming and algia means pain . . . pain . . . appropriate, don't you think?"

"It'll pass," Earl said, "and without pills."

"Ha, ha."

We were silent for a while as we sipped our drinks out of the plastic cups. It was as late as we had stayed up in years—two in the morning—and I was amazed to hear so many night birds calling out to the stars.

"We never had a tenth reunion or a twenty-fifth," I said, looking over at Earl to make sure he was still up. "Maybe at those reunions people come with scores to settle and eager to show off. But fifty is whole different ball game. It's a strange one. I've been thinking a lot about it."

"No kidding," Earl said, as much to show that he was listening as anything else.

"Right. Anyway, by the fiftieth it's not about who you are or what you're doing. It's more about how you are, how you're feeling and what lies ahead . . . in the not too distant future. We're all in the same place now . . . whether we're rich or poor, happy or sad, alone or together . . . there's nothing any of us can do about it."

"If you're trying to depress me," Earl said, "you're doing a good job."

I took another sip of my scotch. It felt good going down, even at this hour of the night.

"Join the club," I said.

"You've got a lot of years left," Earl said. "And you're not in the same place as Michael was. His hard life is not yours . . . or your fault."

"What if I'd seen him that day at college or sensed something in high school and gotten him to tell me the truth? Insisted he get help."

"Then my life would have been the hard one. Instead of leaving a legacy of grandchildren and great-grandchildren, I'd have wound up a lifelong bachelor being toasted at my funeral by a handful of old golfing buddies."

"I'd have attended," I said with smile, "if there was a free lunch afterward."

Earl opened two more bottles. There was no more scotch left so we switched to vodka.

The best antidote to my troubling night was our first tumble in the sack in quite some time . . . nice hotel rooms have always turned me on.

CHAPTER ELEVEN – DAISIES AGAIN

Michael's mother died without ever coming back to the moment, at least according to her aide. She certainly did not reappear during any of my visits over the next year. I never heard her speak again. I wondered when I sat with her . . . her eyes clouded over . . . if she saw herself in Michael as he got older and felt helpless to do anything about it. That had to pull her further down into her rabbit hole.

I told Sandi about Michael's letter. She didn't sound all that surprised. She said Fran told her about Michael's spells, which is what she called them, when he wouldn't leave the house and stayed in the dark in their bedroom. After a while she did get him to see someone and take some medication. It helped, but it would have been better, the doctor said, if he'd addressed his issues earlier. Although he did say the episodes should become less frequent and milder as he got older . . . and easier to live with.

Apparently, the doctor was wrong about that, especially once Michael found himself alone again.

"They were right on top of it with Doug," Sandi said. "He started seeing someone at an early age, but I think it was a different kind of problem for him. It was more a function of his peers, the friends he hung out with . . . the drugs and the alcohol, although I could be wrong. Who knows why someone that young turns to that."

With all of Michael's money, and there was a lot of it, I started a foundation named after Doug that focused on recognizing the early signs of mental illness in children. There were a lot of non-profits I found that focused on treating a problem once it manifested itself, which is why I thought it would be important to start one focused on identifying the problems in the first instance—before they became obvious and overwhelming—by putting out information about things to look for and training teachers, coaches and parents, to be more observant and aware of the signs.

And there were signs: hitting, bullying, hurting yourself, difficulty in school and frequent mood swings. There were more subtle signs to look for as well: angry outbursts, fear, lack of energy, nightmares, difficulty sleeping and concentrating, constant physical complaints, neglecting your appearance, obsession with weight or eating significantly more or less than usual. Obviously, parents have the best radar for this kind of thing. Unfortunately, if your mother has her own problems and your father is focused on her a lot of things can fall through the cracks. That's when teachers and coaches can be important.

Some kids can hide it better than others. Some kids hide it so well that there are no obvious signs. Those are the hardest ones to identify, but we are working on that as well. I thought it would be a fitting way to spend Michael's money.

It's ironic how I looked up Michael on Facebook fifty years after our breakup simply to satisfy my curiosity from a distance and instead wound up connecting with him again. He came back into my life and gave me a new purpose. Writing this book and working on the foundation are a wonderful way to keep busy at my age.

It's certainly a very strange way to reconnect with an old friend . . . especially your first love . . . without so much as a hug, a kiss or a word of conversation. His Facebook postings were basically a lie intended to once again hide from the world his true self, which is why I decided to leave Facebook. I don't want to spend the rest of my life being deceived or deceiving anyone.

Besides, I couldn't bring myself to post anything, to let the world in just to show it what I wanted it to see—photos of meals, trips to the beach and sunsets—as if that was what my life was all about. When it came to meals and sunsets, I preferred to be in the moment and enjoy them with Earl. I didn't want to live my life through a camera lens and I didn't need to post photos of my children and grandchildren. Those were reserved for the people who were really in my life, not some anonymous audience on the Ethernet.

I don't expect to hear from anyone from high school after the book comes out, assuming it gets good reviews and anyone notices, except perhaps for Max and Griff. I'm not planning on telling them about the book. I will leave that up to chance.

My agent thinks the cover should be a field of flowers . . . daisies . . . which I think is quite appropriate.

Now that I've finished the proofs and I'm waiting on the publication date, I keep thinking of that line I remember reading in college—to be young is bliss, to be young and in love is heaven. I know it's a generalization that applies in many cases, probably in most . . . certainly it did in mine. Unfortunately, it wasn't bliss for Michael . . . not heaven at all . . . it was just love and sometimes love isn't enough.

I only wish I had known.

###

SAMPLE: *THE YEAR OF SOUP*

The Preamble – Two Soup Lovers

I decided to open a restaurant on my 30th birthday after three different lovers and the same number of careers. I started after college as a beat reporter for a local newspaper on the New York side of Lake Champlain in Plattsburgh. That lasted for three years. I then became an art teacher at a private school in rural Vermont for another three years, followed by a stint as an assistant to a fashion photographer in San Francisco. It shouldn't be too difficult to figure out how long I lasted in that job—three years. Everything in my life seemed based on threes, including my cycle, which is closer to three weeks than four.

I decided to open a restaurant to break that numerical jinx because I read that it takes at least three years for a restaurant to start making money and with a ten year bank loan I had no choice but to stick with it. Besides, cooking and eating have always been the easiest way for me to forget and move on. I'm not referring to rich, chocolaty desserts or fried foods like homemade potato chips, although both, especially when combined with an old late-night movie, can be a wonderful amnesiac in the aftermath of a break-up, especially when it seems as if you're running out of time. For me, it's always been about soups. I suppose because my great-grandmother was famous for them, as was my grandmother and mother. When my mother died way too young, the victim of a smoking habit she couldn't shake, she left me the family notebook filled with hundreds of handwritten soup recipes that went back across the Atlantic to my great-grandmother's mother and her grandmother.

On those days when I feel singled out and alone, ready to weep if I see one more dark cloud, which has become more and more frequent as my success with relationships has failed to come close to matching my expectations, it's always soup I turn to. It's soup that helps me pull the emotional plug so those feelings can run out my mental drain, and it's more than just the soup—it's the preparation as well that helps make the bitter a bit sweeter.

Take potato leek soup, for example, a basic and simple soup with what seems sometimes like a heavenly reward. First, there's the steady, rhythmic chopping of the potatoes, the leeks, the celery and the onions. The sound of the knife against the cutting board, that old, familiar cutting board given to me by mother as a housewarming gift when I moved into my first apartment, cut and bruised by more emotional mishaps than it deserved, provides a soothing counterpoint to the sharp beating of my sad heart. The focus and concentration that it takes to slice the garlic thin enough to crackle and disappear when sautéed in butter, and it has to be 100 percent butter—margarine can be no substitute at a time like this—always manages to turn those moments of preparation into the only reality.

Browning the ingredients brings an amazing auditory and olfactory comfort. The smell of sautéing onions and leeks, a staple in my mother's kitchen, is like reconnecting with an old acquaintance who remembers me at my best or hearing from a favorite aunt who still holds me up high on a pedestal, regardless of how low I may feel my life has sunk. The onions brown, seemingly alive as they yellow and shrivel with time, always drawing my undivided attention, almost whispering as they simmer, as if to remind me that there is a life force that lives on even when my expectations are lower than they've ever been before. It's a scent that reaches back to my childhood and further connects with my ancestors like some kind of culinary DNA. It's a scent that always helps me empty myself of some of the heartache, at least for a little while, like a narcotic whose high is instantaneous and which takes it time dissolving so the trip back down to earth is slow - the same way the smell of sautéing onion and leeks lingers throughout the house long after the soup has been eaten and put away.

When everything is evenly browned, it's time to add the chicken stock. Now, if I can see the ugliness coming, and often I do, even if it's only subconsciously, I will put up some homemade stock in anticipation. However, when I'm blindsided, as I was in my last relationship, abandoned in complete surprise, and forced to move again this time from San Francisco, then it's canned or out of a box, passable but not nearly as good. The canned soup is always missing something, whether it is patience or passion, it just doesn't offer the same resistance. Good home-cooked stock can make the difference between a long season filled with regret or moving quickly on to forgiveness.

Unfortunately, cooks have to make do with what they have available, as do each of us in life when we are plagued with poor choices. When it came to poor choices I had Nick, Jack and Jolene, and I wasn't planning to make any more.

Now, I've always thought that there is a certain satisfaction that comes with bitterness, which is why we hold on to it as long as we do, even why you sometimes like the taste of it, which probably explains why I like the simmering part most of all. It tames the bitterness so that even the worse memories become more palatable. It goes on for hours making promise after promise which, in the case of soup as opposed to people, it usually delivers on.

When the simmering is done, about two-thirds of the soup gets liquefied in the blender and returned to the pot with a drop of cream—heavy for major disappointments, light for the others. The soup then has to cool a bit so it can be served warm, not hot, because you can't distinguish all the flavors when it's too hot, and without all the flavors it will never be able to take hold of my despondency and anxiety as I sip it down.

In my experience, good soup is defiant of every mood and always manages to release somewhat that tight grip time and recent memories may have around my heart. It turns wherever I am - the kitchen or the small dining area in my new restaurant - into a place where those veils of troubling thoughts and confusion about who I am and what I want are not quite as suffocating as they often tend to be.

Of course, it helps to be accompanied by a good red wine and the appropriate bread which, in this case, would be sourdough that I always keep frozen at home and have delivered fresh every day at the restaurant. I named it Circa for the last nine years of my life that I'd just as soon forget – especially the two men and one woman who inspired me to disavow any future that might involve romance and to keep the rest of humanity at a safe distance.

Instead of just cooking for my own memories, I decided to

open a restaurant to see if I could help others forget and let go, if only during the course of a meal. What better way to do it than with a restaurant where soups are the only course, hearty bowls and warm, crusty bread. I figured that I couldn't be the only one out there susceptible to soup's medicinal qualities and I was right, although I'm getting a bit off track since this story isn't about soup, it's about me and one of my first customers, my favorite customer actually, an old man named Roger Peckinpaw Beanstock, known as Professor Beany, Professor Emeritus of English at Smith College. He walked in the first week I opened—Thursday night—as he would every Thursday night for a year, until my soup could no longer drown out the voices in his head.

ABOUT THE AUTHOR

A Lover's Secret is Howard Reiss' seventh novel. It was inspired by three very different thoughts . . . the mental illnesses that often went undiagnosed and untreated back in the middle of the twentieth century, especially among children . . . how time moved so slow when we were young and seems to speed up as we age . . . and how the internet (and Facebook) sometimes changes our relationship with the past.

The Texture of Love, Howard Reiss' sixth novel, was inspired by his love of Nabokov. On the 50th anniversary of Lolita, he decided to reverse the story and have a younger woman obsessed with an older man.

The Old Drive-In, Howard Reiss' fifth novel, is a nostalgic reflection on what could have been. If we can't really go home again, can we discover something everlasting if we try? Readers' Favorite wishes they could give this book "more than 5 stars." IndieReader says this novel has "richly defined characters and weaves in themes of regret and nostalgia throughout this nuanced romance."

P Town, Howard Reiss' fourth novel, was inspired by a lifetime of visits to Provincetown, a magical town at the tip of Cape Cod. The mix of people, the art, the street music, and the color make it a great place to hide in plain sight. *P Town* is a multiple award winner; winning the Silver Medal in the 2016 Readers' Favorite Awards in the Contemporary Romance category, as well as the 2016 Los Angeles Book Festival in the Spiritual category. IndieReader says *P Town* is "beautifully written from beginning to end" and Readers' Favorite calls it an "unforgettable read."

The Laws of Attraction, Howard Reiss' third novel is an insightful and quirky legal thriller about a courtroom battle over the estate of the elderly patriarch who leaves everything to his young wife who claims to be the reincarnate of his first wife. It leads to a rather unusual and somewhat comical trial to determine whether or not there is life after death. This novel is a Readers' Favorite 5 star "guilty reading pleasure."

Howard Reiss' second novel, *The Year of Soup* was inspired by a dinner at a small restaurant in Northampton, Mass. when an old professorial looking gentlemen with a bottle of wine in a paper bag sat down at a table in the corner and was immediately joined by the young, female proprietor and chef. Although he couldn't hear their conversation, he tried to imagine it, and their stories as well. This novel received the Silver Medal for Best Fiction in the North-East Region at the Independent Publisher Book Awards in 2013.

Howard Reiss' first novel, *A Family Institution,* published in 2011, was based on a true incident involving the discovery of an aunt hidden from the family who spent most of her life in Pilgrim State Hospital. The main character's quest for the truth about what happened takes him to Pilgrim State where he takes a job in the records department, learns a lot about how the mentally ill and, in particular, his aunt was treated in the 1950s, and in the process turns his life and family upside down. It's a serious subject approached with a strong comic touch and has been a growing favorite of book clubs around the country.

Howard Reiss is a graduate of Dartmouth College and Columbia Law School. He co-founded a soup kitchen in Nyack, New York where he lives and runs.

Connect With Me Online

Website: http://www.HowardReiss.com

Facebook: http://www.facebook.com/HowardReissAuthor

Twitter: https://twitter.com/horore

CPSIA information can be obtained
at www.ICGtesting.com
Printed in the USA
BVHW031702230119
538500BV00001B/14/P